This book is dedicated to the memory of H. Roberts Bagwell

FEAR ITSE[LF]

'One of America's most gifted wr[iter]
Mosley's mastery of authentic dialog[ue]

M[...]

'Walter Mosley packs his dialogue tight like a fist, but the econ-
omy of language is beautifully lifted by the blues cadences of
the characters'   Erin Baker, *Daily Telegraph*

'The pace is brisk, the dialogue razor-sharp, the humour droll.
Mosley at his best'   *Good Book Guide*

'Mosley's most provocative and impassioned novel yet'
Kirkus Reviews

'A fast-paced thriller that is effortlessly cool'   *Woman2Woman*

FEARLESS JONES

'Sexy and oozing attitude, this is so cool that it even makes
Shaft look sad'   *Daily Mirror*

'A book to buy, beg, borrow or steal'   *Literary Review*

'Mosley is a master of economic description, each phrase perfectly crafted to pack a weighty punch'   *The Times* Metro

'A slick, expressive narrative so atmospheric you can almost see
the sweat drip from their brows and smell the cordite from the
spent bullet cases'   *The List*

Walter Mosley is the author, among other works, of the acclaimed Easy Rawlins series of mysteries and two collections of short stories featuring Socrates Fortlow, *Walkin' the Dog* and *Always Outnumbered, Always Outgunned*, for which he received the Anisfield-Wolf Award. He was born in Los Angeles and lives in New York.

By Walter Mosley

FEATURING EASY RAWLINS
Devil in a Blue Dress
A Red Death
White Butterfly
Black Betty
A Little Yellow Dog
Gone Fishin'
Bad Boy Brawly Brown
Six Easy Pieces

FICTION
RL's Dream
Blue Light
Fearless Jones
Futureland
Fear Itself

SHORT FICTION
Always Outnumbered, Always Outgunned
Walkin' the Dog

NON-FICTION
Workin' on the Chain Gang
What Next: A Memoir Toward World Peace

FEAR ITSELF

Walter Mosley

PHOENIX

A PHOENIX PAPERBACK

First published in Great Britain in 2003
by Serpent's Tail
This paperback edition published in 2004
by Phoenix,
an imprint of Orion Books Ltd,
Orion House, 5 Upper St Martin's Lane,
London WC2H 9EA

First published in the USA in 2003
by Little, Brown and Company,

A CIP catalogue record for this book
is available from the British Library.

ISBN 0 75381 836 1

Printed and bound in Great Britain by
Clays Ltd, St Ives plc

www.orionbooks.co.uk

A SUDDEN BANGING ON THE FRONT DOOR sent a chill down my neck and into my chest. It was two thirty-nine in the morning. I was up and out of my bed immediately, though still more than half asleep.

I had to go to the bathroom but the knocking was insistent; seven quick raps, then a pause, and then seven more. It reminded me of something but I was too confused to remember what.

"All right," I called out.

I considered staying quiet until the unwanted visitor gave up and left. But what if it was a thief? Maybe he was knocking to see if there was anybody home. If I stayed quiet he might just break the two-dollar lock and come in on me. I'm a small man, so even if he was just your run-of-the-mill sneak thief he might have broken my neck before realizing that Paris Minton's Florence Avenue Book Shop didn't have any money in the cash box.

I slept in an illegal loft space above the bookstore. It was the only way my little business could stay in the black. Selling used books doesn't have a very high profit margin, except for the reading pleasure. Some days the only customers brought in books to sell or barter. Other days I was the only patron, reading *Don Quixote, Their Eyes Were Watching God,* or some other great novel from sunup to sundown.

Mostly I sold westerns and mysteries and romances. But I rarely read those books. The women's genre wasn't written for a man's sensibilities and popular men's books were too violent.

"Let me in there, Paris," a voice I knew better than any other called out.

"Fearless?"

"Yeah, man. Let me in."

I hesitated a moment and a moment more.

"Paris."

I opened the door and Fearless Jones strode in, wearing a green suit with a white shirt, no tie, no hat, and dark shoes. The tip of the baby finger on his left hand was missing, shot off in a gunfight that almost got us both killed, and he had the slightest limp from a knife wound he'd received saving my life in San Francisco many years before.

Fearless was tall and dark, thin and handsome, but mostly he was powerful. He was stronger than any man I'd ever known, and his will was indomitable. Fearless wasn't a smart man. A twelve-year-old might have been a better reader, but if he ever looked into your eyes he would know more about your character than any psychiatrist, detective, or priest.

"I'm in trouble, Paris," we said together.

Fearless grinned but I didn't.

"I got to go to the toilet," I said.

I walked back through one of the two aisles of bookshelves that made up my store. Fearless followed me into the toilet, unashamed and still talking while I relieved myself in the commode.

"It was a woman named Leora Hartman," he was saying. "She came up to me at the Soul Food Shack."

"Yeah?" I said. "What about her?"

"You know her?" Fearless asked.

"No."

"Oh," he said on a sigh, and I knew I was in deep trouble.

Fearless never hesitated unless he knew that he was going to cause problems for someone he cared for. And that someone was almost always me.

I was washing my hands by the time he said, "She's a good-lookin' woman — Leora. And that little boy was so cute."

"What little boy?"

"She said his name was Son. That's what she said. But come to think of it, that must'a been his name, because even though I think he was part of a tall tale, he was just a child and a child don't know how to lie about his name."

We walked back to the front room of the bookshop. The space up there was furnished with a card table that had three chairs and a sofa built for two. I sat in one of the wood chairs.

"Leora is a pretty woman," Fearless said, following in my wake like a bullet coming after a moth. "Talked like she had some education, you know? And she was refined."

"What you mean by that?" I asked. I had learned over the years that even though Fearless and I spoke the same tongue his limited use of language was often more subtle than my own.

"I don't know really," he said with a frown. "She looked like just a regular girl, but there was somethin' that set her apart too. That's why, that's why I didn't think it would hurt to help her out."

"Fearless, what are you talking about?"

"Leora come up to me with this cryin' three-year-old boy named Son. She told me that his father had left her and that her and Son was in the street on account'a he done taken all her savings with 'im."

"She picked you outta the blue?"

"She said that Son's father is a man named Kit Mitchell. Kit's a farmer from Wayne, Texas. I been workin' for him the last month or so."

"The Watermelon Man?"

"That's him."

Fearless and I received thirteen thousand dollars apiece after we were involved in the shootout that maimed his baby finger. With my money I bought and refurbished a building that had been a barber's shop. When I was through I had a new used book store. I also bought a used Ford sedan and put a few hundred dollars in the bank with a solid two percent interest rate.

Fearless got houses for his sister and mother at thirty-five hundred dollars a go, bought a fancy car, and spent the rest on a good time that lasted about three months. After that he sold his car to pay the rent and took on a job for a man selling counterfeit Texas watermelons. Counterfeit, inasmuch as they came from the seeds of the green-and-white-striped Texas variety of melon but they were grown in Oxnard on the leased farm of a man I only knew by the title of the Watermelon Man.

The Watermelon Man hired Fearless to harvest his melons and put them on trucks that he had fitted with Texas license plates. Then he would send his fleet of six trucks into Watts, where they would sell the giant fruit on street corners, telling everybody that they were getting genuine Texas melons. Texans believe that the best food in the world is from down home, and so they spent the extra nickel for this prime commodity.

"So the woman was the Watermelon Man's wife?" I asked.

"That's what she said. She was his wife and the boy was his son. The whole time we talked, Son was cryin' that he wanted his daddy. You know he cried so hard that it almost broke my heart."

"When did you meet her?" I asked.

"I just told you — the other day."

"You never saw her with this Kit?"

"Uh-uh. I didn't even know that he was married."

"So then how'd you know that she really was his wife?" I asked, wondering at the endless gullibility of the deadliest man in L.A.

"Why she wanna lie to me?" Fearless replied. "I didn't even know the lady."

"Maybe because she wanted to find Kit for some other reason," I suggested. "Maybe he owed somebody some money, maybe he's in a jam."

"Yeah." Fearless ducked his head. "Yeah, you right, Paris. Maybe so. But when I saw her and heard that boy cryin', I was just so sure that she was the one in trouble."

"And she wanted you to bring her man back?" I asked, worrying about what my deadly friend might have done.

"No," Fearless said. "All she wanted was to know if I knew where to find him."

"And did you?"

"No. That's why I believed her story."

That was when I should have stood up and shown Fearless the door. I should have said, *No more, brother. I have to get back to sleep*. That's because I knew whatever it was he saw in her story was going to bite me on the backside before we were through.

"Why?" I asked beyond all reason.

"Because Kit hadn't shown up to work at the gardens on Monday. He wasn't there Tuesday neither. His drivers all came but he never showed. I wasn't surprised. The last couple'a days out there he kept talkin' about some big deal he had and how he was gonna make a whole room full'a money."

"Doing what?"

Fearless shook his head.

"Did anybody call him after he didn't show up?" I asked.

"Nobody knew his number. And we really didn't need him. You know I was the one loaded the trucks anyway. And I never liked the fact that he was pawnin' off those melons like they was real Texas. When he didn't come in on Wednesday I called it quits."

"And when did Leora come to you?"

"Day before yesterday."

It was Monday morning, so I asked, "Saturday?"

"No . . . I mean yeah."

"You want some coffee, Fearless?"

He smiled then, because coffee was the signal that meant I was going to hear him out.

2 | MY KITCHEN WAS AN UNFINISHED BACK porch furnished with a butcher-block table and a twelve-foot counter that held three hot plates, a flat pan toaster, and an electric rotisserie oven. I boiled water and filtered it through a cheesecloth bag wrapped around a five-tablespoon mixture of chicory and coffee.

"Damn, Paris," Fearless said after his first sip. "You sure can make a cup'a coffee taste good."

The back wall of my kitchen was just a two-ply screen. It was the tail end of summer and not too cool. Moths and other night insects were bouncing off the screen, trying to get at the light. A thousand crickets hid our words from any spy that might be hiding in the darkness.

I sat up on the table while Fearless leaned his chair against the wall.

"What about this Kit?" I asked.

"Like I said, Paris. The boy was hollerin' and cryin' for his daddy. I felt bad for him. Leora said that she didn't know what to do, so what was I supposed to say?"

"That you don't know where the man is," I suggested. "That you wished her luck."

"Yeah. Maybe that's what I should'a did, but I didn't. I told her that I'd ask around, and that if I found him I'd tell her where to go."

"Then what?"

"Well, you know I'd been out there in Oxnard most the time. Harvestin' all day and camped out on guard at night —"

"Guard for what?"

"Kit had a lease on the property, but it was way out in the middle'a nowhere. He was worried that somebody'd come steal his trucks. So he paid me seventeen dollars a day to keep guard and pick melons."

A dark shadow appeared at the screen door, about the size of a sparrow. After a moment I realized that it was a bat come to feast on those juicy bugs. The bat bobbled and dipped in the air like an ungainly puppet. But as silly as he looked, I felt that chill again. This time it made its way down into my gut.

"Come on, Fearless," I said then. "Let's go drink our coffee in the front."

He kept talking while I led him back to the sitting room.

"The men drove out in their own cars every mornin'. Most of 'em got there about five-thirty. One of the men was a guy named Maynard, Maynard Latrell. More often than not, Maynard was the one drove old Kit up to the farm. At least on the days he came up."

"So he didn't come every day?"

"Naw. He used to but lately he been takin' days off here and there. But never Wednesday. Wednesday was payday."

I returned to my wooden chair. Fearless slumped back on the couch.

"How would he pick up the money for the day's sales?" I asked.

"He'd go to each truck at the end of the day, count the melons, and take what they supposed to have."

"How'd he know how many melons they supposed to have if he didn't ask you?"

"I give a count sheet to Maynard and he give it to Kit. But Kit was gone since Monday last. The drivers just kept what they collected."

"Why didn't Kit stay at the farm?" I asked.

"He had spent months growin' them melons. He said he was goin' stir crazy and that he was afraid his girlfriend was runnin' around."

"He was afraid his girlfriend was runnin' around but he didn't say nuthin' about his wife?"

"You gonna let me talk, Paris?"

"Go on."

"Anyway, Leora told me where she lived and I said that I'd get a line on Kit. I asked around until I found out where Maynard was, and then I went over to see him."

Fearless sprawled out on the couch. Upset as he was, he made himself comfortable as a plains lion. I was hunched over and at the edge of my seat. That was the difference between Fearless and me. He was relaxed in the face of trouble, where I was afraid of a bump in the night.

"Maynard didn't know too much," Fearless continued. "He said that he used to pick Kit up at a bus stop on Western at four A.M. I asked him if he ever said about anyplace he might hang out. At first Maynard didn't remember, but then he thought about Mauritia's country store on Divine."

Mauritia's was a hole in the wall that sold clothes and beauty products for Negro women. They carried hair irons and skin lighteners, fake fingernails and different brands of makeup designed for various hues of dark skin. I had only been in there once. I remembered that it smelled of coconut and rubbing alcohol.

"So you went to Mauritia's?" I asked, trying to urge him on.

"Maynard said that early one morning a week before, Kit had three boxes and that he had Maynard help him drop them off at Mauritia's front door. So I went over there to see maybe if he worked for them part-time or somethin' like that."

Fearless sat up, took his coffee cup from the floor, and brought it to his lips. He made a loud smacking sound and grunted his approval.

"It's after three, Fearless. What did they say at Mauritia's?"

"They said that they remembered a man looked like Kit come over to their place a couple'a times but that's all they knew. He was just droppin' off for the man usually bring 'em their Madame Ethel's supplies. A guy name of Henry T. Orkan."

My eyes were sore. I had been up until midnight reading *To the Finland Station* by Edmund Wilson. I had just gotten to the end of the section on Fourier and Owen when I fell asleep.

"Orkan lives out past Compton at the end of a lane that didn't have no other houses on it. I called up a cabbie I knew and had him drive me out over there for a favor yesterday."

"You mean Sunday," I said.

"Yeah. Orkan is a crazy old guy. He come outta his house with a shotgun cradled in his arm, askin' me what I wanted on his property. It was nutty, Paris, like he was some kinda moonshiner in the back country instead of a man livin' in the middle of a big city."

I knew that Fearless hadn't been afraid of that man sporting a shotgun. Fearless had never been afraid of anything.

"Did he tell you where Kit was?"

"At first he was all cagey, but when we got to talkin' he warmed up. He told me that Kit just showed up one day with a receipt for the boxes of beauty supplies. He dropped by after that pretty regular for two weeks, and then he didn't come anymore. But he had got a number for Kit, though."

"So this Orkan is a beauty product distributor?" I asked.

"I guess he is. That place'a his looked like a shanty down at the Galveston shore. No paint on it and all lopsided and messy." Fearless shrugged. "I called the number Orkan gave me. A woman name of Moore answered. I asked her about Kit and she said that she wouldn't talk on the phone but that I could come by if I wanted to."

"Why didn't she want to talk on the phone?"

"Superstitious I guess. You know country people's scared'a all these machines they got today."

"So you went there?"

"It was a big old ramblin' house. Must'a had a dozen tenants or more. They told me that Kit had taken a room on the top floor, but that he hadn't been back there since the first day he didn't come in to work."

"Wait a minute, Fearless," I said. "If Kit got a room on the top floor of a rooming house, then how could he walk out on his wife and child?"

"That's what I went to know from Leora," he said. "I went over to her apartment and asked why didn't she know that Kit had another place. But she said all she knew was that Kit had been away at his watermelon farm. So I told her where he had been stayin'." Fearless hesitated again.

"What?" I asked.

"The funny thing was, all she had was a room and a half. And Son wasn't there with her. She said that she left the boy with her mama, but you know, Paris, there wasn't even one toy or buildin' block on the floor. It wasn't like a child had ever been in that house."

"Did you say somethin' about that?"

"No. I didn't even think about it really. Later on I did but right then I was just doin' what I promised I would. After that I went down to Marmott's on Central and listened to Lips McGee and Billy Herford until almost midnight. Then I went home. I didn't think about Leora again until my landlady Mrs. Hughes told me about the cops."

"Cops? What cops?"

"They was askin' about me and if anybody around there had ever heard of Kit Mitchell. They told her not to tell me they were there, but Mrs. Hughes likes me so she was waitin' by her door for me to get in."

"What do the cops want, Fearless?" I asked, sounding more like a doubting parent than a friend.

"I don't know, Paris. But it don't sound good. I mean, she said that they were in suits, not uniforms, and they called themselves detectives."

My mind slipped into gear then.

"Why'ont you go upstairs and take my bed, man? I'll sleep down here."

"No, Paris. I don't wanna put you out your bed."

"Just do what I say, okay? Go on upstairs. I'm going to want to talk to you more about this thing with the Watermelon Man, but we should wait until we're both sharp. You get a good night's sleep and we'll get into it again in the morning."

3 | WITHIN TEN MINUTES I COULD HEAR my friend snoring. He had spent three years on the front lines in Africa and Europe during the war, but he claimed that he slept like a baby every chance he got.

"Me worryin' about them big shells and bombs wasn't gonna help nuthin'," he'd said one drunken night. "But a good night's rest meant that I was sharp when I had to be."

Many a day I had curled up on the front sofa and slept for hours, but not that early morning. Fearless didn't know what those cops wanted, but that didn't matter to him. All he needed was a corner to sleep in, and if in the morning he had to pull up stakes and leave California he'd do that, looking forward to a new life in Seattle or Memphis or Mexico City.

Fearless was sleeping the sleep of an innocent man but I couldn't get that chill out of my chest. I wasn't guilty of any crime, but just being in the house with a man wanted by the police put me in a state of high anxiety.

At four I turned on the lights, pulled out the dictionary, and looked up random words. *Leaf lard* was the first one I lit on. That meant lard rendered from the leaf fat of a hog. *Leaf fat,* I read, was fat that formed in the folds of the kidneys of some animals, especially the pig.

I liked looking up words in the dictionary. It calmed me, because there was no tension in the definitions. Definitions were neutral: facts, not fury.

When the sun came up I went down to the corner to buy the *L.A. Times* from the blind man, Cedric Jarman, who sold papers near the bus stop. I knew that Fearless would sleep late because of the time he got to bed, so I sat on the front porch and read the dreary news.

Ike was still declaring victory in Korea two years after the war was over. We had halted communism in its tracks, but A-bomb testing continued just in case we had to have a real war with somebody like Russia or Red China. A white woman's body had been found by a hobo in Griffith Park. She had a German-sounding name. There was some flap over a Miss L.A. beauty contestant, something about a Negro heritage that she didn't declare with the pageant officials. The president, a Mr. Ben Trestier, said that they weren't disqualifying her because she was Negro but because she lied. "It is the lie, not the race, that shows she isn't our kind of queen," Trestier was quoted.

"But if she told the truth you wouldn't have let her compete in the first place," I said aloud. Then I laughed.

That's what we did back in 1955, we laughed when we pierced the skin of lies that tried to disguise racism. I'd be down at the barbershop playing cards in a few days, and we'd discuss the fate of Lana Tandy, the light-haired, fair-skinned Negro who tried to be the beauty queen of L.A. We'd laugh at the pageant and we'd laugh at her for thinking she could make it that far. Mr. Underwood, the retired porter, would get angry then and tell us that we shouldn't be laughing but protesting like they were doing down south. We'd say, "You're right, George. You're right." And he'd curse and call us fools.

After I'd made it through the headlines I went back inside.

The new bookstore was larger than the last one I had, the one that my neighbor burned down. The room was twenty feet square. I wandered from wall to wall, serenaded by the cacophony of Fearless's snores while running my fingers over the spines of books.

I had bibles, cookbooks, science fiction paperbacks, and *National Geographic* magazines. In a special section I had all of the books by black authors that I could find; from Sterling Brown to Phillis Wheatley, from Chester Himes to Langston Hughes, from W.E.B. Du Bois to Booker T. Washington.

I liked touching the stock. It made me feel like I was somebody; not just passing through but having a stake in the world I lived in. People knew me. Customers came to the store and asked my advice on books. They gave me their money and I sold them something of value.

After a while my fingers went across an old copy of *Candide*. I took it from the shelf and curled up on the sofa again.

I was asleep before finishing the first paragraph.

I DREAMT ABOUT A MAN IN A FARMER'S HAT. The short and stocky farmer was leading me down a long and dark hallway, whispering about money, lots of money. Finally we reached a door.

"Open it up," the farmer said. "Open it up and you will have all the money you'll need for the rest of your natural-born days."

I was trembling, scared to death.

"No," I said. "No."

"But you're right here, Paris," he said, "next to the gold mine. You don't even need a key. Just turn the knob and push it open."

I didn't want to do it but still my hand reached out. When I grasped the doorknob I thought it would burn me but instead it was chilly. The refreshing coolness washed over my body. Feeling more confident I pushed the door open. Green light flooded the hallway. The room was full of money, piles of it. And on the biggest pile sat Lana Tandy, naked and spread-legged, smiling at me.

"Come on, baby," she said. "It's all yours."

My fears melted away and I ran toward her. The door slammed behind me but I didn't care. It wasn't until the money rose up like a wave behind Lana that I realized I was trapped. She screamed as the wave of green slapped against me. I was submerged in millions of dollars, suffocating under the weight of that great wealth.

I struggled wildly against the heavy cash, but it was too much for me. Lana let out a strangled cry. She grabbed me by my shoulders and said, "Paris, help me. Help." She pounded against my chest, but instead of feeling the concussions of her fists I heard a hollow knocking. Even when we were separated by the crashing waves of money, I could still hear the echo of her knocking against my chest. A tide of bills washed over me and I couldn't breathe. I struggled and screamed, realizing that I was about to die. When I stroked down with both hands to propel my head toward the surface, I came awake sitting upright on the couch, gulping air and trembling.

Lana was still knocking on my chest. Knocking on my chest?

The sun was shining into the store through a window set high on the wall. Someone was rapping on the front door for the second time that morning and, also for a second time, I was afraid for my life.

4 | "PARIS MINTON?" a white man in a brown jacket asked.

His pants were brown too, but they clashed with the hue of his sports coat. He had spaces between his teeth and freckles on his forehead. His black hair looked like it was painted on and his eyes were both too low and too close together. He should have been a short man, with those goofy features, but he was at least six foot four, two inches taller than Fearless.

Something was missing. At first I thought it was something about my visitor, but then I realized that it was a sound. Fearless was no longer snoring.

"Yeah, that's me," I said.

"My name is Theodore Timmerman. I'm looking for Fearless Jones."

"Last I heard Fearless was somewhere up near Oxnard, workin' on a farm."

Theodore frowned and I realized that I should have asked him why he was nosing around about my friend. I wasn't fully awake. I tried to cover my mistake by yawning and asking, "What you want him for?"

"Can I come in?" he replied.

"I don't even know you, man," I said. "The bookstore don't open till ten, and I already answered your question."

"I need to find Fearless Jones. Maybe you have some idea about how I can locate him."

"No. I mean you might try cruisin' up and down Central. Fearless is workin' for a guy sells watermelons off the back of a fleet of Texas trucks around that way. If you see one'a them, they'd prob'ly have an idea of where he is."

"You don't have a number?" Timmerman asked.

"He don't have a phone."

"Oh."

"What's this all about?" I asked.

"Mr. Jones has come into an inheritance," he said, masking the lie with a foolish grin. "I'm representing the estate."

"Oh? Who died?"

"That's confidential, Mr. Minton. Only to be revealed to Mr. Jones himself. But I can tell you that it would be well worth his while to contact me."

"Maybe if you gave me a way to get in touch with you," I suggested. "Then if I ran into Fearless I could tell him where to call you."

The tall white man looked up over my head into the bookstore. For a moment I think he was considering pushing me aside and looking around for himself. At any other time I would have been afraid that he would harm me or my stock. But I knew that Fearless was upstairs and Fearless, at least in my mind, was proof against any danger.

Timmerman pulled out his wallet and shuffled a small stack of cards until he produced one that read,

Theodore T. Timmerman
Mutual Life of Cincinnati
Claims and Investigations

The phone number was local, however. The ink on the bottom line was slightly smeared.

"Is there a finder's fee if I can get this to Fearless?"

"Yes," he said. But I could see that the idea was novel to him. "Sure. Two and a half percent."

"That don't sound like much."

"Out of fifty thousand that's over twelve hundred dollars."

"Oh," I said. "Damn. Well, let me ask around and see if I can come up with something."

Timmerman grinned again. "Can I use your toilet, Mr. Minton?"

"Sorry, but I got a girlfriend in the nude back there. Well, she's not exactly a girlfriend. I mean, we just met each other last night. There's not too much privacy and I don't wanna get her all upset with some big man walkin' in. You see what I mean."

We were both liars. Almost everything we'd said to each other was a lie.

He nodded, looked up over my head again. I got the feeling that he wanted to catch a glimpse of a naked black girl.

"Well," he said, still hesitating, still looking for a way in. "You have my number."

The big man in the poorly chosen clothes walked away, taking the six wooden stairs of my front porch in two strides.

"Mr. Timmerman."

"Yes, Mr. Minton."

"Fearless got a lotta friends. How come you came to me?"

The white man looked at me a moment. He was trying to figure out where I stood in his business.

"Sweet," he said at last. "Milo Sweet was listed as a contact for Mr. Jones. When I went to him he gave me your name."

It was time for me to think. Was the bail bondsman holding paper on Fearless? Was that why Fearless was on the run?

No. Fearless wouldn't lie to me. Not unless it was to protect me, or maybe he was protecting someone else. No. The story was too complex for his style of lying. Fearless's lies were no longer than a few sentences, sometimes no more than a word or two.

"Good-bye, Mr. Minton," the man who said he was in insurance said. "Call me the minute you hear from Mr. Jones. Time is money, you know."

He crossed the street, climbed into a brand-new, maroon-colored Pontiac, and drove off.

"Who was he?" Fearless asked at my back.

I hadn't heard him come up behind me but that was no surprise. Fearless's job in World War II was to get behind German lines at night and "neutralize" any military man or operation that he came across.

"I don't know," I said. I closed the door and walked back toward the porch. "But he said that Milo gave him my name so that he could ask me about you."

"Me?"

I went back to the kitchen to fix breakfast, but when I got there I realized that my appetite had gone with Theodore T. Timmerman.

"Did you jump bail, Fearless?"

"No."

"Does Milo have any reason to be after you?"

Fearless shook his head.

"He said his name was Timmerman, Theodore. You ever heard of him?"

Fearless could exhibit the blankest stare imaginable.

"He said that you inherited some money," I said. "You got any rich relatives or friends that care for you like that?"

The ex-assassin hunched his shoulders. "Who knows? Maybe."

"Probably not."

"Why you say that, Paris?"

"He called you Fearless, not Tristan. Seems to me that anybody care enough about you to leave you fifty thousand dollars would at least know your legal name."

"Fifty thousand. Damn. I hope you wrong, Paris. You know I been lookin' for fifty thousand dollars my whole life."

That made me laugh. Fearless joined in. I pulled a box of Shredded Wheat from a shelf on the wall and some milk out of the ice chest that stood in for the refrigerator I planned to buy one day.

After we sat down to breakfast I started asking questions in earnest.

Questions is what I do. I read my first book two weeks after learning the alphabet. It wasn't that I was smarter than anybody else, but it's just that I wanted to know anything that was hidden from me. My mother used to offer me candy if I'd be quiet for just ten minutes. But I could never stop asking why this and why that, not until I learned how to read.

Somebody might think that a man who's always probing — *putting his nose where it doesn't belong,* as my mother says — would be somewhat brave. But that couldn't be further from the truth about me. I'm afraid of rodents and birds, bald tires, fire, and loud noises. Any building I've ever been in I know all of the exits. And I've been known to jump up out of a sound sleep when hearing a footstep from the floor below.

That's why I own a bookstore full of books, so that all my questioning can be done quietly and alone. I didn't want to ask questions about Fearless's whereabouts or activities. But after that big white man showed up at my door, I needed to know if my friend's problems were going to spill over onto me.

5 "... NO, PARIS," FEARLESS SAID. "I told you all I know about it. Leora and Son were lookin' for Kit, and the next thing I know the cops are askin' around about me."

"And you haven't talked to Milo in two months?"

"Maybe three," he said. "Last time I saw Milo was at The Nest. He was there with a nice-lookin' woman. I think her last name was Pine."

"What about Kit?" I asked. "Did you find out anything else about him?"

I had asked it all before, but I'd learned from long experience that Fearless didn't have a straightforward way of thinking. He never remembered everything all at once. I asked him questions the same way the police questioned a suspect: with the hope of finding what wasn't there rather than what was.

Fearless rubbed his hand over the top of his head. His ideas, though often deep and insightful, came from a place that he had very little control over. If you asked him, "How did you know that man was going to pull out a knife?" he might utter some nonsense like, "It was the way he lifted his chin when he saw me walk in the room."

"Somebody said about the Redcap Saloon," Fearless said.

"O'Brien's Bar?"

"Yeah."

"Who said about it?"

"It was that man Pete."

"Dark-colored guy?" I asked.

"Naw. Yellah. High yellah at that. Him an' Kit was friends. At least I seen 'em together more'n once. Pete's got a hot dog cart over in MacArthur's Park. I asked him if he'd seen Kit and he said about the Redcap Saloon."

"Maybe we better go over there and see what we can see."

Fearless grinned. "I knew you wouldn't let me down, Paris. We connected at the hip, you an' me."

"Unless they put you up on the gallows, unless that."

"It ain't gonna go that far, Paris. Naw, man. It's probably just some questions them cops want answerin'. 'Cause you know I ain't even broke a sweat in over a month."

"What about that white man lyin' an' lookin' for you?" I asked.

"Who knows? Maybe he don't have nuthin' to do with it."

"Anyway," I said. "Let's be careful. You go out and climb the back fence. I'll pick you up in five."

Fearless just nodded. He went out the screen door, which I latched behind him.

• • •

MY FORD WAS A SICKLY BROWN COLOR that might have
gone well with Theodore Timmerman's suit. But that was all
right, because the poor paint job helped cut down on the price. It
was a used 1948 model and only cost me two hundred and fifty
dollars. It ran well and gas was cheap, so transportation was no
problem at all. I pulled around Mace and drove up the alley
between Seventy-first Place and Florence. Fearless was nowhere
to be seen as I approached, but when I got to the back of my place
he jumped out, opened the passenger's door, and hopped into the
seat like an eel gliding into a resting place between stones.

After a few blocks Fearless said, "It's nice to be ridin' again.
You know it took me so long to get to your place last night 'cause
I had to walk."

"You don't even have bus fare?"

"Not right now, Paris. You know the day Kit skipped out was
my payday."

"I can't believe it. Don't you have a bank account?"

"What for? I make money and I spend it."

"But you don't have anything."

"I got as much as any other man, more than many."

If anybody ever wrote a book about our friendship they would
have called it *The Businessman and the Anarchist.* Fearless lived
from day to day and here to there. His life in California was the
dream that so many others had been shattered by. One night he
slept on the beach, snoring by moonlight, and then he'd spend a
week lying in some pretty girl's bed. If he had to work he could
swing a twelve-pound hammer all day long. And if work was

scarce he'd catch a dozen sand dabs from a borrowed canoe, come over to my house, and trade that succulent entrée for a few nights on my front room sofa.

o'brien's was up on cockbarrow, a few blocks from the train station. The entrance was no wider than a doorway, and the sign could have been for a professional office rather than a bar. But once you got past the short hall you entered a large room built around the remnants of a large brick oven that had once been used to make bread for Martinson's Bakery in the twenties.

The oven had been twelve feet in diameter. Hampton James, the bar's owner, cut the bricks down to waist level and installed a circular mahogany bar around the inside. On busy days he had as many as four bartenders working back to back, serving the colored employees of the railroads.

O'Brien's was the place that colored train professionals patronized. All porters, waiters, restroom attendants, and redcaps went there when the shift was finished or when a layover began. There were a dozen cots in a back room where, for three bucks, a porter could get a nap before heading off on the next outbound train.

There were no windows in the walls but the roof was one big skylight, and so the room was exceptionally sunny. Hampton used the exhaust fans left over from the bakery to keep the place at a reasonable temperature. And he had a red piano on a wide dais for one jazzman or another to keep the mood cool.

Hampton was the only bartender working at that time of morning. A solitary customer sat at the bar. That patron was dressed in a porter's uniform, drinking coffee.

"Hampton," I said as Fearless and I approached.

He winced, straining to find my name, and then said, "Paris, right?"

"Yeah."

"What you boys drinkin'?"

"That coffee smells good."

If it had been later Hampton would have told us to go to a diner. But he was just getting warmed up at eight-thirty. We could have ordered ice water and he wouldn't have cared.

"Regular?" he asked.

Regular in California meant sugar and milk, so I said, "Black."

"Nuthin' for me," Fearless added.

"You're Fearless Jones, right?" Hampton James asked.

"Yes sir."

Hampton was a nearly perfect specimen of manhood. He was five eleven with maple-brown skin. He was wide in the shoulder, with only ten pounds more than he needed on his frame. He had a small scar under his left eye and eyebrows that even a vain woman wouldn't have touched up. His lips were generous and sculpted. And his oiled hair was combed back in perfect waves in the way that Hindu Indians draw hair on their deities.

"I saw you get in a fight one night down on Hooper," Hampton said to Fearless. "Down at the Dawson's Market."

"Yeah?"

"Don't you remember?" Hampton asked.

"Did I win it?"

"Oh yeah. Yes you did. It was a big dude named Stern but you put him down and they had to carry him off."

"I don't remember any fights but the ones I lost," Fearless said in a rare show of pride.

"How many you remember?"

"None comes to mind."

Hampton had a sharp laugh, like the chatter of a dozen angry wrens. I laid down two dimes for my twelve-cent coffee. He pocketed them, keeping the change for his tip.

"What you boys want?" Hampton asked. He was looking at me.

"Why you think we want anything other than coffee?" I asked him.

"No Negroes drop in here for coffee, brother. An' even if they did, it's cause they work for the trains. Any civilian knows about my door would come at night or on his way to someplace else."

"We could be on the road somewhere," I speculated.

Hampton looked at my clothes, which were only made for working, and shook his head.

"Dressed like that," he said. "And with not even a valise between you. I don't think so."

"Yeah," I admitted. "You right. The reason we've come is that Fearless here owes me twenty dollars."

"So?"

"He don't have it, but he told me that his friend Kit owed him for a week's work he did out in Oxnard. Kit was supposed to pay him Wednesday last but he never showed up."

Hampton's only imperfect features were his eyes. They weren't set deep into his head like most people's. They were right out there competing with his nose for facial real estate. As a result even I could easily read the hesitation when it entered his gaze.

"What's all that got to do with me?"

"Light-colored man name of Pete," I said. "You know, he has a hot dog cart downtown. He said that he'd seen Kit in here more than once."

"Kit who?"

"Mitchell," Fearless said. "Kit Mitchell. Sometimes they call him Mitch. One'a his front teeth is capped in silver."

It was always good to ask questions when in the company of Fearless Jones. Women liked answering him because of his raw power and sleek appearance. Men stopped at the power. They didn't know that a man as dangerous as Fearless would never bully his way through life. All they knew was that if they had that kind of strength and skill they'd never take no for an answer again.

"I don't know really anything," Hampton James said. "I mean, Kit ain't been in here since he started that watermelon business. But I heard from one of the bar girls that he took her up to a room he had at the Bernard Arms over on Fountain."

"Sounds like a white place," I said.

"Yeah," the bar owner said. "That's why she was talkin' about it. She said that he went in an' asked for Hercules and they showed him up to a penthouse apartment that was all nice with a stocked bar and everything."

"Hercules?"

"That's what she said."

The bartender glanced at the porter and moved in that direction. He seemed worried. Looking at him, that all but perfect sampling of humanity sidling away fearfully, gave me my third chill of the day. It was as if he were scuttling away from some danger that was coming up from behind me. The feeling was so strong that I turned around.

There sat Fearless Jones, staring up innocently at the skylight.

6 | MY EYES WERE WATERING and I couldn't stop yawning by the time Fearless and I got to Ambrosia Childress's house. We went to the front door together because I needed her phone number to stay in touch with my friend.

She answered in a bathrobe that was open just enough to snap me out of my lethargy. She had deep chocolate skin, dark red lips, and bright brown eyes. When she looked at Fearless her lips parted.

"Hi," she said.

I might just as well have been a tree.

"Hey, Ambrosia. I'm sorry to drop in on you like this but I need a place to stay for a day or two."

"Okay," she said. No question why. No coy hesitation. I do believe that her nostrils widened and her chest swelled.

"Thank you, honey," Fearless said.

He was swallowed up whole by her doorway and I was left at the threshold with a scrap of paper in my hand.

We'd decided that it would be dangerous for Fearless to travel the streets with so many people looking for him. I could make the rounds asking questions while he suffered the four walls of Ambrosia's protective custody.

"GOOD AFTERNOON. BERNARD ARMS," a friendly young woman said in my ear.

I was down the street from the residence hotel, closeted in a sidewalk phone booth.

"Brian Letterman," I said in a tone completely drained of my Louisiana upbringing. "Pasternak Deliveries. With whom am I speaking?"

"Susan Seaborne. Yes, Mr. Letterman. What can I do for you?"

"I got a new guy at the front desk here, Sue. You know how it goes. Some guy in a hundred-dollar suit came in and dropped off a parcel without leaving the proper information. Lenny didn't know. And now I have a problem."

"Oh," Susan Seaborne said. "I see."

"I'm glad you do, because my boss wants to fire me. Can you believe that? Lenny takes down two lines for an address and Pasternak wants to put it on me."

"I really don't see what we have to do with your trouble at work," the young woman said.

"Oh, yeah. I'm sorry. It's just that my wife's pregnant, and if I lose this job —"

"Are you looking for a new job?" the operator asked, trying to urge me toward clarity.

"I got two lines here," I said. "Actually three words. Hercules and Bernard Arms. That's all the address that the suit gave Lenny. If I don't get a proper address my new baby will be suckling cheap wine on Skid Row."

"Lance Wexler," the woman said brightly. "You're looking for Lance Wexler. He's got a penthouse suite."

"Is there a number on that suite, dear?" I asked in the wake of a deep sigh.

"P-four. That's his apartment."

"P-four," I said, pretending to write it down. "Can you connect me to his room, please? I need to see when he wants to take delivery."

"We can take the package at the front desk."

"I know," I said. "But Mr. Pasternak wants me to go there myself and get the man's signature. Either I put the package in his hand by four o'clock today or I can kiss sweet butter good-bye."

"But Mr. Wexler isn't here," my new friend Sue said.

"Are you sure? Or is it that he just doesn't want to be bothered?"

"No. He's out. I'm sure of it. No. He's definitely not here. He hasn't been in for a few days."

THE BERNARD ARMS RESIDENCE HOTEL was nowhere near any colored neighborhood. They wouldn't have rented a toilet to Kit Mitchell.

Next door on the right was a florist's shop called Dashiel's. On the left was a stationery store with no name posted. I went into the stationery store and bought a big blue envelope and a small stack of gummed labels. I attached one of the labels to the envelope and wrote the name Mr. John Stover. Beneath that I penned The Bernard Arms.

With the envelope under my arm I went around to the alley behind the building.

The back door of the residence hotel had a concrete platform in front of it. On that dais stood six large metal trash cans. Next to that was a double doorway. The doors were unlocked. They opened onto a hallway that smelled of garbage with a hint of freshly hatched maggots. The walls down that passage were painted dark brown to waist level and light blue the rest of the way up. It was as if the management had decided to make the working environment as hard and ugly as they possibly could.

At the far end of the unsightly corridor was a doorway that had a red-and-white sign that read FIRE EXIT attached to it. The stairwell beyond the door was also of utilitarian design. Filthy bare wood stairs led me past rough plaster walls that were painted a shade neither yellow nor green but a color that took on the worst aspects of both hues.

With the blue envelope securely nestled under my arm, I walked up the zigzag stairwell until it came to an end. I opened the door and came out on a tar paper and gravel roof. Realizing that I had overshot my goal by one floor I was about to turn back, but then I heard a sound, what a poet on my bookshelves might have called a susurration.

I looked around the side of the small structure that housed the doorway and saw the tan shoes and bare butt of a very white man humping away between a woman's shuddering legs. She was wearing a maid's uniform and he was most likely the valet. They were going at it on a sheet spread out over the gravel and tar.

"Warren. Oh, oh, Warren," the woman moaned.

It was her calling out a name that was common but not someone I knew that struck me. The name Wexler came back to me.
Hercules's name suddenly seemed familiar.

I backed toward the doorway and descended a floor to the
penthouse.

The penthouse hall had emerald carpeting and muted lime
walls. There were potted ferns between the entrances to the
suites and crystal chandeliers hung every six feet or so. The window at the end of the hall looked out over the tops of trees. It
was more like a view of Paradise than some upstart brick-and-
plasterboard city.

I thought about the lovers wrestling above me — Warren and
the woman who called his name. Again I thought of the name
Wexler. Where had I heard that name before?

My heart was thumping by then. I had made it all that way by
using stealth that would have been better suited to a much braver
man. I had planned my steps carefully, all the way down to the
envelope under my arm. Hercules wasn't home but Kit might be
up there with some railroad prostitute. And all I had to do was
mention Fearless's name to keep him from doing something violent. Everyone who knew Fearless also knew not to cross him.

But the lovers on the roof had disconcerted me.

The cream yellow door sported the characters P4 cut out of
mother-of-pearl. I felt my heart leap when I knocked. A moment
went by. I knocked a bit harder. More time passed.

I sighed out loud. What the hell was I doing there anyway? I
wasn't Fearless Jones's father. What did I care if he had to leave
California? I had gone further than many a friend would.

But who was Hercules Wexler? I could see his family name printed somewhere.

I grabbed the knob, remembering my nightmare, and turned it. The door was unlocked. There was nothing left to stand in my way but common sense.

I entered Suite P4.

7 | THE LARGE ROOM WAS STIFLING, filled with sunlight pouring in from at least a half-dozen closed, unshaded windows. The walls were yellow cream and the carpet royal blue. The ash furniture was heavy and bright. Glass-door cabinets exhibited fine china and porcelain knick-knacks. Copies of Renaissance paintings in ornate gold frames hung here and there. A glossy finished dining table in the middle of the room supported a large vase with at least three dozen long-stemmed, once-red roses displayed like peacock feathers.

The only problem was that the roses had blackened and died and the hot room smelled sour.

I didn't know what I was looking for exactly. Maybe some envelope or receipt that would give me and Fearless a line on Kit Mitchell. Just something so that when the police came down on Fearless he could give them a lead.

I could have been arrested for burglary, but I only planned to spend five minutes searching.

The first thing I did was to locate the fire escape. Then I leaned the back of a chair under the front doorknob. If somebody tried to get in I could be down in the street and off before they saw my face.

The dining room had a wide doorway, with no doors attached, which connected it to a living room that was two steps down. This room was also yellow and blue with windows and light. The paintings here had the same garish frames, but these copies were from the Postimpressionist period. Cézanne and Lautrec, Manet and Monet, but no Van Gogh or Gauguin. I knew about paintings. I once got a whole boxful of art books discarded by the Santa Monica library. They were mostly in black and white and had been thrown out in favor of the color plates found in newer texts.

There were no books or bookshelves anywhere in Mr. Wexler's home.

There was a swinging door that was partly open. The temperature in that apartment must have been at least ninety-five degrees, but the wedge holding the door ajar made me cold enough to crave a sweater.

The foot that kept the door from closing was bare, connected to a large white man with a butcher's knife buried in his chest. All he wore was a pair of brand-new blue jeans. His arms and legs went in all directions. His eyes were open and he was beginning to stink. His wrists were bruised and bloody, as if he had been struggling with tight bonds. There was a balled-up knot of white cloth wedged in his mouth. The open mouth, puffed-out cheeks, and bulging eyes made him look somewhat like a gasping fish.

My first instinct was to run. I even turned and took three steps. But then I stopped myself. The man was obviously dead. From the smell he had been there awhile. A killer wouldn't stay around the body, I thought. And I'd seen worse. Less than a year before, I'd searched a room full of slaughtered men, looking for the fingertip that Fearless had gotten shot off.

The man was partly on his side, so I didn't have to move him much to get the wallet out of his back pocket. There was a driver's license for a Lawrence Wexler.

"Hercules," I said to no one.

He was big enough for a Hercules. Well over six feet and bulky with both muscle and fat. And he was bloated from many hours of being dead in that heat. There were bruises and burns all down his right arm. I suppose he gave up whatever information it was that he had before the left arm had to be mutilated.

The wallet was real alligator. Even back then it had to cost fifty dollars or more. It held three twenty-dollar bills and a packet of business cards bound together by a rubber band. There were liquor stores, furniture movers, and Madame Ethel's Beauty Supply among the cards. There were also six business cards for the same man — Lawrence Wexler. It seemed that he was a salesman for Cars-O-Plenty, a used automobile business.

My stomach started churning and I ran to find a bathroom. I told myself to wait, but the call of nature was too strong. A door leading from the kitchen went into a small toilet. Seated there on the commode, I placed the wallet on the floor before me. Madame Ethel's sounded familiar to me, but at first I couldn't place it. Then I remembered that Kit had done a delivery for that company.

I considered taking the wallet with me. I didn't care about the money but maybe there was something in there that I needed.

But what if I got caught?

I'd tell the truth.

That thought made me laugh.

It seemed like I was on the commode for hours. The fear in my gut was worse than many intestinal viruses I had contracted. I felt relieved and weakened when the bout was through. I'd had enough time to check everything, so I just took one of Wexler's business cards and returned the wallet to the dead man's pocket.

I passed through the house wiping every surface that I had touched and many that I might have touched. I put the dining room chair back in its place and moved out of Suite P4 with less fuss than a butterfly leaving a dank cave.

I made it down the stairs without taking a breath. I was at the swinging doors to the back alley entrance when a man yelled, "Hey you!"

I turned, seeing a tall and slender white man dressed all in white. He wasn't a cook but it certainly was a uniform he was wearing.

"Yes sir," I said. The words just came out of me. Betrayed by four centuries of training, but I didn't worry about that right then.

"Who are you?" the white man asked.

He had a pencil-thin mustache and a crooked face, though you could see by the tilt of his brimless hat that he thought he was handsome. There was a thin gold band on the ring finger of his left hand.

"Cort Stillman," I said, hoping that he didn't wonder about a Negro named Cort.

"What are you doing here?"

"Looking for a Mr. John Stover." I handed over the blue envelope.

Lance Wexler's business card felt like a bomb in my pocket.

"There's no John Stover living here," he said, twisting his already ugly mouth. "And even if there was, what are you doing out back?"

"The lady out front said that there was no Stover. And I told her that I knew that he was staying with a woman on the fourth floor. That's what they said when they brought the package in. You know it's my job to make sure the package gets to the man it was addressed to. They told me at the front desk that they wouldn't take it, so I came in the back way to sneak up and knock on some doors."

Sweat dripped down my spine. I hoped that my face was still dry.

"Let's go down to the front desk and ask them about this," the man said.

He was taller than I and probably stronger. At any rate, I'm not good at hand-to-hand combat. No good at fighting, period. I looked around, hoping for a miracle.

I found it on his feet. I was sure that there weren't three men in six square miles wearing that particular hue of tan shoe.

"Listen, Warren," I said. "We could do each other a favor here."

"How you know my name?"

"If they call my boss and tell him that I snuck in like this, he'd be forced to fire me. You know I cain't have that," I said, ignoring his question.

"How you know my name, man?"

"And there's a certain young lady who would be very thankful that you kept it quiet about what you were doin' to her up on the roof."

Old Warren turned as white as his jacket.

"I don't know if she's married, but I bet your young wife might be upset with you bein' unemployed and a cheat all at once."

Warren looked like he wanted to hurt me, so I grabbed the envelope from his hand and walked out through the swinging doors, leaving him to consider the consequences of lust.

8 I MADE IT TO THE CAR and headed down toward my own neighborhood. As soon as I saw black faces on the street I parked and practiced breathing. My gut was still writhing, and my heart knocked against my chest like Fearless Jones at the door.

Fearless Jones was my best friend and more trouble than a white girl on the prowl in Mississippi. Here I thought I was smart, sneaking into a white residence, ringing a white man's bell. But I should have known — whatever the worst could have been behind that door, it would have to come to pass if Fearless brought me there.

It was September. September is often L.A.'s hottest month. Eighty-five degrees. And still I was shivering on the inside.

Fear is the motivating force behind most of my actions. Whatever it is I'm most afraid of takes all of my attention. Right then I was afraid that the cops could place me at the scene of a murder.

Forget that the man had been dead at least two days when I was caught by Warren at the back door. Forget that I had probably erased any scrap that might have put me in the dead man's suite. If the police liked me for the murder, then I would be the murderer in their book — and their book was the only one that mattered.

I had to know why Kit Mitchell was missing, why Leora and Son were looking for him, and why he would have had free entrée to a murdered car salesman's apartment.

To answer these questions I pulled back into traffic and drove off toward the office of the bail bondsman — Milo Sweet.

MILO HAD MOVED from his Hooper address, over the illegal chicken distributors, to an apartment building on Baring Cross Street between 109th Street and 109th Place. Loretta Kuroko — Milo's secretary, girl Friday, and final hope — was sitting in the little front room of the domicile-turned-office. She was forty with the skin of a twenty-year-old and the eyes of some ancient sage. She lived and worked down among black people because of her hatred for the white men who imprisoned her and her family during the war. And she adored Milo with a passion that could not be understood in contemporary terms. It wasn't sexual, or at least I didn't think it was. Their bond was like some ancient myth about two ideal characters carrying on their labors through the centuries, living out the drama and foibles of the whole human race.

"Hello, Paris," Loretta said. "How are you?"

"Fine, Loretta." I proffered a bunch of dahlias that I'd bought from a florist on Century Boulevard.

"Oh," she said with light in her deep eyes. "Thank you so much."

Milo never brought Loretta flowers or chocolates or even a paper cup of coffee — that wasn't a part of their mythology.

"He's back there. Go right on in," she said. "I'll put these in water."

The hallway, from the front room to the back, was exactly two and a half paces. On the way you passed the door to a toilet on the right. That was where Loretta would get her water.

The back room was larger than the front, but it seemed smaller because of the eight file cabinets that Milo had against three walls. In those archives he had the records of his days as a lawyer — before he was disbarred — and as a restaurant owner, bookkeeper, and car insurance salesman. He'd also been a fence and a bookie, but I doubted if those records were still intact.

"Paris," Milo shouted. It was his normal voice, but even Milo's whisper was loud. "Have a seat."

"Thank you, Milo," I said.

He was sitting behind a maple desk, in a red leather recliner, under a naked hundred-watt bulb dangling from bare black cord. The chair in front of the desk looked like some sort of starved four-legged animal. I was afraid that even my few pounds would be the last straw.

But I sat anyway. The legs strained but held.

"What can I do for you?" Milo asked.

Milo's skin color wasn't as dark as Fearless's, but it was close. He was a couple of inches taller than I and a few inches shorter than Fearless. His feet and hands belonged on someone who was much larger, and his body was naturally powerful. But Milo wasn't a physical man. He was a thinker, a reader, a man who understood power but who was forever blocked from holding its reins.

Milo could quote passages from a thousand poems, do problems in calculus and trigonometry, but if you waved a stack of hundred-dollar bills under his nose he would forget his own name.

"Kit Mitchell," I said.

The delay between hearing the name and his next breath was enough to let me know that Ted Timmerman had something to do with the Watermelon Man.

"Who?"

"Don't fuck with me, Miles," I said. "You know as well as I do that you done sent Fearless down a dangerous road. You know it."

Milo pulled out a cigar.

If I didn't know that I was in trouble before, that stogie was the final proof. Milo smoked to hide his nervousness — and he never got nervous until the walls were caving in.

"Talk to me, Milo."

"What do you know, Paris?"

"Enough to put you in prison."

The bail bondsman's eyes widened. I liked that for two reasons. One was that I had gotten to him, raised the stakes. And also I liked to see bright white eyes against black skin — it made me feel like home.

"I don't know nuthin' 'bout no prisons," Milo said. "I know money and I know power, that's all."

"So which one did you send Ted Timmerman out after?"

"You met Mr. Timmerman, then?"

"Milo, do I have to go get Fearless? I mean, do you want to do this song and dance with him?"

"I'm not afraid. I haven't done anything wrong."

I snorted.

Milo blew out a cloud of smoke.

It was hot in that room. I was sweating even though all I had on was green gardener trousers and a white T-shirt. Milo wore a three-piece suit with a red tie knotted up to his throat, but he was still dry as a bone.

"What's goin' on, Milo?"

"Money, son," the dark-skinned ex-lawyer proclaimed. "Only money, and nuthin' else."

"I got twenty-three dollars seventy-five cents in my pocket," I said. "And compared to Fearless I'm a millionaire."

"I know you got money in the bank," Milo said. "Money in the bank and papers on that bookstore. You ain't broke."

Milo had been an equal third partner when Fearless and I got our thirteen thousand dollars and almost killed. His money was gone too. But Milo had squandered his cash on foolish investments. He wanted to be rich so bad that he never had a dime.

"Winifred Fine come to see me four, no five, five days ago," he said.

"And?"

"That's Winifred L. Fine." Milo pronounced the name as if he expected me to faint dead away.

"Yeah. I know her. The one own that fruit market down on Avalon."

"And three gas stations, two hardware stores, and Nathan's Bakery," Milo added.

"She own Nathan's too?"

"She also make Madame Ethel's Beauty Supply line."

"Never heard of it," I lied.

"Black women all over Georgia, Tennessee, Florida, and Alabama use Madame Ethel's."

"When did you get to be such an expert on women's beauty products?"

"I'm an expert on money," Milo said. "Money, boy. Big money. And when Miss Fine come to me five days ago and says that she needed to locate her nephew, I knew that big money was on the rise."

"What nephew?"

"Bartholomew Perry."

"BB's her blood?"

"You know him?"

"Seen 'im around. He come down Watts all the time, thinkin' he's slummin' just 'cause his daddy owns that used car lot." An alarm went off in my head but I didn't let it show.

"So you know where he hangs out?"

"Naw. I just seen him. At Baptiste's mainly. That's all."

"What was he doin' when you seen 'im?"

"Stuffin' his fat face," I said. "He'd bring his high-yellow and white girlfriends down there."

"All right now," Milo complained. "Ain't no use tryin' to run a man down like that. I'm sure he got black girls too."

"Not that I ever saw."

"But you don't know everything. You don't know shit."

"Whatever you say, Miles."

"How would you like to have a real bookstore?" he asked me. "New books on finished oak shelves with a real cash register, not just some cigar box with the lid ripped off?"

"Sure." My pulse quickened in spite of common sense.

"Winifred L. Fine can do that for you. She can take a hole in the wall like you got and make it into a co-orporation."

"What you sayin', Milo?"

"Like I said — Miss Fine asked me to find Bartholomew."

"He jump bail or sumpin'?"

"No."

"Then how did Miss Fine get to your door?"

"You might not know it, but I got a reputation for finding people, Paris. Most the times it's bail jumpers, but I do other kinds of searches too. I can be discreet."

"Discreet about what?"

"Miss Fine needs to have a private talk with her nephew. I didn't ask her why."

"So you agreed to find a man for somebody and you don't even know what for?"

"She wants to talk to him. That's all I need to know."

"And what's she gonna pay you for that?" I asked.

"This ain't about no fee," Milo said. He shrugged just as if he had already made it rich. "This is gettin' in good with the richest black woman in Los Angeles, maybe even the whole country. A man could become a millionaire behind a woman like that."

"Listen, Milo. A missin' nephew ain't no million dollars unless there's somethin' serious goin' on."

"There isn't," he said.

I sat back in my spindly chair. The joints creaked and the backrest sagged, but I started to get the feeling that that little chair would hold up under a man Milo's size, or bigger.

What I had to figure was how much to tell Milo. How much could I trust him?

We were friends — after a fashion. I had done some work for his bail bonds business when men awaiting trial went on the run.

Usually I'd just find out where they were hiding and tell Milo. Nothing dangerous.

We played chess now and then and had political and philosophical debates. But we didn't share the life-and-death kind of friendship that Fearless and I had.

"What does BB have to do with Kit Mitchell?" I asked.

"I don't know," Milo said. "I hired Timmerman to find BB and he came up with Kit and BB hangin' out together a few months ago. I think they were doin' some kinda business."

"What kind of business?"

Milo pursed his lips and rubbed his thumbs and forefingers together.

"BB might'a crossed the line a li'l bit, but that don't have nuthin' to do with Miss Fine and why she wants to talk to him," the bail bondsman said.

"What kind of business?" I asked again.

"Kit needed some trucks for his melon business and BB knew how to get 'em on the cheap."

"Hot?"

"There ain't no proof of that one way or t'other," the lawyer turned skip chaser said.

"Is that why the police are lookin' for Kit?" I asked.

Milo shrugged. "Kit's a businessman and black. You know all businessmen cross the line now and then. But when a black one do it the cops on him like white on rice."

What Milo said was true but it didn't explain the dead man nicknamed after a Greek demigod.

"You know a woman named Leora?"

"Never heard of her."

"She has a young boy-child named Son. Says she's Kit's wife."

"I don't have any personal information on Mr. Mitchell. He could have five wives as far as I know, and two heads for all I care."

As Milo sat back in the red leather I wondered if he knew anything more. I couldn't ask him about Wexler because I shouldn't have known anything about a murdered man. As far as I knew, Lance Wexler was still decomposing in secret, his foot holding open the door.

"Where does this Winifred L. Fine live?" I asked.

"Why should I tell you?" Milo said.

"All I can say is that you have to trust me. Fearless might be in some trouble around Kit and I agreed to help him out. If I run across BB along the way I'll make sure you know about it."

"What kind of trouble?" Milo asked.

"This woman Leora come around and asked Fearless where was Kit," I said. "She said that she was his wife. She said that he abandoned her and his child. After Fearless asked a couple'a questions the cops come around his place and asked about him. Now the next morning your boy Timmerman comes to my house askin' about Fearless too. You know neither one of us believes in coincidence, Milo."

"Maybe not," he said. "But if there's a word for it in the dictionary then there's a chance that it could happen."

"Tell me where I can find Miss Fine."

"But you could get to Winifred if I give you her address. You could make all her fortune work for you."

"Milo, I wouldn't even know what to do with a beauty product distribution company. All I care about is my books."

Milo frowned for a full fifteen seconds before calling out, "Loretta!"

"Yes, Mr. Sweet."

"Write down Winifred L. Fine's numbers on a card for Paris. Call her and tell her that I'm sendin' him by." And then, "You better not be messin' with me, Paris."

"I was thinkin' the exact same thing about you, Mr. Sweet."

9 | THE FINE FAMILY LIVED ON BRAUGHM ROAD, which occupied a strip of land between Santa Monica and Los Angeles. It was a big yellow house, a mansion really, flanked by strawberry farms that have long since disappeared. It had a southern look to it. The driveway was long enough to be called a road. It led to an electric fence equipped with a buzzer, a microphone, and a loudspeaker — all of them held together by black electrical tape.

"Who is it?" a man's voice asked a minute or so after I pressed the buzzer.

"Paris Minton," I said.

"Who the hell is Paris Minton?"

"Friend of Milo Sweet."

"Who?"

"Listen, man," I said. "Tell Miss Fine that Paris Minton is out here, that I work for Milo Sweet and I need some information to get the job done."

The loudspeaker went silent and I was by myself out there in the almost country of L.A. There were five different birdcalls that I made out but could not name. Flitting insects were everywhere. A big beetle thumped down on my hood. He sported a shiny black-and-green carapace and seemed to like the heat from the engine rising through the hood. His long legs weren't strong enough to lift him above the surface, instead they moved like the oars of some ancient galley making its way across the vast brown sea of metal. A blackbird flew up and landed so quickly it was as if she had appeared out of nowhere. She swiveled her head to get a good look at the beetle and then lunged at him with her beak. I could see its oars waving in the air for a moment and then two gulps and he was gone. The blackbird cocked her eye at me and then, in less than an instant, she was gone too.

"Who is this?" a woman's voice asked from the loudspeaker.

"Paris Minton," I said.

"And who is Paris Minton?"

I told the new voice about Milo Sweet and my working for him.

"I don't know nuthin' about a Mr. Sweet sendin' no man up in here," the voice said.

I didn't respond because she hadn't asked a question.

"Well, come on in I guess," the voice said.

The electric fence, made from simple wire gating, rolled half the way across the entrance and then seemed to get stuck. It was still trying to roll but something, somewhere, was an impediment. I got out of my Ford and helped the gate move along its track. Then I got back in and drove the S-shaped driveway up to Winifred L. Fine's front door.

The house was four stories with an extra turret on top of that. It would have been impressive if the owner had it painted and did something about the front yard.

Really, I guess you would call it the grounds. The lawn in front of the fading house was at least five acres. The grass was overgrown but I could see why. There was a refrigerator, a stove, various canisters, and less identifiable refuse in among the long blades of grass. A gardener would have gone crazy trying to mow. And even if he managed, the lawn would have looked worse because all the trash would have been more visible.

There weren't only discards in the yard, however. There were trees too. Fruit trees mainly. Two apples — which is one of the only fruit bearers that don't do well in the southern California clime — a dying peach, a dead pomegranate, and a date palm that had only one living leaf.

I saw no place set aside for parking, so I just pulled as far to the right side of the road as possible and stopped the car.

The front door was green with a picture of Mary and baby Jesus laminated to its center. I wondered if knocking on Mary's forehead was considered a sin.

A middle-aged black woman opened the door. She was quite short and wore a full-length formal black gown that had shiny black buttons from the throat down to the hem. The sleeves went all the way to her wrists. The head of an unblinking red fox peeked at me from her right shoulder.

"Miss Fine?" I asked.

"Yes," she said. Her eyes didn't waver, they hardly blinked. It was almost as if I were staring into the face of two dead animals, the fox and the woman.

The foyer behind her was as much in disarray as the grounds. There was a large ceramic pot in one corner filled with peacock feathers that were coated in dust. Above this was a large painting of a white woman astride a white stallion galloping away from a squat stone castle.

"May I speak with you, ma'am?"

"Certainly, young man," she said.

With that she led me to the left, down a long and wide corridor made narrower by stacks of cartons labeled Madame Ethel's Beauty Supply along the walls. There were also piles of documents, newspapers, ledgers, and manuals of all kinds. We came to a room that had a barber's chair and a park bench for furniture. By then I was pretty sure that I was in a madhouse, or at least in a house that was in the process of going mad.

"Sit down, sit down," the woman said, waving at the park bench.

She struggled with the barber's chair. The long skirts and stiffness in her joints made the necessary movements difficult, but she finally managed to seat herself upon the cracked grandeur of the golden leather cushion.

"Miss Fine . . . ," I said.

She held up her hand to stop me and then shook the same hand. A tinkling accompanied the motion. I saw then that there was a tiny silver bell attached to her wrist. The old woman then stared at a bookcase to her left with great concentration.

The room was quite odd. First of all, it wasn't so much a room but the dead end of the cluttered hall. There was nothing that seemed normal in there. Besides the park bench and barber's chair there was an unfinished sawhorse and a high table on which stood three miner's lanterns. The bookcases were crowded with handmade papier-mâché figurines. There were statuettes of black men and women shopping, kneeling in prayer, two men fighting with knives, and dozens of other tableaus.

"Miss Fine," I said again.

"Shh!"

A man came out from behind the bookcase then. He wore black slacks and a long-sleeved white shirt that was one size too big. His coloring was equal parts brown and drab green, and his eyebrows were thicker than some men's beards.

"Yes?" he asked with undisguised disdain.

"Oscar, this is my guest," she said.

He glanced at me with similar condescension.

"Yes, I know. Mr. Minton, who, I am told, was sent by Mr. Milo Sweet."

"What do we have to offer my guest?" she asked.

"What does he want?"

"Why I . . . ," she said. "What do you want?" she then asked me, as if some request I had made was the cause of her embarrassment.

"Nothing. Thank you, ma'am."

"You have to have something," she said. "You don't just walk into somebody's house without accepting their hospitality."

Miss Fine was staring at me. Oscar was staring at me.

"Tea?" I said.

"Hot tea or ice?" Oscar asked.

"Ice."

"Milk or lemon?"

Miss Fine giggled and bounced a little in her chair.

"Milk," I said.

"Sugar?"

"Okay."

"How many teaspoons?"

"Half of one."

Oscar's immense eyebrows rose like two bales of black hay giving way to a great subterranean upheaval.

"Don't have much of a sweet tooth," I apologized.

Oscar gave a slight shrug.

"And you?" he asked Miss Fine.

"The usual."

"It's rather early, don't you think?"

"The usual," she repeated.

Oscar shrugged again, turned, and went back behind the bookcase. For all I knew there was a closet back there where he lived with a maid, a chauffeur, and a cook.

"Now, Miss Fine," I said.

"He's not a very good servant, is he?" she asked.

"I wouldn't know," I said. "Never had a butler and never been one."

"Are you here on business?"

"I'm working for Milo Sweet, like Oscar said."

"Oh, Mr. Sweet. You know I like that name. Sweet. I love sweets, and so I liked his name right away."

"You asked Mr. Sweet to look for Bartholomew Perry."

"Bartholomew? I did?"

"That's what he told me."

"He did? Well then he must be right."

By that time I was completely lost. Either Winifred Fine was senile or so wily that there was no way for me to understand her motives.

"Why do you think you might have wanted him to find BB?" I asked.

"What did Mr. Sweet say I wanted?"

"He said that you wanted to have a secret talk with Bartholomew."

Miss Fine grinned and ducked her head as if we were exchanging confidences.

"Your tea," Oscar said.

He had come in from behind the bookcase with a silver tray supported by his left hand. The tray held a slender tumbler of milky ice tea and a squat glass filled with amber liquid. I took my glass. Oscar then proffered the tray to his mistress. She took the liquor with eagerness.

"Miss Fine will see you now," Oscar said to me.

"What?" I said.

"She's waiting for you in her sitting room."

"Isn't this Miss Fine?"

"Rose Fine," Oscar said. "Miss Winifred is waiting for you in her sitting room."

"But he's my guest," Rose Fine whined. "I'm all dressed up."

"I'll be back in just a little bit," I said.

I took the old woman's hand and kissed it.

She gasped and yanked the hand away.

10 "I AM WINIFRED FINE," the woman standing in the doorway said.

She was almost my height (which is five foot eight) and slender, the color of twilight after a storm. She had been beautiful as a young woman. She was handsome today.

"Paris Minton," I said.

I extended my hand and she turned her back on me, gliding into the large sitting room that Oscar had led me to.

This room was immaculate. The custard-colored walls, edged in dark wood, were twenty feet high. From the ceiling there hung a crystal-and-amber chandelier the like of which I'd never seen before or since. The light through the different crystals was both brilliant and warm. It seemed like a fireplace blazing from the ceiling.

"Have a seat, Mr. Minton."

Along the walls there were several framed landscape paintings, hung all in a line. At the end of the room were full-length purple curtains. There was a large desk before them and then four red-and-blue-striped sofas that formed a square. I took a seat at the corner of one of the sofas. At the edge of the couch opposite me was a toy gyroscope, the kind that had a slender pump at the top with a bright red handle made from wood.

"A child?" I asked the lady.

"Yes," she said with a happy smile that bordered on being a grin. "My grandson had been staying with me for a while. He's away for a few nights with some friends on holiday."

I wondered what kind of friends millionaire black women had.

Oscar took up a post at my side. I got the feeling that if I made any quick movements he would shoot me before I could be of any threat to the lady.

Winifred did not sit.

"Why are you here, Mr. Minton?"

"To get information."

"But I thought you worked for Mr. Sweet? Certainly he told you all you need to know."

"I like to do my own investigations," I said.

"I don't understand." She inclined her head.

Winifred Fine was wearing a two-piece suit that was deep blue in color. When I had first seen her I thought that she was in her late forties. But seeing her figure under that thin material I figured that she was closer to sixty.

"I got questions," I said.

"What questions?" Oscar asked me.

"Like for instance. Do you know a friend of BB's called Hercules Wexler?"

The lady seemed unperturbed but Oscar straightened up a bit. His boss noticed this too.

"Who is he?" Oscar asked.

"Big white dude that BB's been doin' business with." I figured they might have worked together, seeing that they were both in the used car business.

"Why do you bring this information to me?" Winifred asked. "Why not tell the man who employed you?"

"Milo is the excitable type, Miss Fine. When things get rough he goes all to pieces. He asked me to look for BB because I'm a little more levelheaded."

"What do you mean, 'when things get rough'?"

"Why are you looking for Bartholomew?"

"That is none of your business."

"You're right about that, ma'am. But I was sleepin' in my bed this morning and suddenly I found myself all involved in your business. People started knockin' on my door and talkin' to me about your troubles. Some of them lied, others were just confused. One man even said that someone could get killed if he looked too deep into the whereabouts of BB or his friends. Two men have already disappeared."

"What men?" Winifred asked.

"Kit Mitchell, for instance."

That got the spinster's attention.

"What about him?"

"That's what I wanted to know from you. Seems like Kit and BB's two peas in a pod."

"What have you found out, Mr. Minton?" Winifred asked.

"I already told you just about everything I know," I said. "Now it's your turn."

Winifred stole a glance at Oscar and then strode toward the great curtains. She went to a corner and pulled on a braided golden rope. The rope must have been connected to a weighted pulley, because the heavy drapes opened effortlessly. The twenty-foot windows revealed a sun-soaked garden I would never have suspected after seeing the desolate front yard.

Great pines and eucalyptus trees made the walls of Winifred's private Eden, protecting pomegranate and loquat trees that bore fruit in the midst of golden and scarlet flowers. Birds flitted from bough to bough as a huge tiger-striped cat watched motionlessly from the base of a marble fountain. The fountain gave off a continual spray upon the nude figure carved from an onyxlike stone. The sculpture was of an obviously Negro woman. She had small breasts and a largish butt. With one hand she attempted to maintain her modesty and with the other she was reaching for some unknown goal far above.

I could feel myself become sexually aroused, but I wasn't sure if it was because of the woman depicted or the wealth the garden represented.

"You like my garden, Mr. Minton?" Winifred asked me.

I realized that I had gotten to my feet and approached the window. Oscar was standing at my elbow.

"It's beautiful," I said.

"That woman was me," she said proudly.

I could see it, mainly in the shape of the face.

"It's surprising," I said.

"That I was once young and beautiful?"

"That the front yard is in such a mess but back here is like a paradise."

"The front of the house is my sister's responsibility," Winifred Fine said, rather petulantly for a woman of such power.

"About BB Perry," I prodded.

"I saw you looking at the paintings along my walls," she said instead of answering. "They are all by Edward Mitchell Bannister. Do you know his work?"

"I'm not really up on my painting," I said. "I mean, I've seen a lot of them in art books but I don't know the artists' names as a rule, except the Postimpressionists. They're so wild it's easy to tell the difference in styles."

"Bannister was a great landscape artist of the nineteenth century. He was a black man. The first truly great landscape artist that this country ever had."

I'm a well-read individual. It's unusual that I meet a man or woman who has gone through more books than I have. I've met English teachers who didn't know as much about literature. But for all my stores of knowledge I'd never heard of Bannister before that day.

Winifred Fine saw that knowledge and wealth impressed me.

"Bartholomew is my nephew by blood," she said. "His father, Esau, was my sister's husband."

"Uh-huh."

"Esau is a fool, and his son takes after him."

"So why do you want to talk to him?"

"I think he's in trouble."

"Why?"

Oscar cleared his throat. Winifred turned her gaze to him.

"Make me a chocolate malted, Oscar." It was the last thing in the world I expected to hear from her.

"Yes ma'am."

The butler, or whatever he was, turned and left.

When he had gone from the study Winifred said, "Oscar is very protective of me."

"That's a good quality in an employee."

Winifred smiled and said, "He doesn't like you."

"He tell you that?"

"I can see it in his eyes."

"You were going to tell me something while he was gone," I suggested.

"Esau Perry is a fool. He's a gifted mechanic. Anything made from moving parts he can fix. He knows watches and steam engines, cotton gins and hydraulic lifts. But put a deck of cards in his hand, a woman on his lap, or a bottle anywhere within reach and he loses his mind."

I was enjoying the way the tall old maid put together sentences. You could tell by her grasp of the language that she was formidable and in control.

"So what?" I asked.

Winifred's stormy eyes washed over me. Then for a moment the squall subsided.

"Bartholomew is just like his father. Good under the hood but a mess out in the street. He'd be in jail today if I hadn't helped out. Now I think it was a mistake. Maybe he would have done better in prison."

"No ma'am," I said.

Lance Wexler was dubbed with a demigod's name, but Winifred Fine held herself like a real deity. Her high cheekbones and sleek face seemed to bring her eyes to the great heights of heaven.

She considered me and then nodded; maybe I knew more about the pedestrian doings of the world.

"Whatever you say, Mr. Minton. All I know is that Bartholomew has done something that could be very embarrassing to this family. And I want to talk to him before the damage becomes irreversible."

"What damage?"

"That is none of your concern."

"It is if it's illegal and I'm out there up to my neck in it."

"Who said anything about illegal?" she asked.

"Nobody," I said. "But you got all the elements there. Foolish men around wild women, gamblin', liquor, and cars."

Winifred smiled. It was a wonderful thing. Beautiful. She opened her mouth, showed two rows of almost perfect teeth (one on the bottom was missing), and said, "Go to the desk, Mr. Minton, and open the top right drawer. There's a brown envelope there. Take it and go find Bartholomew for me."

The desk was made from some knotty, light-hued wood. The shallow drawer slid open with ease. There were three items inside: an antique dagger with a seven-inch blade, a new Luger pistol, and a light caramel-colored and sealed envelope that was stuffed with some sort of paper.

"What is this?" I asked.

"A small sum," she said. "For your services."

"I didn't come here looking for a job."

"If you are working for Mr. Sweet I want you to remember who the real client is. If you find out anything, a personal report to me will earn you another such envelope."

I shoved the fat letter into my front pocket.

"Uh-huh. One more question, Miss Fine."

She sighed deeply and asked, "Yes?"

"Kit Mitchell."

"What about him?"

"Do you know him?"

"He did some mechanical work for us a while back, two or three months ago, I think. Bartholomew had suggested him."

"You seemed to be upset when I mentioned his name."

"He wasn't a very good worker," she replied coolly. "I should have known better than to take a recommendation from Bartholomew."

I didn't believe a word of what she said, but Winifred L. Fine wasn't the kind of woman you called a liar. Her breeding prohibited any such intimacy.

"Does Bartholomew's problem have anything to do with Kit?"

"No," she said with all the finality of Creation. "Go now, Mr. Minton. Come back when you have knowledge of my nephew."

"Can I get a phone number?"

She pointed with her baby finger to a small stack of cards on the lower left corner of the desk. The card had two lines. The first one read W.L.F. and the second one had her number.

"You can show yourself out," she said.

"What about Oscar?"

"What about him?"

"Isn't he going to bring your malted?"

"I'm allergic to milk products," she said. Then she turned her back on me and stared out upon the stone image of her younger, more vulnerable self.

11

"WHO IS THIS?"

"It's Paris, Ambrosia. Fearless there?"

"He's sleep."

It was two in the afternoon.

"Wake him up for me, will ya? We got to be movin' soon."

"Who do you think you are, tellin' me what to do, Paris Minton?"

"Listen, honey. I know you thought that you'd have him longer than this but playtime is over for a while. Fearless needs me to help out with a problem he's got. It's a big problem, and you would not want him thinkin' that you kept him from me at an important point like the one we at right now."

Love might be light in someone's eyes, but hatred is silent and dark. Ambrosia didn't say a word for a full thirty seconds, and then she put the phone down — hard. She yelled a few well-chosen curses, and then Fearless picked up an extension somewhere in the house.

"Paris?"

"... and tell that skinny-ass mothahfuckah that he bettah not show up at my door to get ya, neither!" Ambrosia yelled on her line. Then she slammed down the receiver in both our ears.

"Yeah, Fearless. It's me."

"You find Kit?"

"Meet me at the Emerald Lounge."

"Why'ont you pick me up?"

"Because Ambrosia said she don't want me there."

"You scared of a woman, Paris?"

"No," I said. "It's just that I'm respecting her wishes."

"I won't let her hurt you."

"Just get over to the bar soon as you can. All right?"

Fearless laughed and hung up the phone.

I leaned forward over my butcher-block table and recounted the five-dollar bills that had been stuffed in the envelope Winifred L. Fine gave me. There were 186 notes. Nine hundred and thirty dollars. Not the millions Milo was talking about, but a pretty big payday for a man who had never earned over two dollars an hour on a regular job.

The name Wexler was still nagging at me. It was as if I had heard it before calling the Bernard Arms. The newspaper was in the trash, the column heading WOMAN FOUND DEAD in plain sight. I remembered that when I thought about the name Wexler it was as though I had read it before. . . . And there it was — Minna Wexler. The corpse of the young woman in Griffith Park. Wexler. Could it be a coincidence?

She had been found by a hobo, Ty Shoreman, who had been living in the park for a few weeks. She was stripped to the waist at the time of her death. Strangled. There were signs that she had been tortured before her demise. I thought about the burns up and down Lance's arm. The hobo was held for questioning and then released.

Wexler.

There were three sharp raps on my front door. I shivered in response.

BOTH WHITE MEN WORE DARK SUITS and frowns. One was going bald and the other had hair nearly down to his eyebrows.

"Paris Minton?"

"Yes, officer?"

"Why you think we're cops?" the hairy one asked.

"Guilty conscience?" his partner chimed.

"How can I help you?" I replied.

"We're looking for a friend of yours," baldy said. "A man named Fearless Jones."

"He ain't here."

"Do you know where we might find him?"

"No sir."

My face went blank. The life drained out of my voice. My arms hung down at my side and I was willing to do anything those policemen wanted — except tell the truth.

"When's the last time you saw him?" the ape-man asked.

I stared out at the sky between their faces, pretending to concentrate. "Maybe four weeks. He's been up north working for a man grows watermelons."

The cop with the advancing hairline took out a small leather notebook and the nub of a yellow pencil. He jotted down something and smiled at me. I remember being surprised that the one with all the hair was also the man in charge. That seemed unfair somehow.

"May we come in, Mr. Minton?" he asked.

"Sure." I stepped backward, pulling the door with me. "Have a seat."

They entered my front room but neither one took me up on the offer to sit. They scanned the room like dog-pack brothers, looking everywhere. The balding cop stepped into the bookstore, checking for surprises or infractions.

"Sorry for the intrusion," the other cop said. "I'm Sergeant Rawlway and this is Officer Morrain."

"Pleased to meet ya."

"Nice place you got here," bald Morrain said from the left aisle. "You sell a lotta books?"

"Yes sir."

"That all?"

"I don't understand you, Officer Morrain."

He walked back into the room and looked down into my eyes.

"Lots of times we find that people down around here set up places that are supposed to sell one thing but really they have some other business."

"Like what?" I asked, simple as a stone.

Morrain smiled and sucked in air through his nostrils.

"Where is this watermelon farm?" Sergeant Rawlway asked.

"Up near Oxnard," I said. "Fearless harvests them for these street salesmen that work all over Watts. Is Fearless in trouble?"

"Why don't you worry about yourself?" Morrain suggested.

"Well, yeah," I said. "Sure."

"When did you say you saw Fearless last?" Rawlway asked.

"About a month . . . almost that."

"Are you good friends?"

"Yeah. Uh-huh. I met Fearless when he was discharged from the service, after the war."

"Has he always been a farmer?"

"No sir. Fearless works at whatever. Day labor, farming, you name it."

"If you're such good friends," Morrain asked, "then why haven't you seen him in so long?"

At that moment I thought about the five-dollar bills on the counter in my kitchen. If the police came across that cache they'd arrest me on suspicion. I could feel the moisture breaking through my pores.

"He, he's been on that watermelon farm, like I told you. I run this store and don't have time to drive up there. And even if I did, Fearless is workin'."

"Where is Fearless?" Rawlway asked again.

"I told you," I said. "I don't know. He was up on that farm. He haven't called me. I guess he's still there."

I was wily but numb. That was my defense against the law. I didn't have the slightest antagonism toward those peace officers. That might come as a surprise to anyone who hasn't had the experience of being a black man in America. I wasn't angry, because we were just actors playing parts written down before any one of us was born. Later on, at the barbershop, I'd laugh about my answers with other black men who had grown up playing dumb under the scrutiny of some other man's law.

"He was seen in the past few days by various witnesses not a mile from your door," hairy Rawlway reported.

"Witnesses?"

"Where is he, Mr. Minton?"

"I'm tellin' you the truth, man. I ain't seen Fearless. I don't know anything about what he's been doin' or about any witnesses either."

"What about Bartholomew Perry?" Rawlway asked.

"I know him to say hi to," I said. "I mean, we ain't friends or nuthin' and I don't even remember the last time I saw him."

"Are he and Fearless friends?"

"Not that I know of."

"I could take you down to the station, Paris," Rawlway said.

"You could, sergeant, but that wouldn't change what I said. I don't know where Fearless is. I don't know Bartholomew Perry more than to tell you his name. I'm in this buildin' here all day sellin' books. That's all."

"And you expect us to believe that you sell books for a living?"

"Why not?"

Morrain stepped back into one of the aisles.

"Who wrote . . . um . . . ," he said, holding a book at arm's length so that he could make out the spine. "Let's see here, oh yeah. Who wrote *Madame Bovary*?"

"Gustave Flaubert."

He picked out another book.

"How about the, *The Mysterious Stranger*?"

"Mark Twain."

"You think you're smart, nigger?"

"I'm just trying to make a living, officer. Fearless is my friend but I haven't seen him. That's all I know."

It was always a tough part to play. They saw themselves as the foremen of the neighborhood. I was a lazy worker, a liar looking to cheat them out of what was their superior's proper due. My job was to make them believe in their picture of me while at the same time showing that today I wasn't shirking or lying or lining my pockets with their boss man's money.

"You remember our names?" Rawlway asked.

"Sergeant Rawlway and Officer Morrain," I said.

"If you hear from this Fearless, call us. Because if we find out you didn't, there's nothing in any of these books that will save your ass from me. You understand?"

"Yes sir."

12

THE EMERALD LOUNGE WAS AN OASIS of sorts in the Negro community. It was run by a Jamaican named Orrin Nye. He had an American wife and three little kids. Orrin only allowed classical music on the record player. Because of this aesthetic only a certain kind of customer frequented the place. Members of the church, especially the choir, older ladies who were scandalized by boogie-woogie and rhythm and blues, pretentious white-collar professionals, and world-weary lovers, muggers, and thieves were the regulars — them and Fearless Jones when he was in love.

Fearless was a killer of men but that didn't keep him from being sappy sometimes. Love made him think about church and church for him was somehow represented by the German masters, especially their arias. And so in those rare moments that he fell for some girl, he would bring her to the lounge. I think it was because he wanted the woman he was with to see, or maybe hear, the contents of his heart.

The last woman he fell for was Brenda Hollings. She was an overweight, nearsighted girl who had come from Tennessee with her parents at the tender age of seventeen. Her parents came out to live with an uncle who owned a Laundromat and needed workers he could trust.

Fearless met Brenda when she was nineteen.

"Paris," he told me, "that there's the woman I want to bear my sons and daughters."

I didn't say anything. She was awkward and not friendly, plain looking by the best light and sharp-tongued to boot. Add those drawbacks to the fact that Fearless had never lived in the same place for more than three months during his entire adult life and one could see why I didn't hold out much hope for his dreams of domestic tranquillity.

But he got a steady job at Douglas Aircraft and rented a nice little cottage on Ninety-second Street. Whenever Brenda would snap at him, he'd hop to and do whatever it was she wanted.

Beautiful women were always throwing themselves at him, but he never gave in to temptation for the six months he and Brenda were engaged. Then one night I got a phone call. I was staying in a rooming house then, on Vernon. That was about a year before I opened my first bookstore.

"Hi, Paris."

"Brenda."

"Is Fearless with you?"

"No. He's probably at his place. Is something wrong?"

"I need to talk to you. Can you come over here?"

"Sure. I guess so. You at your mother's place?"

"No. I got my own apartment now."

I was wary, but I agreed because I thought that Fearless would want me to help his fiancée if she needed it. Brenda gave me an address on McKinley and I was there in less than fifteen minutes.

It was the bottom floor of a three-story apartment building that looked something like an incinerator, with its gaping front doorway and shadows like soot up the walls.

Brenda answered the door and invited me in. It was a neat little place with thick maroon carpeting and powder blue walls. The furniture was simple but it was homey.

"When did you move out from your parents?" I asked after being seated and served a beer.

"I don't know," she said. "Sometime last month, I guess."

"But I thought that you and Fearless . . ." My words trailed off then. The walls began to feel like they were leaning in.

"My old boyfriend from Tennessee, his name is Miller, well . . . he came out to see me," Brenda said.

She was ungainly and lumpy, wore glasses with lenses thicker than Coke-bottle bottoms, but still men swarmed around her like gnats. There are some things about the human animal that I will never understand.

"He wanted me back and I decided to go with him," Brenda was saying.

"Does Fearless know?" I asked.

She shook her head and looked down at the blood-colored floor. "I'm afraid to tell him."

"He's gonna find out sooner or later," I said.

"I was wondering if you could help."

"Me?"

"You're his best friend. He'll need you to be there for him. You know I'm worried that it will break his heart."

Or Miller's spine, I thought.

"I'm sorry, Brenda, but you know how it is. I mean, I don't think Fearless would want me tellin' him that it's over between you two. No ma'am. He wouldn't like that at all."

She tried to convince me, but when she saw that I wasn't going to budge her face hardened and her tone turned surly.

"Well," she said. "If you don't wanna help me, at least you can give me a ride over to the Emerald Lounge. I'll call Fearless and talk to him there."

She made the call. I overheard her saying *baby* this and *honey* that. We drove over to the lounge at about nine-fifteen.

"Paris," Orrin said. "Brenda. Where's Fearless?"

"He's on his way," I said.

We sat down at a small table near the speakers. Beethoven's Seventh Symphony was just beginning and Brenda ordered a grenadine and vodka, the fanciest drink Orrin served. I made do with beer. When the symphony was almost over, and Brenda was on her fifth drink, I started to get worried — I was shelling out the money for her drinks and Fearless had yet to make his appearance.

"I don't want to hurt him," Brenda said sadly.

Tears came to her eyes and she took my hand.

"It's just that my parents made me leave Tennessee because my father hated Miller's father. But I always loved Miller. And now that he's here . . ."

She cried on my shoulder and maintained her grip on my hand. Fearless never showed up. But that wasn't unusual. Time often got away from him. He might have come across a stranded motorist. He might have gotten himself arrested.

I took Brenda back to her apartment and went home myself, wondering where I was going to come up with the money for food that month now that Fearless's ex-fiancée had swallowed down my last twelve dollars.

A week later I was in Marie's Diner because that was the only restaurant in town that let me run up a tab. Fearless came in and sat down across from me. I had decided to stay away from him while he and Brenda worked out their problems. Fearless was as even-tempered as they come, but a broken heart might let his darker side gain control. And Fearless Jones's dark side was a terrible thing.

"Hey, Fearless," I said. "How's it goin'?"

He was wearing a black T-shirt, black trousers, and black cloth shoes. Looking at him, you might have thought he was a weak sister being so thin. But, as I've already said, I had never met a stronger man in my life.

He took out a pink envelope and handed it to me.

I opened the letter already knowing, or at least thinking I knew, what it would say.

Dear Fearless:

I do not want to write these words but there is no other way. I cannot look you in the face and tell you the terrible thing that I have done. You are a good and sweet man and I am no kind of woman for you. I have been with another man while wearing your engagement ring. I have slept with him. Paris came to

me. He took me to the Emerald Lounge and bought me drinks,
saying that we were celebrating my marriage. But we got so
drunk that when he took me home I brought him inside to
make some coffee. I did not mean to sleep with him. I do not
think he meant it either. And maybe I would not ever have said
about it, but now I think I am pregnant and I could not be
with you not knowing if it was your child we was raising. I am
going back down to Tennessee now.

I am sorry.

I will always love you,
Brenda

Upon finishing the letter I was certain that I wouldn't live to
walk out of Marie's. Fearless would kill me with his bare hands
before I could rise.

I put the letter on the table and looked Fearless in the eye.
I wanted to say something but the fear Brenda's letter instilled
made me mute.

"I went to Orrin's," Fearless said.

I made a choking sound and held up my left hand.

"What were you doin' there, Paris?"

"She tricked me, man. She said that she wanted me to take her
to meet you over there. I thought you were coming but, but you
didn't."

"And then you took her home?"

"All I did was wait to see that she got in the door. I swear. I
swear."

Fearless's face was drawn. He grabbed my left forearm. The
pain shot up into my shoulder. I didn't make a move though. I
just stared into his intense eyes.

As the seconds passed my arm went numb. Fearless blinked and then a tear escaped. He let me go and hung his head.

"I know," he said. "I know you wouldn't do me like that. And even if you would, you wouldn't go to my favorite place. No. I figure there's somethin' down there in Tennessee she wants. An' she just point me at you 'cause she worried I'ma mess it up for her."

"Fearless —"

"You don't have to say nuthin', Paris. I know you know sumpin', but that's okay. If she wanna end this with a lie then I'll let her. 'Cause the only thing that matter is that she don't want me."

He looked up at me and smiled then. It was a deep, hurting smile. After shedding that tear his life would go on. Before the bruise on my arm was gone he had buried his pain.

13

THE FIFTH SYMPHONY WAS PLAYING when I entered the Emerald Lounge that afternoon. Fearless sat at the same table where Brenda had cried on my shoulder. His face was tilted upward, taking in the deep percussion of that long-ago music. I was sure that he was thinking about Brenda.

"Fearless."

"Paris."

I sat down and he brought his gaze back down to earth.

"We got deep trouble," I said.

"Let's hear it."

I told him about Hercules Wexler first. Then I went into Bartholomew Perry, Milo Sweet, and Winifred L. Fine. After that I told him about the cops' visit, and finally I mentioned the dead woman in the park who had the same last name as Hercules.

"Damn, Paris. What's it all about?"

"I don't know. I mean, some parts make sense. BB and his father sell used cars, and so did the Wexlers, at least Hercules. Winifred must have heard something, and so she's looking for BB. The cops lookin' for Bartholomew because of Minna Wexler."

"Why you say that?"

"What?"

"About BB and the dead white girl."

"You ever see BB when he wasn't with a girl either white or look like she was?" I asked.

"No . . . but that don't mean he was with her."

"I'd lay odds that he was, though."

"But even so, what's that got to do with me?" Fearless asked.

"Kit bought his used trucks hot from BB. I got that from Milo, who heard it from that man lookin' for you — Timmerman. Kit also knew Hercules, and he'd been to a rich black woman's house. That woman is BB's auntie and she's the one hired Milo in the first place."

"But does that tell us why the cops are after me?"

"You looked for Kit. Maybe somebody mentioned it somewhere along the way when them cops was lookin'."

"Damn, Paris. You know I have broke the law a time or two and the cops never got me. Wouldn't be a kick in the head if I went down for somethin' I don't even know about?"

"Did Kit have any partners in the business?" I asked. "I mean, leasin' the land and gettin' those trucks must'a cost somethin'."

"Maybe Maynard'd know."

"That's the guy used to ride Kit in?"

"Uh-huh. He might know sumpin' 'bout that Hercules too."

"I don't know, Fearless. If he didn't tell you I don't see why he'd tell Maynard. Were they good friends?"

"Not really."

"What about that big payday Kit was braggin' on?" I asked. "Did he say anything more about that?"

Fearless pulled his lips into his mouth and shook his head.

I sat back then, letting the brass horns wash over my recent memories. I remembered being scared awake by Fearless and then by the white man.

"And then there's Teddy Timmerman," I said.

"What about him?"

"Milo is the one that sent him after you. So it just stands to reason that Milo knows more about you than you do."

"So then we got to go ask Milo some hard questions," Fearless said.

"But he ain't gonna open up unless we have the right words."

"What's them, Paris?"

"First we got to get a little closer to BB. Best way to do that is to go out and see Esau."

"Who's that?" Fearless asked.

"That's BB's father. He's the man owns that used car lot down near Compton."

"Your car or mine?" Fearless asked me.

"You got a car now?"

"I took Ambrosia's Chrysler."

"I thought she was mad at you."

"No, Paris, she's mad at *you*." Fearless grinned.

"Let's each of us drive," I said. "'Cause if the cops drop down on you, at least I'll be free to get you out."

"Okay."

"So let's get goin'," I said.

"Hold up, Paris. Ludwig is playin'. Might as well let him finish the number."

So we sat through the movements of Beethoven's Fifth in Watts, California, 1955. While listening I smiled thinking about the balding Officer Morrain. If he had come into the lounge, he would have suspected it as a front for some devilment because of that music. That's why the police had so much trouble with the Negro community: they refused to see us as we appeared right there before their eyes.

ON THE DRIVE OVER I WAS BEHIND A BEAT-UP DODGE that didn't have much pickup. The Dodge pulled out as the light turned amber, entering the intersection. The driver obviously thought he could make it before the crossing traffic made its move. Maybe he was used to driving a car with more pickup. But an oncoming Pontiac was already into a left turn and a Ford had come to the light moving fast. Between those two automobiles the Dodge was bent nearly into an L. I stopped but a few pedestrians got to the accident first. They dragged the body of the driver out and then his passenger, a middle-aged white woman. Blood covered her face and she was speaking rapidly.

I wanted to help but the sight of blood repelled me. I don't have a strong stomach or a brave heart. One of the reasons I remained friends with Fearless was that he never looked down on me for being scared.

"Scared as you are," he'd tell me, "you still get up every day just like men think they brave."

I pulled up to the curb a block from the accident to compose myself. Sirens were wailing from somewhere far off. People streamed toward the scene of the crash. I sat in the car massaging my temples and thinking of reasons that Kit Mitchell would have easy access to a white car salesman's penthouse. I also wondered how a car salesman, regardless of his race, could afford such a nice house.

ESAU HAD AN UNPAVED LOT down on a dirt street off of Aprilla in the county. There was no sign or flagpole to mark it. There wasn't even a fence, just twenty or so cars parked every which way, with an unpainted hut set somewhere near the middle.

When I got there Fearless was already at the hut, talking to Esau.

"Hey, Paris," he hailed. "What took you?"

"Mr. Perry," I said. I held out my hand to the elder man. "My name's Paris Minton."

"What's up, Mr. Minton? Your friend Fearless said that you wanted to talk to me. You wanna buy a car?"

"No sir. I've been hired by your ex-sister-in-law, Miss Winifred L. Fine, to locate your son, and I was wondering why she didn't ask you." I decided on the direct approach partly because I didn't trust anyone I was dealing with and partly because I liked the way Esau looked.

He had shiny black skin and tight eyes. His hands were thick but he was a lightweight. At sixty he probably could wear the same pants he put on when he was a twenty-year-old. He wore a gray pair of coveralls that had an emblem for the defunct Oklahoma Star Oil Company over the left breast. He was the kind of man who lived in my New Iberia neighborhood in

Louisiana; the kind of man who could make a living with just two sticks and a cupful of spit.

"She hired you to find him, huh?" Esau said. "She tell you why?"

"No sir, she didn't. And so I wanted to make sure that there wasn't some bad blood between the two families that I was gettin' mixed up with."

"Well," Esau said. "Winnie never liked me too much. When her sister and me got married she refused to come to the wedding. Then, after Honey left me and went back to Winnie, they didn't even tell me she was sick until after she died."

"Your wife died and they didn't even tell you about it?" Fearless asked.

"By that time we was already divorced. Honey had moved back with Winnie and I kept BB."

"Why would Miss Fine want to see Bartholomew now?"

"She always liked the boy. More because he was blood than anything he did, I think. Every now and then they'd get together at her place out in the desert. She got what she call a cabin outside of A Thousand Palms."

"But you've never seen her?" I asked.

"She used to invite me and BB for a Thanksgivin' dinner. I'd go when BB was a boy, for family, you know. But now he's grown I stay home." Esau shrugged and pulled a pack of cigarettes from the pocket of a T-shirt under his coveralls. "Want one?"

Fearless shook his head but I accepted the cigarette, and the light that came after.

"But you're not bothered that she hired me to look for him?"

"Naw. She wanna find him, that's okay by me."

"Why didn't she just call you?"

"She did. At least that Oscar did."

"When?"

"Week ago. 'Bout that. Maybe eight days."

"And what you tell him?"

"That I don't know where BB is. He met some girl a few months ago. They go off together all the time. The two of 'em."

"White girl?" I asked.

"I see you know my Bartholomew."

"You know her name?"

"Me an' BB didn't talk all that much about his personal life. I didn't ask an' he didn't say."

"You know somebody who might know?" I asked.

"Them peoples down at Hoochie's might could know," Esau speculated.

"That place on Hoover?" I asked, just to be sure. "The dance club?"

Esau nodded.

"Did he ever say anything about a man named Kit Mitchell?"

"No," Esau said, a little too fast and a little too sure.

"You got any cars for fifty bucks, Mr. Perry?" Fearless asked.

"Couple'a Fords like your friend's the cheapest I got. Lowest price is two twenty-five, though."

"Lemme think about that for a while." Fearless put his hand on my shoulder then and I nodded.

"Guess it's time to go."

"Mr. Minton," Esau said.

"Yes sir?"

"Tell BB I'd like to talk to him before he sees Winifred. Tell him, well, just tell him that I'd like to talk."

14

"WHAT YOU THINK ABOUT MR. PERRY?" I asked Fearless.

We were a few blocks away at a small park that was like an island at the intersection of Slater Avenue and 127th Street. There was a picnic table with the benches attached under a shady oak tree. The grass was dead. One lone sparrow eyed us sidewise from the nearest bough. He was waiting for a crumb to drop and so was I.

"He's lyin' about Kit."

"You sure'a that?"

"No question there."

Fearless Jones could have been Buck Rogers's lie detector. He could tell if someone was lying even if he didn't understand the language they spoke.

"What about the rest?" I asked.

"Cain't tell. But I'm sure that he wants to talk to BB. He wants to talk to him bad."

I could read Esau for myself. Still it was good to have Fearless confirm my conclusions. But what difference did it make? I could go out looking for BB, but there was no promise that I would find him. And even if I did find him, it was a dangerous game turning a man over to somebody with the police breathing down your neck. If I confronted him, Milo would lie, and so would the white man he sent to my house to find Fearless.

I shared these pessimistic thoughts with my friend.

He took it all in and nodded.

"Then maybe I better go down to them cops questioned you," he said.

"Turn yourself in?"

"Why not? They gonna get me sooner or later — that is, unless I skip town. And you know that little taste of Ambrosia reminded me of just how sweet she is."

"You don't know why they after you, Fearless. They might could put you in jail for months."

"I didn't do nuthin' except sit out with those gourds in Oxnard for weeks. They mad, but what they gonna charge me wit'? Why shouldn't I go?"

"Because we don't know what they want."

"And we ain't gonna know unless I turn myself in." Fearless grinned at me. I knew that grin. It said, *Sometimes you have to be a fool if you want to make it in this world.*

I knew that I couldn't talk Fearless out of his decision, so I asked, "What should I do?"

"Go on home and wait for my one phone call," he said. "It may not come for a while, but you be there and I'll get what we need."

• • •

WE SEPARATED THERE. Me going back to my bookshop and Fearless following his name.

My store was hot from the brutal summer sun beating down on it. I opened the front door to let a breeze bring the temperature down into the eighties. I was too jumpy even to read, so I picked up a folio of photographs taken by the New York photographer Weegee. I took this to the front room and sat there perusing the strange and revealing images of a New York that few tourists ever saw, even though it was right there under their toes and noses. Weegee treated the whole city as if it were his backyard. I imagined that he knew ten thousand people by name and that they were so familiar with him that they never had their guard up against his lenses. He roamed from Park Avenue to Harlem with his camera, mostly at night, getting behind all of the lies we tell and showing just how ugly people can be when no one else is around.

"Hello?"

If I could have jumped out of my skin I would have. As it was, I leapt out of the chair and threw out my hands, letting the book fly somewhere back into the store.

"What!" I shouted.

It took a few seconds for me to focus on the young woman framed inside the gray rectangle of the screen door.

If she had a gun you'd be dead right now. If she had a gun you'd be dead right now. Those words repeated themselves over and over in my mind. My heart was thumping. I was rubbing both thumbs against my fingertips, trying to look normal.

The Negro woman smiled.

"I didn't mean to sneak up on you like that," she said. "I thought that you must have heard me coming up the stairs."

"No." It was the only syllable I could manage without stumbling over my tongue.

"Can I come in?"

"Come on." I was getting better.

She tried the screen door, but it was latched. Did I think that I could keep someone from getting at me with a slender latch and a paper-thin screen?

"Let me," I said.

She was wearing a tan dress with a pink scarf. At first it looked kind of like a uniform, but on inspection you could see that the material of both articles was of a finer make than any employer or service would spend. She carried a woven straw purse. This too was a higher quality than it at first seemed.

"Are you Paris Minton?"

She had medium brown skin and eyes a brown so light that they were disconcerting. Those orbs seemed to belong not simply to some other race but to a whole other species of animal.

"Are you?" she asked again.

"Who are you?"

"Leora. Leora Hartman."

"Where's Son?"

"He's with his great-uncle," she said, at once answering my question and telling me that my secret knowledge wasn't of the least concern to her.

"Would that be Kit's uncle or yours?"

"Son is not related to Kit Mitchell."

We were still standing in the doorway. Leora's figure was slight but her bones weren't thin or fragile. She wore tan shoes that were exactly the same hue as her dress.

"Can I have a seat?"

"Sure. Why not?"

We sat across from each other. She put her knees together and let them recline to the side. Her calf was very presentable. She was as composed and elegant as the wife of a diplomat, except for those eyes; they were wild and fearful, watching for the slightest aggression.

"Fearless tell you about me?" I asked.

"He said if I needed to get in touch with him that I should come here."

"Hot day, huh?" I asked this to put her off some, but it didn't seem to work, at least not at first.

"Yes it is," she said. "But at least it's dry. It's the humidity I can't stand."

I smiled and nodded but didn't say anything.

"Aren't you going to ask me why I'm here?" she asked, finally.

"You like my store?" I replied.

She stood up and walked down the right aisle. Looking over the shorter center shelf to the books on the wall, she said, "I see you have a lot of the Balzac oeuvre."

"Eighty-one of his books," I said, coming up next to her. "I got them from a woman in Tarzana. She advertised in a book-buyers' newsletter I subscribe to."

"It really is a lovely store." She looked around a bit more.

"Thanks," I said.

"Do you have a science section?"

"Down there, in the far corner."

Our eyes locked on each other.

"I'm very interested in physics."

"Really? What kind?"

"Theoretical. Theoretical physics, theology, and theater. My mother always says that it's only the first three letters that get to me." Her laugh was nice.

"Why'd you lie to Fearless?"

"It was the only way I could think of to be sure that he'd look for Kit for me."

"What do you want with Kit Mitchell?"

Leora walked back to the front, reclaiming her seat and her composure.

I followed.

"Where is Fearless?" she asked.

"In jail."

"What for?" She didn't even blink.

"I don't even know. Do you?"

This time she didn't respond.

"Two cops, Morrain and Rawlway, were after him. So he turned himself in. They were looking for a young man named Bartholomew Perry." I was wondering if she knew BB too.

There was a momentary tightening of Leora's face.

"Maybe you know what those cops wanted," I suggested.

"No. Why would I?"

"I don't know. Why are you here?"

"Fearless gave me an address for Kit. I went there but they said that he skipped out without paying the rent."

"Really? Did they have any idea where he got to?"

"No. When a man skips out on the rent he usually doesn't leave a forwarding address."

Even though she had the poise of a woman in her thirties, I figured that Leora was twenty-five at most. Her skin was flawless without the help of makeup and she had hands that could have belonged to a child.

"So what does Fearless have to do with all that?"

"I need him, to help me find Kit."

"Why?"

"It's personal."

"So's havin' the cops on your ass because some girl lied and put you on a trail got you locked up in a six-foot cell."

"I'm sorry if I got Mr. Jones in trouble. I didn't mean to do that. But I have to find Kit Mitchell."

"Why?"

"I can't tell you that." Leora Hartman stood up. She wanted to walk out but had nowhere else to go. "What did they arrest Mr. Jones for?"

"Nothing, as far as I can tell. Maybe it's just questions they need to ask. Like why was he looking for Kit Mitchell."

"Kit was doing business with someone. A man named BB," Leora said.

"Bartholomew Perry," I said, nodding and looking for deception.

"Oh. Is that what it stands for? You already seem to know everything I can tell you."

"What I don't know could fill the Library of Congress."

Leora smiled.

"This BB and Kit have gotten into something and I need to tell them to stop," she said. "That's the truth."

"What are they doing?"

"I can't tell you about that, I can't. Only it's something they've stolen and . . . and beyond that it's private."

"I can't help you if I don't know what it is you're looking for."

"I don't know you, Mr. Minton. I feel bad about your friend, and I want you to understand that I had a reason to lie, an important reason. But I can't trust you. You can understand that."

I understood, but I couldn't just let it go. Fearless was my friend.

"Fearless said that Kit had been bragging that he was gonna bring in a whole truckload'a money over some big deal. That was just before he disappeared. Is this thing that him and BB stole worth all that?"

"I don't see how."

"Do you know a man named Lawrence Wexler?" I asked.

"No."

"Any Wexlers?"

"No. Why are you asking me these questions? Do you know where Kit Mitchell is?"

"Why aren't you asking about where BB is?"

"I don't know anything about him but his name. It's Kit Mitchell who stole . . ." She stopped before revealing the secret.

"What's it worth to you if I try and find out?"

"I don't have much money, Mr. Minton."

"You could'a fooled me. Those fine clothes. Straw bag with what looks like real gold ties on the handle. And the thing cost the most, that classical education. There's some money somewhere."

"On my back and in my head maybe," she said. "But my wallet is empty."

"That's too bad," I said. "Mine is too. But I wish you luck."

Leora was surprised by my refusal. Her gentle ways and poise had gotten her a long way in life.

She turned to the door.

"If you give me a number I'll tell Fearless you were here. He's got more free time than I do."

"By the time he gets out of jail I will already have found out what I need to know," she said. "Either that or I'll be beyond help."

15 AFTER LEORA LEFT the only thing I had to do was wait for Fearless's call. I didn't know how long that would be because I had no idea of the particular crime they were investigating. It could have been anything from grand theft to murder.

I imagined that Fearless was locked in a room with men who asked questions punctuated by fists and blackjacks, but still I wasn't worried about him. Fearless had lived the life of a soldier since before he joined the armed forces. He was a one-man army who did his duty. And when the enemy had done their worst he would walk away with no anger in his heart because he would have known that he had won in spite of their weapons and torments.

Fearless rarely bragged about his courage. The things I knew about him had come from long nights of heavy drinking and lots of questions on my part.

One night he told me about how a gang of men had jumped him and brought him to an old abandoned barn outside of Fayetteville, Louisiana. He was sixteen and they were looking for his auntie's boyfriend, who, they said, had stolen a man's watch.

"'Turn him ovah, boy,' the main man told me," Fearless had said. "'Turn him ovah or I will mash your face in like a sack'a mud.'

"'No sir,' I tells him," Fearless said in the words of the sixteen-year-old boy. "'My Auntie Mar wouldn't want me puttin' no drunks on her man.'"

"'Who you callin' drunk?' the main man, his name was Arthur, shout. An' you know, Paris, I wasn't even afraid even way back then. I knew I was in trouble. I thought I might be dead. But there was no way to turn. Arthur slapped me hard enough to knock some other boy down. I knew right then I was gonna get hurt. And it made me mad that them men would pick on a child. So I hit Arthur on his nose and then dived down and rolled. I got a hold on a timber and hefted it. I was swinging like Babe Ruth in that small space. Two of the men got knocked out and Arthur and the rest got away."

"What they do to your auntie's boyfriend?"

"They were so embarrassed by bein' beat up by a child that they forgot that two-dollar watch and stayed outta my whole family's way."

Fearless wasn't overly proud of his strength or his courage. They were just things to him. He was like some mythological deity that had come down to earth to learn about mortals. Maybe that's why I stayed friends with him even though he was always in some kind of trouble. Because being friends with him was like having one of God's second cousins as a pal.

• • •

AT SIX I WENT DOWN TO THE CORNER and bought a small bottle of French brandy, a brand they stocked just for me. It cost four ninety-five even way back then, but it was worth it. I didn't drink hard liquor all that much, but when I did I wanted it to be good. I didn't want any day-old wine, or scotch that smelled like a doctor's office.

I sipped my brandy along with a supper of sliced apples with wedges of cheddar and blue cheese from my ice chest. I had never been to France. And maybe those Frenchmen never heard of drinking brandy with a meal, but that was close enough for me. Maybe I'd never get on a steamship and sail to Europe, and maybe I'd never know the elegance of a fine hotel room on the Seine, but at least I could imagine it in my bookstore. At least I could read about the world and conjure up a feeling of being far away and safe.

Since I was a child books have been my getaway. Even the few times I've spent in jail were made bearable by Conrad, Cooper, and Clemens. I could hear the soft lapping at the banks of the Mississippi or ride the hill-high waves of the South Pacific under a golden moon shining behind long gray clouds. I could pretend to be the great philosopher Aristotle categorizing the world subject by subject, laying out the basis for all knowledge for the next twenty-five hundred years.

Literature came to my aid even when I had to face the hard reality of racism. Like when the bank turned me down for a small improvement loan.

"We don't give improvement loans," the bank officer Laird Sinclair had told me.

"But Ben Sideman said that you just gave him a loan to repave the alley at the side of his building," I said.

"But he *owns* a driveway."

"I own my store."

"You do?" Laird said. He looked down at my folder, maybe for the first time, and added, "But you still owe the balance of your mortgage."

"Everybody owes the balance, man," I said. "But I got eight thousand in equity."

Laird smiled and shook his head.

"It's more complicated than that, Mr. Minton," he said. "The bank has to consider many different factors before making a loan decision."

"Like what?"

"For instance. Are you married?"

"No."

"There," he said, as if I had proved a point for him. "A single man is a bad risk."

"Ben Sideman ain't married either," I said.

"Mr. Sideman has nothing to do with your application."

"I don't see why. Ben's got a third mortgage on his place and he don't have anywhere near the equity I do. He needed to fix his driveway for customers to be able to park. I need to paint my store for it to be more attractive to my customers."

"I have another appointment, Mr. Minton," Laird said.

I went home and reread thirty of the Simple stories by Langston Hughes as they were chronicled in back issues of the *Chicago Defender,* which I kept in a trunk in my bedroom. Simple's view of the world was just what I needed to laugh off the bile that banker filled me with. Jesse B. Semple never accepted the outrageous lies that were foisted upon him, and he didn't have a pot or a bookstore.

DRINKING MY BRANDY, THINKING ABOUT MY FRIEND and the banker named Laird, I fell into a doze on my bed.

In the dream I walked up to a man at a workstation on a vast production line that had thousands of workers busily laboring on either side. The conveyor belt was so long that I couldn't see an end in either direction.

"Hello, Paris," the worker said to me.

"Hi," I said.

"My name is," he said, and then he added something, but I couldn't hear the name over the roar of the machinery around us.

"What did you say?"

"I said," the worker replied, and then he added something I didn't understand.

"What are we supposed to be doing here?" I asked then.

On the conveyor belt were oddly shaped mechanisms made from all kinds of metals, wood, cloth, and paper. Every mechanism was unique. They were obviously pieces of larger, insane machines. The workers moved the devices as they passed without adding anything or making any substantial change to their structure.

The nameless worker was looking at the line too. He was smiling.

"What are we building?" I asked him.

"Nothing," he said.

"Nothing?"

"That's right. You see, this production line has been growing for the last few years because the war is over and all the veterans need a place to work. It's so long that it crosses over the river into the next state, goes north for Lord knows how many miles, and then crosses back over and down to here."

"Past us again?" I asked.

"Yeah."

"So all of these things just go round and round?"

"No. Uh-uh."

"Where do they go, then?"

"Here and there along the way there's checkers," the worker said.

"Checking for what?"

"To see if any of the" — he said a word that stood for the gadgets on the conveyor belt, but I couldn't make it out — "have gone bad. And if they have, then they throw that" — he said the word again — "into the discard bin."

"But that's a waste of time."

"For them," the worker agreed.

"But not for you because you have a job?" I asked.

"Well," the worker said, "that's part of it. I mean, it's not much pay but it's enough for about a half of my expenses. But I live on less, because after the checkers throw out the" — that word again — "I go and pick 'em up and take 'em back to my place."

"But what use are they?"

"None," he said, "right now. But later on, when they run outta stuff to put on the production line, they gonna have to come to me to buy all them that I took home. That's when I'm gonna be rich."

I started laughing then. I laughed so hard that I fell down on one knee. Workers started turning around to look at me. And even though I was laughing, at the same time I was in mortal fear that I'd lose my job.

A bell rang. It was a long, monotonous ring that seemed to be an omen of great danger.

"What's that?" I asked the nameless worker.

"Shift change," he said. "Shift, shift, shift."

I ANSWERED THE PHONE as if I had never been asleep.

"Yes?"

"That you, Paris?" Fearless asked.

"What time is it?"

"Mornin' sometime, but I don't know when exactly."

I was fully dressed. The empty bottle of brandy was on the stool I used for a night table. I could see the last of the morning stars through the one window set in the middle of my slanted roof.

"You still in jail?" I asked.

"Yeah, man."

"They still questioning you?"

"No. They gave up a few hours ago, but they still holdin' me on a parking ticket fine I never paid. I ain't got it."

I took a deep breath. The fear and laughter of the dream still crowded my chest.

"Let me find my shoes and I'll be right down there," I said. "You at the Seventy-seventh?"

"Yes sir, Mr. Minton. I sure am."

I put the phone back in the cradle and sat up. That's when the brandy made its return. My head started spinning and I had to lie back on the bed. The dizziness subsided, but then the roof began a slow turn to the right. When I closed my eyes I could feel the bed shifting under me.

Shift. The word echoed in my mind. I remembered the production line and the would-be entrepreneur's chant.

The phone rang again. How long had it been since Fearless called?

"Hello," I said, the bed moving under me like a river under a lily pad.

"Paris," a bail bondsman I knew said.

"Good mornin', Mr. Sweet. I was just thinkin' about you. It wasn't a kind thought. No sir. It was more like why do you wanna be messin' with me an' Fearless and here we supposed to be friends?" The words flowed out of my mouth just like me going down that river.

"I'm sorry, Paris."

I opened my eyes. Now it was my thoughts' turn to take a spin. Milo never apologized unless he wanted something. Never. If he bumped into you and you stumbled and fell, he'd more likely say, *You shoulda got out my way,* than to proffer an apology. That's because Milo had been a lawyer, and all lawyers know that an apology is tantamount to an admission of guilt. And admitting guilt was the only cardinal sin in the lawyer's bible.

I made it once more to a sitting position. If I sat sideways, with my head down below my shoulders, the room stopped revolving and merely shook.

"What is it, Milo?"

"What is what?" he asked.

"Don't fool with me, man. It's too early and I'm way too hung over to be played with."

"I made a mistake, Paris," Milo said. "I should have shared what I knew about Miss Fine with you."

"You scarin' me, Milo man."

"I'm tryin' to apologize."

"Spit it out, brother," I said. "I got to go get Fearless out of jail."

"What's he in jail for?"

"What all people are in jail for — not havin' the money it takes to keep from gettin' there in the first place."

"Will you come to the office after you get him?"

"What for?"

"I got a phone call last night that disturbed me," he said.

"From who?"

"Just come on over, Paris. I'll pay you."

"All right," I said.

It wasn't the money he offered but the fact that he offered it that made me acquiesce to his request. If Milo offered to put up cash, the situation had to be dire indeed.

I hung up the phone and propelled myself into a standing position. I found that the trick here was also in the shoulders; if I kept shifting them I could stay upright.

I wanted to go back to bed, to take off my clothes, and put my head under the covers. But I knew that was a fool's move. Things were happening without my knowledge or control, and people knew where I lived. Two people named Wexler were dead, and lawyers were calling me before banking hours to admit their guilt.

I went to the stairs even though I believed there was a good chance I'd stumble on tangled feet and break my neck for the effort.

IT WASN'T YET SIX O'CLOCK. Fearless was oblivious of the time. They'd probably questioned him all night. They might have beaten him. He called so early because time for him was just one long day. Milo called because he was scared. He'd probably been up all night fretting over the grief that only greed can bring on a man.

Thinking about Milo brought up a question. How was it that he had involved himself in a problem that Fearless stumbled into on his own? What did Milo have to do with Kit Mitchell? I took a sip of reheated coffee, hoping that the answer was in my sober mind.

There came a knock on the door.

The chill reentered my intestines. The last four times someone had come to my front door my problems had gotten worse. A dog would have stayed away from that trouble after the first time. A stupid dog would have waited for the second bane to start avoiding distress.

I was fully dressed and shod, so I stepped quietly through the screen door at the back of my house. I tiptoed down the wood stairs, hopped the fence into the alley, and ran like a six-year-old.

I didn't slow down for three blocks.

Maybe it was childish to run away from my own home but, I reasoned, who but Trouble could be knocking at my door that early in the morning? Like I said before, I'm a small man. I've been chased, caught, and beaten by big-boned women.

"Runnin' ain't a bad thing, baby," my mother used to tell me. "When you're dead you'll wish you had the legs for it."

THE SUN WASN'T UP and there was still a chill in the desert air. There's a system of alleyways in L.A. that make the streets in some southern towns look like country paths. The alley behind my building was wide and well paved, and it went on for twelve city blocks. There were no rats or cats, not even much trash strewn about. Just one long strip of asphalt with a ribbon of concrete down the middle, a permanent divider line.

After my initial sprint I slowed to a walk. A few streets down from there and I even began to feel safe. Whoever it was at my house had probably gone away. And even if they broke in, there was nothing to steal but books. (One of the books on my bedroom shelf had been hollowed out. That's where I put Miss Fine's five-dollar bills.) For a moment I worried about the fate of my last bookstore. The store owner next door burned me down to get the lot. That had been the worst experience of my life. After a little time fretting I stopped worrying about it. Lightning couldn't strike twice, not even on my unlucky head.

17

"WHAT YOU SAY THAT NAME WAS AGAIN?" the desk sergeant at the Seventy-seventh Street Precinct asked.

I had walked there. It wasn't very far, and being a pedestrian made me feel secure. My enemies, if they were out looking for me, would drive past a man on foot without a second glance.

"Tristan Jones," I said to the sergeant.

"Um, let me see here," the portly, bespectacled white man said as he thumbed through an oversized logbook on his side of the counter. "Oh I see. He owes a big fine, a very big fine."

The sergeant closed the book and reached for the phone. He picked up the receiver, dialed a number, and waited for someone to answer.

"Hello, Jerry?" the sergeant said. "Yeah, it's Rick. What you think about that Barbette, huh? Damn, I didn't think she'd really do it but Frank said that she's wild. . . . Uh-huh. . . . Yeah."

I scratched my ear and waited patiently. Being a cop wasn't a business. He didn't have to make sure the customer was happy. If he wanted to say hello to the jailer before getting my friend, that was his prerogative.

The story he told was long and one-sided because I couldn't hear the parts that the man on the other end of the line added. The gist of it was that this woman, Barbette, had made a wager that she would accompany a group of them to one of their friends' apartment buck naked. She came in and visited with them just as if she were fully clothed. She hadn't gotten embarrassed until a guy came over with his girlfriend.

"Can you imagine that?" Sergeant Rick said. "She didn't mind us seein' her titties and bush but another woman made her shy."

I must have shifted or something, because Rick noticed me again.

"Hold on, Jerry," he said into the phone, and then, "Can I help you?" he asked as if we had never met.

"Tristan Jones," I said.

"I told you he's bein' held over for a big fine he owes."

"How much is it?"

"Why?"

"Because I'd like to pay it and get my friend out of jail."

"I have to call you back, Jerry," Sergeant Rick said. Then he hung up.

Sighing heavily, he reopened the logbook. After turning pages back and forth half a dozen times, he said, "Yeah, yeah. That's what I thought. It's ninety-eight dollars and forty-seven cents."

He slammed the book shut and actually reached for the phone again.

"Do you have change?" I asked, reaching for my wallet.

Sergeant Rick took off his glasses then. His eyes had looked small behind the lenses, but they shrank to almost nothing without the magnifying effect.

"Change for what?"

"Hundred-dollar bill."

I kept the folded bill behind a sepia-tone photograph of my mother. I carried it around with me because I promised myself when I was a child that once I had enough money I'd always have a hundred bill just like a gambler my uncle once knew named Diamond Blackie.

Sergeant Rick held the tender up to the light, rubbed it between his fingers, turned it over and over. He did everything but lick Mr. Franklin's face.

"Where'd you get this?" he asked.

"From the bank."

"It's only seven-fifteen, son."

Fearless would have bridled under that insult. He might have even resorted to violence. But I'm a different sort of man. I found his reaction funny. The only problem I had was keeping the smile off my face.

"I'm a businessman, officer. I find that it is at times imperative that I have a certain amount of cash on hand to meet incidental costs. My associate, Tristan Jones, is aware of this fact, and he called upon me to do him this service. So I appear here before you to meet his debt and obtain his freedom."

Sergeant Rick looked at me as if I had just walked off the

moon. He must have realized that if he had heard my voice and words over the phone he would have thought I was an educated white man. He was stunned, but he had a good comeback.

"I thought you said you got this bill from the bank."

"Originally," I said. "I took this bill from my branch three weeks ago, the last time I found it necessary to use my incidental fund."

"And what was that?" he asked. "Another jailbird?"

"That was the library of a woman who was moving to Seattle. She specialized in French literature, translated of course."

Sergeant Rick stared at me a moment. I began to worry that I'd gone too far. If he was a sensitive man, he might feel insulted by my palaver. His tiny eyes got still smaller and his cheeks quivered slightly. I was trying to think of some way to tone down his anger when he began to laugh.

He laughed long and hard, leaning forward on the ledge before him. Then he sat down and leaned way back in his swivel chair.

"Oh, that was a good one," he said. "You're good, son. Real good."

He stood up again.

"What's your name?"

"Paris Minton."

Hearing this brought on another round of laughter.

"Okay," he said. "Whatever it is. I don't have change, but if that's all right I'll go get your *associate*."

"Thank you, officer. That will be fine."

The cop went through a door down to his left, and I went to a worn oak bench to sit and wait.

The station was a good size. At the front door sat a desk where another policeman had asked me to explain my business. He had sent me to the counter sergeant. Two other Negro men were sitting on the bench with me. They were both young and surly. Neither one had a word to spare, and that suited me fine.

After fifteen minutes Fearless and Sergeant Rick came from some other quarter of the station. I didn't see the door they came out of. I just turned and there was my friend's smiling face.

"This him?" the cop asked me.

"Yes sir."

"Go on, then."

I put out my hand to shake but Rick turned away.

FIVE MINUTES LATER we were in Ambrosia's gold Chrysler, headed for Milo's office.

"You might have to pay that fine again one day," I said to Fearless. He was at the wheel.

"How come you say that, Paris? Didn't you just pay it?"

"Yeah, but that cop didn't give me no receipt. He might'a just pocketed my hundred."

Fearless smiled.

"You always there when I need it, Paris. Don't you think I'ma forget that."

"I'll tell you what," I said. "The next time you need help, remember how I helped you this time and then forget to come and see me."

Fearless had a big laugh for a slender man.

"What did they want?" I asked.

"To know 'bout them white people. Did I know Minna Wexler or a colored boyfriend she'd been runnin' wit'? Did I know why she was going to meet with Kit Mitchell the day she disappeared? I played dumb and they kept on askin' questions. It was like that all night. One time I fooled around and gave my name, rank, and serial number. The bald-headed one acted like he wanted to hit me, but his boss got the joke and laughed."

"Why were they looking for to question you?" I asked.

"I thought it was because I was lookin' for Kit, but really it was because they talked to Maynard Latrell. They knew Maynard drove Kit every mornin', and he told them that I was the man had Kit's trust."

"And they're lookin' for Kit because he was somehow connected with BB."

"That's what it sounded like," Fearless said.

"They say anything we didn't already know?"

"You mean other than Kit havin' a meetin' with Minna?"

"Yeah."

"They said somethin' about an emerald necklace reported stolen."

"What about it?"

"They said that Kit had stoled a necklace and did I know anything about that."

WE GOT TO MILO'S BLOCK JUST AFTER EIGHT.

Fearless pulled up to the curb directly across the street. I was making sure that my door was locked when I noticed a white man coming out from the concrete pathway to the side of the apartment building that housed Milo's office.

Theodore Timmerman was wearing the same mismatched brown clothes he had on at my doorstep.

Something in the way he moved, something stealthy and sly, made me call out.

"Hey you, Timmerman!"

When Theodore turned, the gun was already in his hand.

Fearless's name was stuck in my throat. If that white man's bullet had hit me I would have probably died calling out to my friend. But Mr. Jones was faster than either one of us. He dove low and hit me in the thigh. As I went down I heard the crack of gunfire and made a sound that even now embarrasses me to remember.

I was saved from being shot, but nowhere near safe. Teddy Timmerman fired once again, tearing up turf not two feet from my head, and then he took aim.

Fearless, who was on the ground next to me, reached for something and then leapt to his feet. Teddy swiveled but again not fast enough. Fearless threw some missile that caught the fake insurance man in the chest. I heard his grunt all the way across the street.

Teddy started shooting wild and ran down the street to his car. He must have had another gun in there, because he took potshots through his window. Finally he got the car started and threw it into reverse. The last we saw of him he was speeding backwards down Baring Cross.

"Wanna go after him, Paris?" Fearless asked. He wasn't even breathing hard.

"No, man. Let's go check on Milo."

18

THE DOOR TO MILO'S OFFICE WAS OPEN wide, but Loretta's front room looked none the worse for wear.

Going through the hall to the office I tripped over my own feet and Fearless had to catch me. I held on to him for a moment, because it was hard for me to regain my balance. I was so scared after being shot at that my internal organs were quivering.

Milo's office had seen some violence. One of his files was overturned and the spindly visitor's chair was upside down. Milo was not in sight.

Then we heard a deep bass moan that could have been a sea lion sunning himself in Monterey Bay.

Bloody and bruised, Milo was on the floor behind his desk.

"Thug," he said. "Try and bully me. See what that gets him."

Fearless lifted the portly bail bondsman with one hand and his chair with the other. It was a show of strength that was almost impossible, but he did it with such ease that most people wouldn't have even noticed.

Once he was seated, Milo began to cry. It wasn't fear or weakness but rage at being so mistreated.

"You hurt?" I asked our sometime employer.

"He wanted Miss Fine's name and address," Milo said. "Said he was gonna kill me if I led him wrong."

"I thought he worked for you."

"Me too. I used him before. He's always good if I got a white jumper, and he's even proven all right on Negro cases. But he got somethin' up his nose out there. A way to make some money, you better believe that."

Milo loved money. He would be balancing a checkbook on his deathbed.

"Is he the reason you called me?"

"Yes sir," Milo intoned. "He called up last night and asked me for the client's name. At first he was all friendly, but when I didn't give him what he wanted he got rude. And when that didn't work he said that he'd be down here, like he was the father and me the wayward son."

"What did you have him doing for you, Milo?" I asked.

"Lookin' for somebody," he replied.

"Kit Mitchell?"

"Who it was don't matter," Milo said with an attempt at finality in his tone.

"If it were Kit it do," Fearless said simply.

Milo heard the threat in those words. He knew that he was a small fish and that Fearless was a man-eater. He knew when to back down.

"Yeah. It was Kit," he said.

"And what does Kit Mitchell have to do with that white man?"

"It's all the same thing. Bartholomew, Kit. Miss Fine wanted them both."

"I thought you said that Winnie wanted to find Bartholomew."

"Yeah, yeah. That's right. She wanted to find both of them."

"Why didn't you tell me that?" I asked, trying to get some threat in my own voice.

"Because it wasn't none of your business."

"People shootin' at us on the street is too our business," Fearless said.

"He shot at you?" Milo asked, showing his first inkling of the trouble we were in.

"Uh-huh."

"I didn't know it was gonna come to gunfire, Fearless," Milo said. "I mean, I thought it was just business as usual. Miss Fine wanted Kit and BB. Theodore was on Kit, and when you come in, Paris, I put you on the boy."

"If Miss Fine wanted Kit too, why didn't she tell me that?" I asked the bail bondsman.

"Because I called her," Milo said. "I called her and said that you good, too good to know all her business. I said she could send you out after BB but to let Kit alone."

"So why did you send Theodore to my door?"

"He heard about Fearless workin' for Kit and came to me an' asked did I know where he could find him. I didn't think there was anything wrong with givin' him your address. I mean, he was workin' for me."

"Now why is he after Miss Fine's address?"

"He don't know that he is," Milo said. "He just come in here an' tell me he wanted to speak with my client."

"Why?"

"Because if I didn't, he said he was gonna kill me. But hell if I was gonna give in to that garbage."

"So why you still breathin', Milo?" Fearless asked.

"After I realized that he meant to beat the answer outta me, I decided to send him on a wild goose chase," Milo said. "I did some bail work for a nice white woman used to live up in Beverly Hills. She had a maid that had been with her family for forty-some years. That was Phyllis Noreen."

"Bobby Noreen's mother?" Fearless asked.

"Yeah. You know Bobby be in jail every time you turn around. And every time Bobby went in, Phyllis got so upset that the only way to calm her down was to get her son out. Then the white woman, Belinda Thurman, would call me."

"So you sent a gunman to that good woman's house?" Fearless was not happy.

"Belinda died three years ago last March. They sold her house, knocked it down, and built a six-story apartment building."

"Damn, Milo." That was me. "You lie in the face of Death just to keep that millionaire black lady on your side."

We heard the front door to the office slam open, followed by hard footsteps of more than one man. Fearless swiveled like a big cat while I took a step backward, looking for an exit.

"Police!" an adolescent voice yelled, and the room was invaded by half a dozen pairs of wide blue shoulders.

• • •

FEARLESS AND I WERE IN HANDCUFFS before Milo could convince the cops that we had saved his life.

"No sir, officer," Milo said for the thirteenth time at least. "Paris and Tristan here are freelance operatives. They were comin' over to see if I had any work. The thief shot at them, and then they came in to make sure that I was okay. We were just about to call the police when you busted in."

"Who was the man that attacked you?" a uniformed sergeant asked.

"I don't know, officer. Just a big white man. Said he wanted the bail I'd been collecting. I told him that I don't keep cash on the premises. But he said he didn't believe it and hit me a couple'a times."

"Did you know him?" the sergeant asked again.

"No sir, officer. I did not."

"What about you two men?" the sergeant asked.

"No, man," Fearless said. "We just come lookin' for work. That's all."

"What about you?" The sergeant with the boy's voice turned his attention to me.

"I was um, I came here, um, you know, to see Milo."

"Did you come here looking for work?"

"Man, right now all I'm thinkin' about is that man shootin' at me, Milo laid up behind his desk, and you comin' in here shoutin' at us with guns in your hands." When I get really alarmed like that all I can tell is truth. If that cop had pressed me on Timmerman I would have folded. So instead I just told him how I was feeling, hoping that he wouldn't push any harder.

It worked. Most of the policemen left and a bored detective came by. He questioned us for about half an hour, taking down details of the attack and attempted robbery.

"There's one thing that doesn't make sense in your story," the short and fat detective said to me.

"What's that?"

"If this armed robber was after Mr. Sweet's money, then why would he start taking potshots at you in the street?"

The policeman, I don't remember his name, had a porcine face marked by small ears and tiny, suspicious eyes. When he squinted at me, I got so nervous that my lie reflex froze up.

"I pointed at him, officer," Fearless said. "That must be why he shot at us. Because he knew that he just did somethin' wrong and there I was pointin' at him."

"Did you know him?" the detective asked.

"No sir."

"I don't get it. Why would you point out a stranger just walking down the street?"

"Because he was white," Fearless said. "I don't see too many white men takin' a stroll down by Milo's."

The detective was still suspicious, but he let it slide.

Loretta Kuroko came in at nine. She wore a light emerald green blouse and a darker skirt of the same color. She had been with Milo through all of his different professions and so knew how to keep quiet.

When the detective left, Milo sent Loretta home, telling her not to come back until he had worked out a few "details." Then Fearless and I followed his burgundy '48 Cadillac to his apartment on Grand.

• • •

MILO'S PLACE WAS A STUDIO designed on the same principle as his office. It was dominated by a big oak desk, which was surrounded by oak filing cabinets. The sofa against a far wall might have opened out into a bed. Next to that was a small walnut cabinet that opened up into a bar.

"How do you cook?" Fearless asked.

"Cook? A man cain't cook. I go down on Century when I need a meal, Johnny's Restaurant Grill. I pay 'em twenty dollars a week and they always have something for me — breakfast, lunch, or dinner."

"What if you wake up in the middle'a the night and want a sandwich?"

"I close my eyes and go back to sleep."

"Milo," I said. "Why'd you hire that man Timmerman to look for Kit?"

"I already told you," he replied. "Because Miss Fine wanted to talk to him."

"That's a lie, man. You said you put Timmerman mostly on white cases."

Milo hesitated a moment before saying, "I usually do use him for whites, but he could find a black man too."

"Come on, Milo," Fearless said. "Don't be lyin' an' that man out there ready to kill you. How come you used him and not a colored man?"

"You're a tough man, Fearless. I know that. But I also know you ain't gonna do nuthin' if I don't wanna talk."

"That's true," Fearless said. "But you better believe that I won't show up if you call on me neither. If that man Timmerman is after you, he know where you live. He might already have found out you lied and be on his way here right now."

Milo's eyes moved to his front door.

He shifted in his chair and then clasped his hands together. He pressed his thumbs on the bones just above his eyes and muttered something that might have been a prayer.

"I said I wouldn't tell anybody," he said at last. "You know I like to keep my word."

"Dead man keep a secret like motherfucker," I said.

Milo nodded.

"Miss Fine told me that BB and Kit were messed up in somethin' that could prove harmful to the family name. They stole something from her and she was very upset about it. I made a few calls around and found out that Kit had been seen in the company of a white man name of Lance Wexler. Once I knew that, I called Theodore, because he could cross the color line with no problem. If anybody could find them men it was him."

"And what was that something Miss Fine was talking about?" I asked.

"She didn't say. All she let on was that it was very important to her and that she would be very grateful if I put her in contact with either Kit or BB or both."

"And what about Wexler?" I asked.

"She didn't say anything about him," Milo said. "I just saw him as some kinda background information."

"Did you ever find out who he was?"

"No. I told Miss Fine about him, but she didn't seem to care. But the way I figured it was, if he did turn out to be important Timmerman was my man."

"And just what was it that you were supposed to do, Mr. Sweet?" I used the proper address because I knew that was the way that Fearless liked to comport himself, with respect.

"She wanted me to find them and give her the information I gathered."

"What information?"

"Where they lived, their phone numbers if I could get 'em, and their situation. You know, did they live with anybody, if they had a house or an apartment, like that."

"Sound like a setup," Fearless speculated.

"No, man," Milo said. "This is Miss Winifred L. Fine, the richest Negro lady in the forty-eight states. She's not no thug or gangster. There ain't even no way that you could tell what she's thinkin' about. You know people like that different than you and me."

"I don't know, Milo," Fearless said. "I once had a girlfriend was a millionaire. White girl name of Bell, Solla Bell. She told me that her father had had two men killed that she knew of. She said it so that I would keep my head down when we were around where he had eyes lookin' out. You don't have to be a poor man to wanna kill somebody."

"I don't know about no rich white girls or their fathers, Fearless. All I know is that Miss Fine has pedigree and social standing," Milo said, holding up his right hand as if he were swearing under oath. "She ain't got nuthin' to do with no lowlife element like we used to bein' around."

"Like Teddy," I suggested.

"We got to move you, Mr. Sweet," Fearless said. "Put you someplace that that white man cain't kill you."

"Yeah," the bail bondsman agreed. "I'm beginning to think that Theodore Timmerman is a very dangerous man indeed. Where you think I could go?"

"My mama got a house I bought with the money we made last year. She wouldn't mind you campin' out a few days or so."

19 FEARLESS CALLED HIS MOTHER and we dropped Milo off in front of the house.

From there I had a plan to gather information while keeping me out of harm's way.

"What did you throw at that gunman?" I asked Fearless.

"Brick."

"A brick?"

"Not a whole brick, but just a chunk, like a half like."

"Where'd that come from?"

"I don't know. It was there in the gutter, so I grabbed it. You know I used to like to play ball. I could'a played on the Pumas, but they spend half their lives in a dusty bus and I'd rather stay in one place."

"But how did you know that brick was there?" I asked. "I

mean, you reached down and grabbed that stone like it was put there just in case somebody started shootin' at us."

"It's my army trainin', Paris. That's all. Wherever I am I look around me. I see things. I don't think about 'em or nuthin'. I just see 'em, and then they're there for me when I need 'em."

"So when you got out the car you saw that little chunk'a brick on the ground?"

"I didn't know I saw it but I did, and when that man started firin' I knew it was there and I grabbed it. That's all."

"And what's all this shit about a millionaire white girlfriend?"

"What about her?"

"You ain't never said nuthin' 'bout that to me before."

"I don't tell you everything, Paris. You know I'm a gentleman anyway."

"No, baby," I said. "There's more to it than that."

"Yeah, maybe. But I don't wanna talk about it. Where we goin' anyway?" he asked, trying to change the subject.

"I wanna go over to that rooming house that Kit had been stayin' at," I said. "Where was it?"

"Over on Denker."

"Let's go there."

Fearless made a right turn and then another one.

After five or six blocks I worked my way back to the question about the millionaire white girlfriend.

"I never told you because it's the kinda thing you always said that you didn't wanna hear," Fearless said.

I knew what that meant. I had always told Fearless that I didn't need to hear about anything illegal because I never wanted to be in the position of being blamed for letting the cat out of the bag to the authorities or, worse, to some gangster who wanted revenge. Had that been a regular day with me at my bookshop and Fearless dropping by to shoot the breeze, I would have held up my hand and said, *All right, let's just skip it.* But I had already found one dead body, figured out that another corpse was connected to my friend's problems, and on top of that I had been shot at. It didn't seem that some simple story could be any worse.

"How long ago did you and this girl break up?" I asked.

"More'n six years."

"Let's hear it, then."

"Okay. You heard of a man named Thetford Bell?"

"The aeronautics guy?"

"Yeah. He got a house up there in Beverly Hills. Wife, three kids. One'a them is Solla. Cute girl. Black hair, dark eyes. She climb up on you just like a cat . . ."

"Where'd you meet her?"

"I was gardenin' next door to her place and some young man was pesterin' her. He had hold of her arm and wouldn't let go even though she was yellin'. Wasn't nobody else to help, so I went up and said that I couldn't let him abuse the lady. He called me a name and I broke his nose for him."

"And she did her cat impression to thank you?"

"Not right then. I walked her to the door and then I left. You know I figured that somebody would get me fired over that. But what happened was that Solla asked the head gardener —"

"You mean you weren't the only one?" I asked.

"It was a big place so they had four people on the grounds," Fearless said. "Anyway, the guy whose nose I broke had left and the head gardener didn't even know about the fight and so he gave the girl my address."

"Didn't he think it was strange that some young white girl wanted a colored gardener's address?"

"She said that I had done some work for them on the side but they weren't home to pay me, so that her daddy wanted the address to send me my pay. Anyway, she come over to say thanks and ended up spendin' the night."

"And then she told you about her father?"

"After a while she did. You know I think she just wanted one night to see what a dark man could do. I guess she liked it, because she was always callin' after that. But then we went to the Huntington Library and one of her friends saw us. Solla pretended that she wasn't wit' me, and then later she said about her father."

"So you broke up with her?"

"Naw, man. I wasn't afraid of her old man. Shit, I started takin' her all over the place after that. Then one night a big ugly dude come up on me when I was takin' a shortcut down the alley to my house. White dude. Real fast." Fearless said these last two words with respect. That meant something, because Fearless was possessed of blinding speed.

"What happened?" I was beginning to regret my request to hear the story, but by then it was too late.

"The white guy told me that Solla was off limits and that he was gonna rough me up so that I would remember in the future. I remember he said, *No hard feelings.*"

Fearless was lost in thought for a little while. We were getting close to the Denker address.

"So what happened?" I finally asked.

"He was good," Fearless said with a single nod. "Too good. I killed him right there under a Lucky Strike sign."

"And then you and Solla broke it off?"

"Then I walked home and went to bed. The next day, when I knew Solla was gonna be out, I went over to her house and knocked on the door. I told the colored woman who answered to take me to Mr. Bell. And when I sat down in front'a him I said that the next man I kill won't be his errand boy but him. Then I broke it off with Solla."

"Did you tell her about her father?"

"She already knew about him, man. She the one told me."

We pulled up in front of the boardinghouse and I jumped out with Fearless Jones's story still swirling in my mind.

20

WE DECIDED THAT FEARLESS WOULD GO back to Ambrosia's house while I did my question thing.

"Yes?" a middle-aged, auburn colored woman asked me at the door. She wore a once-black housedress that had faded to a reddish gray. The hem came down to the middle of her shins. Over the dress she had a white apron that hinted at a powder blue heyday.

"Hello, ma'am," I said. "I'm looking for the super or the landlord for the rooms."

"That's me," she said. "Victoria Moore. I'm the owner."

"Well hello, Victoria Moore. Glad to meet ya." I put on my brightest smile. "My name is Thad Hendricks. I'm just in from the Bay Area and a friend'a mine told me that you had a recent vacancy. I'm down here lookin' for work while planning my wedding. She's from down around here, and I thought that I could scout out a job before sinkin' too much money into rent."

The woman's face lit up. Everything I said delighted her: looking for the room, planning to get married, saving a dollar, and applying for jobs. I was the daydream she'd been having two minutes before the doorbell rang.

"Oh, isn't that wonderful," she said.

"So do you have a room available, Mrs. Moore?"

"Miss Moore," she said. "And yes, I do happen to have a vacancy. You know that Kit Mitchell just up and left one morning and never came back. He owed me a week's rent. I'm down twelve dollars as it is."

"That's pretty steep for just a room, isn't it?" I asked, not wanting to seem overly eager.

"It's a very large room, Mr. Hendricks," Miss Moore said. "On the top floor. With a view. And the twelve dollars is for both room and board."

"Can I see it?"

The landlady was short but so am I. She looked at my face and then down around my feet.

"No bag?"

I reached for my wallet and produced my last five- and ten-dollar bills.

"I left my bag with my fiancée," I said. "You know I'll only be staying here a week, and so I'd be happy to add on three dollars to what you usually get. And if you rent the room to me, at least you won't lose a second week's rent while looking for a more permanent tenant."

Miss Moore reached for the money but I held it back.

"Could I see the room first?"

The landlady closed her hand and smiled.

"Of course, Mr. Hendricks. You're going to fall in love with it I'm sure."

THE FRONT DOOR LED INTO A LARGE DINING ROOM with a long table that had fourteen mismatched chairs set at placemats with the dishware and cutlery already out.

"We serve coffee, toast, and hard-boiled eggs in the morning, and dinner six nights a week," Miss Moore informed me as we walked through the dining room and into a long hallway.

Halfway down the hall a door swung open and a large man dressed only in a T-shirt and boxer shorts emerged. He was fat and freckled, lemon-colored and past fifty.

"Miss Moore," he said in an accent that had to be put on. "I distinctly remember you promising me that I would be told when the tub was ready for my bath."

"Oh, Mr. Conroy. You aren't dressed," she said.

This observation caused the big man to fold his arms over his belly.

"I said," Miss Moore continued, "that you were next on the list. But you can't expect me to be watching the tub and then running down here to tell you when it's ready. I've been washing linens all morning. And then there's dinner I have to prepare."

The landlady's gaze drifted to Mr. Conroy's stomach upon mentioning the meal. He hugged himself even tighter.

"This is Mr. Hendricks, Mr. Conroy. He's going to be with us for a week."

"Pleased to meet you," I said.

I held out my hand but he didn't take it.

"It's that wicked girl Charlotta taken my bath," Conroy said to me. "She will take your bath and pick your pocket if you don't lock your door."

"Mr. Conroy, I will not have you bad-mouthing the other tenants."

"But she —"

"Not another word. Come with me, Mr. Hendricks."

The stern property owner led me to the end of the hall, where there was a surprisingly wide staircase. We went up three flights and came to a small landing that had only one door. Miss Moore took a brass Sargent key from her apron pocket and worked it on the lock.

It was a beautiful room, having a ten-foot ceiling and picture windows on either side. The bed was maple and stood two feet or more off the floor. The walls were painted a watery coral. Underneath the coat you could see the dim patterns of wallpaper that the painters had been too lazy to strip off. There was a big stuffed chair in one corner and a simple cherry table that could have been used for dining or as a desk in another. It even had a sink against one wall in case I got up in the middle of the night and needed to wash my face.

Through one of the windows I could see the tops of houses all the way to the hills that separated L.A. proper from the valley. There were pine, palm, carob, and a dozen other varieties of trees and wide asphalt roadways with very little traffic on them. There were children playing in the streets and clotheslines heavy with the day's cleaning in almost every backyard. Here and there an incinerator put out white smoke, and the sky was that deep blue that threatens to suck the breath right out of your lungs.

I couldn't remember the last time I had felt that peaceful. I didn't want to turn around and face the job of lying to the good landlady. My deepest desire was to somehow fly through that window and become a part of everything I saw. I wanted to be those streets and those children's jump-rope song. I wanted to climb with those pale puffs of smoke into the blue sky and surrender like the white flags they resembled.

"I threw out most'a the clothes and trash he left," Miss Moore was saying. "You might find something here or there. If it's trash throw it out, but if it could be sold you should turn it over to me so that I can try and make back the rent he stole."

I handed over the rent money. This left me with three singles and one two-dollar note — that and three Liberty quarters was all I had in my pockets.

"I won't be lookin' too close," I said. "Just sleepin' and applying for work, that's all it'll be for me this week."

"The phone is not for tenant use," Miss Moore said. "Dinner is at seven sharp, and you have to sign up for the bath."

"Yes ma'am."

"The big key is for the front door," she said as she handed over two brass Sargent keys tied together with a dirty bit of string. "You can come in whenever you want but the house goes dark after ten, and you should be quiet when you come in late. I don't like visitors, so if you want to entertain you have to tell me about it first."

"No cards and no girlfriends, Miss Moore. It's the straight and narrow for me."

She smiled and squeezed my wrist and then left, closing the door behind her. I went back to the window and stayed there for a long time. It was nothing like my rural home in New Iberia,

Louisiana, but there was the feeling of home there. I spent so much time in books that the natural world was often a surprise to me. It was a new world filled with people walking and laughing, living lives that didn't seem to have any part of a larger story.

There was a partly padded folding chair at the cherry table/ desk. I took it over to the east-facing window and sat down. Later I would search the room and question Kit's fellow tenants. But right then all I wanted was to enjoy that unique moment where I was completely out of my life. No one but Fearless knew where I was.

Fearless had brought me to that placid window. He drove the car, but he was also the reason I came; to find out what Kit Mitchell had been up to and where he had gone.

Anyone who knew me and didn't know Fearless would have been surprised that I would have put myself in such a potentially dangerous situation. To the world in general I was a law-abiding worrywart. I shied away from drugs and crap games, stolen merchandise and any scheme that might in any way be construed as unlawful. I never bragged (except about my sexual endowment), and the only time I ever acted tough was to shout at caged animals.

But when it came to Fearless I was often forced to become somebody else. For a long time I thought that it was because he had once saved my life in a dark alley in San Francisco. And that certainly did have a big effect on my feelings toward him. But in recent months I had come to realize that something about Fearless compelled me to be different. Partly it was because I felt a deep certainty that no harm could come to me when I was in his presence. I mean, Theodore Timmerman should have killed me on that street, but Fearless stopped him even though it was impossible. But it was more than just a feeling of security. Fearless actually had the ability to make me feel as if I were more of a man when I was in his company. My mind didn't change, and in my heart I was still a coward, but even though I was quaking I stood my ground more times than not when Fearless called on me.

Possibly his strongest quality was calling out the strength in people around him.

"And I'm gonna need that strength too," I said to myself, thinking that if Kit Mitchell went off one day and then didn't come back, the reason was more likely foul play than him running out on the rent.

While I was having these thoughts a soft knocking came at the door.

21

MY HEART SKIPPED AND I STOOD UP from the chair. I opened the window and looked out to see if there was a way down to the street from the roof. There was a drainpipe at the end of a sloping tar paper flange. I weighed under one-thirty, so if anybody ever worked up there, then I could certainly scurry across.

For a moment I considered running but then I took a deep breath. It was probably just Miss Moore coming to tell me about dinner or to make sure that I hadn't found anything valuable between the mattresses or from some ledge that she was too short to examine.

"Kit?" a woman's small voice called.

"Who is it?" I asked.

"Who is that?" she replied.

For a moment I forgot my alias, so instead I opened the door.

The woman and her voice had very little in common. She was large and curvaceous, with dark olive skin.

"Who are you?" she asked with a hint of disdain.

"Thad," I said, remembering as I spoke. "Thad Hendricks. I took over the room since the last man didn't come back."

"That bitch," the woman hissed. "Kit might be dead or in some hospital somewhere, and all she care about is her twelve dollars."

"Is that who used to be in here?" I asked. "I thought it was a man named Mitchell."

"That's Kit's last name," the young woman replied. Then she smiled. A smile on her face was like the morning sun's first rays on a mountainside. One moment she was dark and uninviting and the next she was a breathtaking beauty.

"What's your name?" I asked.

"Charlotta."

"I heard about you," I said.

"From who?"

"Fella named Conroy. Said you stole his bathwater."

"That fat fool. Somebody need to shut him up. Always complainin' 'bout everybody, spreadin' lies an' stuff. What else he tell you about me?"

"Just about the bathwater," I said, "and that you picked his pocket or somethin' like that."

"Them high-yellah niggahs run around thinkin' their shit don't stink and everybody wants what they got. You know the only thing in his pockets is past-due bills and a busted watch. Now who would wanna take that?"

"What's your last name, Charlotta?" I asked.

"Netters. I'm from the Tennessee Netters. Where you from, Mr. Hendricks?"

Charlotta's words were merely a question, but her tone and expression, even the way she stood, held the offer of something that kindled a spark way down in the pit of my stomach.

"I'm a Louisiana boy," I said. "Down where the peppers burn out your mouth and the gators grab children right offa their swings."

"I love hot food," she said, with a lingering emphasis on the word *love*.

I reached out with a single finger, touching her forearm ever so slightly.

"And I love spicy women," I said.

Charlotta speculated on the sensitivity of my touch.

"You wanna go down and get some dinner?" she asked.

"No," I said. "But I think I might need my strength."

We walked side by side down the stairs and through the hallway. She bumped up against me now and then, not by mistake. When we got to the dining room all the seats but two were taken, and they were not together. I went to a chair between an older woman and a young man, while Charlotta made her way to a seat on the opposite side. She caught my eye now and then, smiling and pushing out her already protruding lips.

Miss Moore sat at the head of the table while a young girl of thirteen or fourteen brought out the food on large serving trays. People were talking amongst themselves softly. The room was filled with the aroma of buttermilk biscuits that had been brought out and placed along the center of the table in three baskets. Miss Moore hardly had to raise her voice to get their attention.

"Everybody," she said. "I would like you to meet Mr. Hendricks. He's only going to be with us for a week or so. He's down from the Bay Area, looking for work before he gets married . . ."

The last words raised Charlotta's eyes a bit, but she didn't seem bothered.

". . . he's taking Kit Mitchell's old room, and I hope the rest of you will help him out if he needs it. Mr. Hendricks, these will be your neighbors for the next seven days."

She went around the table with her eyes then, introducing my housemates. I didn't remember most of their names, even then. There was Charlotta and Melvin Conroy, a young man merely named Brown, and an older gray-headed woman called Mrs. Mulrooney.

"Welcome to the congregation, Brother Hendricks," Brown said as he reached for a biscuit.

"Brown, please," Miss Moore said then. "Wait for grace."

The young man, who had a flat face and expressionless eyes, smiled and leaned back in his chair.

"Mr. Hendricks," Miss Moore said then. "Will you lead us?"

I bowed my head and everybody around the table, and the serving girl too, bowed theirs.

"Lord," I said. "Bless this bounty and bless this house. Bless the people at this table who give thanks for your gifts, and bless the poor son lost from your light. Thank you for keeping us together and keeping us strong while we worship in your name and your teachings. Amen."

"Amen," fourteen voices agreed.

When I opened my eyes I saw Miss Moore smiling, Charlotta grinning, Mr. Conroy grimacing, and everyone else reaching for food.

Dinner was comprised of chicken and dumplings, collard greens, creamed corn, and peach cobbler for dessert. Every bite was delicious and there was more than enough to go around.

I found myself feeling sorry that I had used a false name to get my room. I would have gladly paid twelve dollars a week to eat like that every night. Living alone, I often settled for hamburgers or canned spaghetti.

"That was a beautiful prayer, young man," the older woman to my right said. "You must spend your Sundays with the Lord."

"I spend every day with him, ma'am."

"Brenda," she said. "Mrs. Brenda Frail."

"Pleased to meet you, Mrs. Frail," I said.

There was a lot of talking and jocularity at the table. It was the friendliness of strangers. The only thing we all had in common was our race. There were Negroes from one setting to another and not any three who were the same color. There was nothing unusual about that, though. Being black in America was the simple fact of not being white. From the high-yellow Mr. Conroy to almost black Brown we ranged. Anyone looking at me would say that I was dark of color, that is, unless I was standing next to Fearless, who had retained every pigment of his African heritage.

Not one roomer was from Los Angeles originally. Most were from the South, but a few hailed from the Midwest. Everyone had at least one job. Most of the men had two. Even old Mrs. Mulrooney and Brenda Frail had part-time jobs, one at the five-and-ten and the other taking tickets at the Grand Avenue Cinema during the matinee.

"How do you like your room?" a man whose name I'd already forgotten asked.

"It's fantastic," I said. "I can't imagine anybody not wantin' to come home to that."

I was hoping to get a dialogue started on Kit Mitchell, but all I received was a grunt from Miss Moore.

There were eight men, six women, and one girl. The oldest was seventy-four, that was Mrs. Mulrooney, and the youngest was Trina Harper, the serving girl. There was a mechanic, a chef, two domestics, two janitors, two waitresses, and a dry cleaner.

After coffee I followed my new neighbors through a door into the sitting room. This room was furnished with three couches, a few stuffed chairs, two small gaming tables, and a rabbit-eared television set. There was also a rather large built-in bookcase with at least a couple of hundred books jammed in. I made a mental note to peruse the collection before moving on.

"You look like a smart man, Mr. Hendricks," the youth called Brown said to me.

"Why thank you, Mr. Brown."

"Just Brown. That's what everybody calls me. You play chess?"

"I have played," I admitted, "from time to time."

Brown held out two fists and smiled. I tapped the left one and he turned over a black pawn.

"My favorite color," I declared.

Brown led us to the gaming table that had an inlaid checker and chess board. There he started setting up the board eagerly.

"Nobody around here really play chess too much," he said. "Mostly it's just checkers and bid whist. Cards can be kinda fun, but you know chess is pure brain."

I felt a feathery touch on my forearm. Before I turned I knew it was Charlotta returning my earlier caress.

"Can I talk to you a minute?" she asked me.

She walked me to a small doorway that led into what can only be called an alcove.

"You wanna have a drink with me?" she asked.

"Yeah but I just started the game with Brown."

"That's okay. I got to go buy a li'l bottle first anyway."

"Oh," I said. "Good, I mean, I'd love to have a drink with you."

"I need two dollars for that and some pork rinds."

I forked over my last three singles and said, "Get yourself somethin' sweet too, baby."

She smiled and brushed my lips with hers.

I had to walk carefully back to the chess table to conceal the erection that Charlotta raised.

22 | BROWN KNEW HIS CHESS. He beat me the first game because I underestimated him, gazing around the room and trying to overhear conversations as we played.

That game was fast, us taking no more than thirty seconds for each move. But I got serious in the second go-round. I took my time at strategic moments and outmaneuvered him so that he had to give up when half the men were still in play.

He won the third game. It was rare that anyone beat me twice in a night.

Brown had worker's hands and a hard look when he concentrated. At first glance I thought he was in his twenties, but then I could see where he was at least ten years older than that.

"Where you from, Brown?"

"Illinois originally," he said. "But they tell me I was born in Mississippi."

"Jackson?"

"Greenwood."

"Delta boy."

"I got the blues in my spit," he agreed.

"How long you been in L.A.?"

"Two years. Most'a that time I lived down at Redondo Beach, workin' on this mackerel fishin' boat they got down there."

"How come you left?"

"When I realized that I was gettin' seasick on dry land, I knew it was time to leave fishin' behind." He had a nice, friendly laugh. "So I moved here to Miss Moore's just a few days ago and got a job cleanin' tuxedos and silk dresses."

Charlotta had returned from the store and was sitting next to Brenda Frail. They were working on a quilt together.

Deciding to play with Brown turned out to be a mistake because of my pride. We traded wins back and forth for two hours, until the late news came on.

Good evening, this is Bob Benning with KTLA news. The police were summoned to a grisly scene late this afternoon at the Bernard Arms Residence Hotel on Fountain. The body of Lance Wexler was found by police, who had been trying to get in touch with Mr. Wexler for the past three days. There was no sign of a break-in. Just two days ago Wexler's sister was found dead in Griffith Park. She was also the victim of foul play. When asked about a connection between the two crimes, Captain Howard North told reporters that the police were looking into every detail of both homicides. . . . Maestro Wexler, oil

distributor and real estate developer, offered a reward of ten
thousand dollars for information leading to the arrest and con-
viction of his children's killers. . . .

My heart was thundering by the end of the report. I wondered
if the randy porter Warren had put together the delivery Negro
at the back door and the death of his tenant. I worried that I
might have left a fingerprint or maybe my wallet fell out on the
toilet floor. I actually reached for my billfold to make sure that I
still had it.

As bad as I felt, I was still able to beat Brown. That gave me
hope. Maybe fear gave me clarity.

"Another game?" Brown asked.

"You good, man," I said. "Tomorrow."

Brown stuck his tongue in his cheek and smiled. The grin
stopped at his mouth, his eyes bearing no relation to mirth. That's
how it was for so many displaced southern, and even midwestern,
Negroes in those days. Coming to California, they had to dig out
from under nearly a century of white oppression. Everybody,
black and white, was a potential enemy. People that had been
mired so deeply in poverty that that's all they could ever expect.
And so when faced with hope, many became distant and watch-
ful. Even when relaxing, people like Brown were on guard, ready
for any threat.

"MR. HENDRICKS," CHARLOTTA CALLED AT MY BACK.

I was halfway down the hall, headed for my room. You know
I had to be shaken by that news report to have forgotten her in
the sitting room.

"Hey."

"Did you forget our drink?"

"No, baby," I said. "I just didn't want to give people the wrong idea. I mean, what would it look like if I just walked up to you and said let's go upstairs?"

Charlotta was slightly taller than I and a few pounds heavier. She pressed me up against the wall and kissed me, hard. She knew how to kiss. The worry was still in my head but all the details fell away. When she stepped back to see my reaction, she had a smile on her face. I took a stutter step to keep on my feet.

"I like bein' treated like a lady," she said.

We kissed down the hall and up the wide stairway. It took me three minutes to unlock the door because Charlotta had worked her hand down the front of my pants. When she found what she was searching for her eyes opened wide.

"Is that real?" she asked me.

"Does it feel real?"

"Yeah."

"Then it is."

There are only three things that I've ever had pride in: my intelligence, my bookstore, and my sexual endowment.

Charlotta and I barely made it to the bed. Once there, we hardly let go of each other.

Somewhere in the middle of our passion I realized how much I needed the release. It wasn't lovemaking, but that was all right. I needed to be pushed around in a situation where I could push back. She didn't need to love me but just what I was doing — how hard and how long.

"Again," she whispered for the third time.

"You got to gimme a couple'a minutes, girl," I said. "Just a couple."

Charlotta smiled at me. She held both physical love and victory in her mien. It was a battle I didn't mind losing.

I got up and lit two cigarettes, placing one of them between her lips. Then I lay down, putting my head on her thigh. We smoked for a while in the afterglow of our passion.

"You used to come up here when Kit had this room, huh?" I asked as nonchalantly as I could.

"What you mean by that?" She flexed the hard muscle of her leg.

"Nuthin' really," I said. "I mean, it's just that when I opened that door and looked at you, I thought that whoever it was you were comin' to see was a lucky man."

"Oh." Charlotta's leg relaxed. "You don't have to be jealous, Paris."

"Wha, what did you call me?"

"That's what your driver's license says your name is."

I had only gone to the toilet once since we'd been together. I couldn't have been out of the room for more than a few minutes.

"Yeah, well, you know, honey. Sometimes a man needs to be a little on the sly. I know I told Miss Moore I was marrying somebody, but really I'm tryin' to get away from some guys wanna do me harm."

"I knew it," Charlotta said.

"How you gonna know all that?" I asked just to put her a little on the defensive.

"I didn't know about no men or nuthin', but I could tell by the way you loved me that you wasn't engaged."

"How?"

"A man gettin' married don't have it stored up like you do, baby. I done had men just got outta jail less hungry than you."

"Where you think Kit went?" I asked. She probably thought that I was changing the topic because of being embarrassed by the way she had mastered me sexually.

"I don't know," she said. "He told me that he might be gone one night. He promised to take me to the show by Friday, but he never came back. You like the movies, Paris?"

"Don't call me that."

"Oh, yeah. I'm sorry, Thad." She kissed me.

"What did he do for a living?"

"Who?"

"The man who lived here."

"Why you wanna know?"

"It's just this feelin' I got ever since comin' up in here," I said, and then I shivered.

"What kinda feelin'?"

"Somethin' bad," I said. "I get like that sometimes. Once, when my uncle Victor was up in Jackson, Mississippi, I woke up in a sweat callin' out his name, and then a week later we found out that he had been killed that very night in a juke joint around there."

I figured that either Charlotta would think I was crazy or her superstitious side would come out — either way she'd stop being suspicious about my questions.

"You know I got a bad feelin' about Kit too," she said. "Before he left he told me that he was about to make a whole lotta money. So much that we could go to the show seven nights a week. He said that he was gonna buy a proper farm and hire people to do all the work for him."

"He was gonna make money on a farm?" I asked.

"No, stupid. He was gonna buy the farm with all the money he made."

"What money?"

"I don't know," she said. "But you better be sure that no poor niggah livin' in a roomin' house gonna make money like that the honest way."

"Were you scared to be with him?" I asked. "I mean, knowin' he was maybe stealin'."

"I didn't know nuthin'," she said in a rehearsed sort of way. "Nuthin' for sure. And anyway, he didn't have the money yet. He only said that he was about to get it."

Damn, I said to myself. Then to Charlotta: "You let white people get in your business and you know it's a fifty-fifty chance that you ever make it back home again."

"What you mean about white people?"

"I never heard'a this Kit friend'a yours," I said. "And maybe if he says a lotta money he really just means the twenty-fi'e cent it cost to get into a movie house. But if he was talkin' about real money, then you know it's got to be a white man somewhere in it. White peoples got all the money and they hang it in front'a our eyes just like I used to hold a sugar beet out ahead of my mama's mule."

"Maybe you do have some premonition in you, Thad," Charlotta said.

I was glad that she used my made-up name, but at the same time I realized that she was bound to let my secret out before the week was over.

"You know," she continued, "Kit said that him and this friend'a his knew some white man that was gonna give 'em the money."

"I knew it," I said. "That's the way it always is. White man come an' tell a whole lotta lies, and then the next thing you know your house is up for sale and you lookin' for a hole to hide in."

"If you lucky," Charlotta agreed.

"Did you call his friend?" I asked.

"Say what?"

"Did you call Kit's friend? The one who was in business with him with the white man."

"Why I wanna go an' do that?"

"I don't know," I said, making a big gesture with my hands. "I mean, I thought you was all worried that he might be in the hospital or dead. Maybe if you found out somethin' from this friend'a his then maybe Miss Moore wouldn't be so fast to give away his room."

I could see that Charlotta hadn't considered looking for Kit herself. She was a fair-weather friend; glad to drink your whiskey and lie in your bed, but not concerned with washing the sheets or ironing your shirt for work the next morning.

"Why you so worried about Kit in the first place?" she asked me. "He ain't blood to you."

I had pushed as far as I could without taking Charlotta into my confidence. So I decided to let it go.

"You right, baby," I said. "Why I wanna be all in some man's business when I ain't never even met him, and here I got a beautiful woman lyin' in my bed?"

I let my fingers trail over her nipples and a ripple of pleasure went down her body.

"Yeah," she said, urging me on and agreeing with the same word. "Why you wanna be worried about BB when you here with me?"

My heart was already thumping. Charlotta's fingers were tickling my thigh. But I had to pull away.

"You not talkin' about Bartholomew Perry?"

"Yeah. You know him?"

"Always hang around with white girls? His father sells used cars?"

"That's him."

"He owe me fifty dollars," I declared. "Fifty."

"Over what?"

"He was out with some white girl, at the Python Club. She wanted champagne for her and her girlfriends, and the niggah just had to act all big and say okay. You know he wanted to get in her drawers so bad you could smell it."

Charlotta hummed her disapproval at BB's depravity.

"Anyway," I said. "He didn't have the cash, and they don't take personal checks at the Python because they get stuck with a service charge if it bounce. So I ponied up the forty-two bucks I got paid that afternoon and BB promised to pay me back fifty. That was six months ago at least. You know I called the mothahfuckah but he moved. I went to his father but he told me he didn't keep up with his son. Fifty dollars."

I was sinking deeper and deeper into the role I had made for myself. The cursing might have disturbed Charlotta, but she had to believe in who she was talking to.

"I thought you said you was from up north?" Charlotta asked then.

"You thought my name was Thad too," I said. "I just told Miss Moore that so nobody would know who I am. Them men after me want some money. But you know, if I could get that fifty dollars I might be able to buy me a few more days."

"I don't know," she said suspiciously. "Here you in Kit's room and you just happen to know his friend . . ."

"I know a lotta peoples," I said. "And that mothahfuckah BB owe me fifty dollars."

"How much you owe them men?"

"Three hunnert dollars."

"How much would you pay if you could get to BB?"

"Pay? Nuthin'. Shit, I need every penny. Even if I turn over the whole thing, it might just only buy me a week as it is."

"You could give me twenty and take the rest and leave town. The fifty ain't gonna help anyways, and you only got two dollars in your billfold."

"If I'ma leave town I'ma need more than thirty-two dollars," I reasoned. "Bus ticket to San Diego cost eight forty-five. Then I need to pay for a room till I get a job."

"If you don't find BB you only got two bucks," she reminded me.

"You know where he is?"

"Maybe."

"I could give you fifteen, Charlotta. That's a lot for just a couple'a words."

She pretended to consider my offer. I could have talked her down to five bucks, but it was all make-believe anyway. Why not be generous with a payoff that would never come?

"Okay," she said. "But only 'cause you so sweet. Ooo, look. All that talk about money made you hard again."

She was right.

"You wanna lie back down a little while?" I asked her.

"No, baby," she said. She stood up too. "I got to get up early to get to work."

"What am I gonna do about this?"

"Either take care of it yourself," she said with a sympathetic smile, "or wait till tomorrow afternoon when I get home with BB's numbers."

"You don't have 'em in your room?"

"Uh-uh. No. But I know somebody prob'ly know where he is."

She looked down on my hopeless excitement and issued a deep grunt of appreciation. Then she walked out the door, leaving me to the foolishness of manhood.

23

I LAY BACK IN THE BED after Charlotta left. It had been a good night's work. Even if it was only loving that young woman, it would have been worth it. She was right, I hadn't been with a woman in over four months. I didn't like the clubs because they were too loud, and I couldn't keep a girlfriend because I didn't make much money selling books and my favorite pastime was sitting alone and reading. Women lived with me the same way that they'd go on a vacation: after a week or two they were ready to get back to the lives they knew and loved.

The truth was that I had become a man of moderate means after my last adventure with Fearless. I owned my building and had money in the bank, but I never bragged to anyone about it. I loved my little business and I would have been selling books for a nickel profit even if I had to do it off the back of a truck. That being true, I thought that any woman who wanted to be with me had to believe in the man she saw.

Sometimes I went out to a few nightspots with Fearless. Women gathered around him, and so if I was somewhere in the neighborhood there was always the chance that some lonely girl would take me in for the ride home.

But going out with Fearless often turned out to be a dangerous undertaking. There were always rough men in the bars around Watts. Rough men often do things that might be seen as rude or intimidating. And Fearless would not suffer a bully. So what might have been a night of drinking, laughter, and women often ended up as a ride in the back of a police wagon.

I DIDN'T KNOW WHAT MIGHT HAPPEN in the morning, so I decided to search the room while I had the chance. I went through every drawer and looked under the bed. I searched the closets, cabinets, and windowsills, and crawled around on my hands and knees looking for a loose board or nail. I pulled down the window shades, thinking that he might have taped some note somewhere on the roll. I did the best job of searching that any detective would ever execute. And the only thing I could say when I was finished was that Kit Mitchell didn't hide a thing in his rented room.

FORTY-FIVE MINUTES LATER I WAS STILL THINKING of Charlotta's sweet kisses. I considered easing the pressure by pleasuring myself, but after being with a real woman for the first time in months I didn't have much heart for it.

It was almost one A.M. when I remembered the bookcase downstairs.

Nobody was awake in the big, rambling house. They were all working people who were up before the sun each morning. And when they worked they worked hard. Even Charlotta had to go off to bed before eleven.

I TURNED ON A SMALL LAMP and pulled a burgundy hassock up to the double shelf.

Most of the books were romances and westerns. There were a few magazines stacked on the bottom shelf, *Life* and *Men at War* made up the most of them. A lot of the books were old and smelled of decaying paper. I loved that smell. Ever since I was a child that odor meant excitement and knowledge.

I found one interesting novel written by a man with the unlikely name of Amos Amso. The book was called *Night Man*. It was the story of a man who conducted his life only at night. He slept in the daytime and kept all of the shades and curtains in his house tightly drawn during the daylight hours. He'd had many jobs. Once he worked for the phone company as an emergency technician, then as an operator. Later he got a job as a cook in a twenty-four-hour restaurant in a downtown San Francisco hotel. Whenever any employer tried to change his position to some hour that bordered on morning or sunset, he'd quit and look for something else. He rarely saw his family or made professional appointments. He hired a man to impersonate him when he had to show up for important meetings that could only be scheduled during the day. When he wasn't working, he took long walks in the wee hours, noting the furtive and feral life that lived beyond the hell of the sun.

Finally the main character, who was also called Amos, came across a woman who was attempting to throw herself off of the Golden Gate Bridge in the early hours of the morning. He saved her and talked to her. He convinced her that her life was worth living. Her name was Crystal Limmer and she was a painter, a watercolorist.

That was about the first hundred and fifty pages of the book. I'm a fast reader, but I never finish a book if I don't see a reason for it. Mr. Amso's book would either have the hero being pulled out of darkness by this bright gem of a woman or he would lose himself to a gloom he'd never known before finding love. Either way I wasn't interested, so I put the book back on the shelf.

At least I tried to return it. The books had been packed so tightly that *Night Man* no longer fit in the space I took it from. I pride myself in organizing space on bookshelves, so I took out a few other books in order to accommodate the full complement.

I removed three Zane Grey westerns. But before I could do anything else, I noticed that there was something behind the first row of books. The shelves were quite a bit deeper than I thought. They were actually set deep into the wall. There was a good six inches of space behind the first row of books.

There was another book back there. A thick book with a hard leather cover that had an embossed design but no writing on it. It was thicker than a bible and the pages were not made of paper but of animal skin. The cover and back were wood with cow's leather stretched over it. And each page was scrawled on with handwriting from various hands in differing kinds and colors of ink.

The first line of the first page read:

I am Gheeza Manli daughter of Menzi and Allatou born into slavery in the year of the devil seventeen hundred and two . . .

Much of what Gheeza wrote was difficult to make out, while many sections were completely impossible for me to read. She wrote in extraordinarily small script. Her entries went on for about forty pages, telling something of her impossible tale and interrupting that story now and then to tell of births, deaths, and smaller or larger crimes committed against her or that she committed against her masters. Gheeza had a daughter named Asha. Asha took over the duty of maintaining the entries on page forty-two.

Asha was called Mary by her slave masters, as her mother Gheeza was called Tulip by the same owners. The book was their story, kept secret from the world of their masters. The book was bound by Tellman, who had been from a long line of binders of prayer books for the people of the kingdom of Ethiopia.

A floorboard creaked somewhere in the rambling rooming house. I pushed the westerns and Mr. Amso's book back into the shelf any way they would go, hugged the handmade book to my chest, and covered it with a pillow from the sofa. Then I hurried down the hall and up the stairs with the treasure clutched so tightly that my arms ached from the effort.

Once in my room I wedged a chair against the doorknob, remembering for a moment that I had done the same thing in Lance Wexler's apartment. I turned on the overhead light and pored over the three hundred pages of animal skin that had been scrawled upon by more than a dozen hands. Now and then there were drawings of plantation houses and slave quarters, of agricultural machines and torture devices used on slaves. From 1781 to 1798 Moses, the only male diarist, also drew and painted pictures of his parents, grandparents, his wife and children. He entered twenty-three colorful pictures in all, and while they were crude there was still something poignant and dignified about the dark faces in their slave clothes and quarters.

The last entry was in 1847 by Abathwa, daughter of Elthren, daughter of Moses. All of these names were secret appellations given in private ceremonies when the masters were sleeping. On the last page Abathwa referred to another book that would be used to continue the memories of the kinfolk of Africa.

At first I thought that the book was some kind of fiction, that it was created by some artist, or more probably artists, trying to create a history out of the tragedy of slavery. But there was no questioning that the book was at least over a hundred years old. And there was no reason to doubt that it went all the way back to the eighteenth century as it claimed.

But what was it doing in a boardinghouse library in black L.A.?

It couldn't belong to Miss Moore. She wouldn't have left such a treasure in a public room. Maybe the house belonged to someone else, or maybe the previous owner had inherited the book from a long line that stretched all the way back to the ancient African kingdoms.

As the hours passed I put together what I felt was the probable history of the book. It was definitely an artifact from the days of slavery, though possibly not as old as it seemed. It had been passed down with subsequent volumes to some man or woman who came into possession of Miss Moore's house earlier in the century. This man or woman had hidden the book and then grew old and senile. So the book sat there in its hiding place behind the ever-changing row of popular novels until I came upon it.

So if it wasn't Miss Moore's book then it was fair game for me.

It was nearly five in the morning when I closed the covers and still I hadn't worked out ten solid pages of text. I imagined spending the next year in my little shop deciphering the entries of those long-ago slaves.

I forgot all about Fearless and Milo, about the murderous Mr. Timmerman and the dead Wexler siblings. I forgot about the Watermelon Man and the strange Fine sisters who lived in luxury and in squalor. That's what a good book will do for me. It doesn't make me into a brave man exactly but just erases all vestiges of fear.

24 I FELL ASLEEP WITH THE SUNRISE, amid the sounds of the tenants getting ready to go off to work. The smell of coffee wafted up into my room, but I was too tired to climb down the stairs. And even if I hadn't been so weary I wouldn't have left my book. It was the most precious thing I had ever seen or touched.

I slept until after nine o'clock. When I had to go to the bathroom I took the book with me, wrapped in a pillowcase. I didn't go out of the room except for that one time.

Thieves are the people most afraid of being robbed.

I put the book under the bed and sat at the window, waiting and planning. I figured out how I was going to smuggle my treasure out of Miss Moore's rooming house, and where I could hide it until Fearless's problems had been solved.

After that I started to think about Bartholomew Perry. If I could find him what should I do? Milo would want me to report to him. Winifred L. Fine would also expect an accounting. Of course, there was Leora Hartman, Kit Mitchell, and, most of all, the Los Angeles Police Department that I had to be concerned with.

I needed BB to talk to me, and that meant I needed Fearless. Fearless to keep BB from running away and Fearless to help me understand. That was because even though I knew the majority of words in the English dictionary, it was Fearless who understood the twists and turns of the human heart.

But before any of that came to pass I needed Charlotta.

She came to my door at three. I gave her a weak kiss. That's because my passions weren't under the covers but under the bed with my book at that particular moment.

"Did you find out where he is?" I asked her.

"Don't you wanna kiss me some more, baby?" she replied.

"After I get my fifty dollars I'll kiss you from your toes to your ears and everywhere in between," I said. "But let me get this pistol from out my back first."

"You promise?" she asked.

"You got skin like honey," I said, "only it taste better'n that. I just need to make sure I live long enough to enjoy it."

She gave me a small piece of paper that had an address and phone number on it.

"I had to lie to a man to get that," she said.

"To whom?" I asked, falling a little bit out of character with my language.

"Well, you know Kit told me that BB loves Sister Sue's Chicken and Ribs. An' they deliver. I went over there an' told

Rooney, the delivery man, that BB had made me pregnant and I had to get to him to help me fix it before it was too late."

"And he believed that?"

"You got his numbers in your hand."

"Well, it's gonna be worth it," I replied. "But can you do me one more favor?"

"What?"

"You got a suitcase in your room? Just a small one, or maybe a hatbox?"

"Yeah. How come?"

"I'll make your cut twenty dollars if you let me borrow it."

I once read a book that claimed mathematics is the universal language of mankind — but I never believed it. Money is the talk of the world. Charlotta ran down to her room and got back with a small powder blue suitcase that had red heart decals along the side.

I kissed her and hurried her off. Then I packed my bound booty under one of Miss Moore's spare sheets.

MY EFFORTS WERE NOT WASTED. The landlady was waiting at the front door when I got there.

"Are you just getting out of bed, Mr. Hendricks?" She used a sweet voice to ask her question, but I could tell from the way she spaced her words that it was a test of my moral fiber.

"I spent the whole day writing wedding invitations on paper I borrowed from that nice Charlotta Netters," I said, "one hundred and nineteen. She let me use her suitcase to take 'em down to the post office."

"She already started her mess on you, huh?" Miss Moore asked and answered.

I knew that bringing up Charlotta would keep the landlady from questioning my suitcase. No older woman would ever like Charlotta. She was like an overripe peach on your favorite table-cloth — bound to leave a stain.

I CALLED AMBROSIA'S HOUSE from a phone booth a few blocks away and got Fearless after only a few curses. I told him where to pick me up. He was there in less than ten minutes.

"Open up the trunk, Fearless."

"What for?"

"I need to keep this suitcase back there while we runnin' the streets."

"What you got in there?" Fearless asked.

"A book I picked up for my antiquarian collection."

"Your what?"

"The collection I just started. This is the first book."

IF CHARLOTTA'S INFORMATION WAS RIGHT, then Bartholomew was staying in a room above a drugstore on Jefferson. Fearless and I went to the address and sat out front in Ambrosia's Chrysler. We didn't have much to talk about on the ride over. Fearless had spent all his time in bed with Ambrosia and I had spent the night worried about somebody stealing the book I had stolen.

"What now, Paris?" Fearless asked.

"I guess we should go up there."

"Okay."

"You got a gun, Fearless?"

"Yeah. In the glove compartment."

"Maybe you better pull it out, then."

"You scared'a Bartholomew Perry?"

"Somebody's been killin' people, man," I said. "The Wexlers got killed and Timmerman almost wasted us. It would just make me more comfortable to know that we had some firepower on our side."

"Why don't you take it then?"

That was Fearless's way of teasing. He knew that I was useless with guns. I couldn't shoot straight and just holding a gun made me nervous. I had been disarmed more than once by men I had drawn down on.

Fearless laughed and pocketed the pistol.

We crossed the street and went through a side entrance, climbed three flights of stairs, and came to a door with the number eight stenciled on it.

"Friendly?" Fearless asked.

"Neutral, I think," was my response.

I knocked on the door. We could hear a heavy man's footsteps. He approached the door and then remained silent for a full five seconds.

"Who is it?" Bartholomew called out.

"Plumber," I said in a loud voice I rarely use.

"I ain't called no plumber," came the reply.

"There's a leak in the walls," I said reasonably. "Landlord wants me to check every floor until we find it."

"I don't see no water."

"It's in the walls," I said again. "If it goes on, he's gonna have to spend a whole lotta money tearing out the side of the building."

The lock clicked and the door came open four inches, held fast by the security chain. That was my cue to stand back.

"Let me see you," Bartholomew said.

Fearless rammed his shoulder against the door. BB shrieked and the chain broke. The door flew inward, throwing the bulbous occupant to the floor. Fearless rushed in and grabbed Bartholomew by the neck as I hurried the door shut.

"Don't say a word," Fearless warned BB, and then he let go of the young man's throat.

"What you want with me, Fearless Jones? I ain't done nuthin' to you."

"Where's Kit Mitchell?" I asked.

"I don't know."

"You don't wanna lie to us, son," I said. "This is serious business and a man could die takin' the wrong stand."

"I don't know where he is. I ain't seen him in almost a week."

"What about that girlfriend'a yours?" I asked.

"What girlfriend?"

"That white girl, that Minna Wexler."

It was the only way it all made sense to me. BB had a few dollars and he liked white girls. A white girl and her brother had been killed and now BB was on the run.

"I don't know anybody by that name," BB said. Then he let out a loud belch.

"It'd be easy enough for us to find out if anybody saw you with her," I said.

He belched again, frowning as if this one hurt him on the inside. He let himself down into a wooden chair that sat at a small maple table.

It was a room of single items. He had a couch that was folded out into a bed, the chair he sat in, and the table it sat at. There was also a chest of drawers upon which perched a butt-ugly pink ceramic lamp made into the shape of a melting rooster.

"Why you men messin' wit' me?" BB asked us. "I ain't done nuthin' to you."

"Yes you have," I said. "You just don't know it. Because of you the cops ran down Fearless. Because of you a man shot at us for no reason. Because of you I can't go to my own home because men are lookin' for me to do me harm."

"I didn't do nonc'a that."

"Where's Kit?" I asked again. "And why does your auntie want me and Fearless to bring you to her house?"

Bartholomew's eyes widened and his left arm began to quiver. "Aunt Winnie?" he said in a trembling voice. Then he stood straight up and took a swing at Fearless!

I was amazed. BB knew that throwing down on Fearless Jones was tantamount to suicide. Why would he do such a thing?

Fearless moved his head, easily avoiding the blow. But BB swung again, catching him in the ribs.

"Slow down, Barty," Fearless said. "You know I don't wanna hurt you."

Instead of listening the crazed fat man threw a wild uppercut. Fearless sidestepped the haymaker and caught his attacker with a straight right hand. Bartholomew Perry was unconscious before he hit the floor.

25

FEARLESS LIFTED BB onto the sofa bed and I searched the room. He was on the run but managed to bring five shirts, six pairs of socks, three pairs of trousers, two suits, and twelve changes of underwear. He even had an extra pair of shoes. He was like a young prince in flight. All that was missing was his retinue of guardian Beefeaters.

He had no weapons, one hundred and nineteen dollars in a wallet on the bureau, and a tiny phone book — mostly containing the phone numbers of women. No books or papers in Bartholomew's room. No TV or radio. He didn't even have a newspaper. There certainly wasn't any information about Kit Mitchell.

Going through his pockets was my last hope. In the secretary wallet of his dark green suit I found a wrinkled slip of paper that had an address on Olympic Boulevard. The single word *Tonight* was written below the address.

"Let's wake him up," I said.

Fearless went into the bathroom and came back with a glass of water, which he poured on the young prince's face.

BB didn't sputter or jump up like they do in the movies. He put his hand to his head and moaned. When he opened his eyes I could see the string of thoughts run across his buff-colored face. At first he didn't recognize us, then he remembered who we were from running into us around town, then he remembered our breaking in, and finally the fear of his auntie came into his eyes.

"Throw down again and we gonna tie you up like a Christmas goose and leave you on your auntie's doorstep," I said.

"No, man. Don't call Aunt Winnie. Don't. I'll pay you."

"Where's Kit?" I asked.

"I ain't seen him," BB said. "I got money, man. Money enough for all three of us."

"How much?"

"A thousand dollars."

Fearless grunted. "That's a whole lotta change," he said.

"If you guys could find Kit we could make it fifty."

"Thousand?"

"Yeah, brother. Fifty thousand dollars American." BB was shivering, burping, and trying to smile. It was a sickening display.

"How?" I asked.

"She didn't tell you?" A wily look came into the playboy's eyes.

"Tell me what?"

"Why she lookin' for me and Kit?"

"You can tell me that."

"If I did, then you could cut me out right here."

"I could cut you out anytime I wanted to, son," Fearless said in an impartial tone.

"I'll give you guys a thousand dollars," BB said. "A thousand, and five each if you get me to Kit and Kit give me what I want."

"Let's see the cash," I said.

"I got your word you'll help me find Kit?" BB asked. Then he looked at Fearless. "And that you'll take my deal and leave the rest of the money to me?"

I looked to Fearless for direction, knowing that any deal I made without him was subject to revision anyway.

"Why not?" he said, answering my wordless question. "Maybe you could hold on to the cash for me and I wouldn't have to sleep on the street no more."

"You said it now, Mr. Jones," I said. "I'ma keep you to it."

"Okay, Paris."

"Then it's a deal?" BB asked me.

"You got to come up with a thousand dollars first," I said. "Do that and we'll work wit' you. That is unless you killed one'a the Wexlers."

"I ain't killed nobody, man."

"But you did know her, right?"

"Yeah."

"And she and her brother got somethin' to do with all this mess?"

"They, they did, yeah. But I cain't tell you about how until you find Kit."

"We gave you our word, BB," I said.

"I know," he said. "But I just wanna keep my secret until we got Kit here with us."

"Who killed Minna and Lance Wexler?"

"I don't know, brother. That's why I'm hidin' here. Somebody's out to kill us."

"Kill who?"

"Me and Kit and anybody else messed up in this."

The chill returned to my gut then. I was messed up in BB's business. I didn't even know what was going on and I was still on a hit list somewhere.

"Where's the thousand?" Fearless asked BB.

The young man went to the ugly pink lamp and unscrewed the bottom. A thick roll of twenty-dollar bills fell out. He handed the wad to me. The moment the money changed hands a fearful shudder went through BB. He'd given us the money, now we could kill him or turn him over to his auntie. Why should he have trusted us?

"Why you so scared'a your auntie?" I asked BB.

"Who said I'm scared?" he asked, trying to achieve some approximation of bravery.

"You goin' up against me to keep away from her tell us you scared," Fearless said.

"I cain't tell ya what we lookin' for," BB said. "But believe this: my auntie would see me dead before she'd let me get away wit' what Kit done did."

I could see that BB wasn't going to let up on his secret, but that didn't matter right then. At least I knew that Winifred Fine's problem went deep enough to make her own blood afraid of her.

"You better find a new place to hide out, Bart," I said. "'Cause you know if we could find you then somebody else can too."

"Where?"

"Wherever," I said. "But don't call nobody. Don't tell nobody where you are. Don't go out the door. Make sure you don't order no chicken from Sister Sue's. And when you light, call Milo Sweet's office, he's in the Yellow Pages under bail bonds. You'll get an answering service. Tell them where Paris can find Honeyboy."

"Who's that?" BB asked.

"I'm Paris. You're Honeyboy."

"Oh. Okay. You guys ain't gonna turn on me, right?"

"Not unless you do it first," I said.

"WHAT NOW, PARIS?" Fearless asked when we got to the car.

"I got to eat, man. Let's go over to that gumbo house you love so much."

Fearless grinned. Blue crab gumbo was his reason for living. Henrietta's Gumbo House was on Slauson just down the street from Paloma. Henrietta's served three kinds of gumbo, jambalaya, and red beans and rice. She also offered vodka drinks flavored with sugary lime and always had sweet potato pie for dessert. I was so hungry that I had it all — twice.

We started eating at about eight o'clock.

"So what now?" Fearless asked me.

"You said that that man, that Maynard Latrell would drive Kit in to work every morning?"

"Just about," Fearless said. "Maynard always tryin' to get on the good side of whoever he's workin' for. I wouldn't go so far as to say he was kissin' butt. But you know he gets close enough for a good whiff."

"Maybe he got close enough to know something that will let us on to where Kit went to."

"I guess," Fearless said. "But you know I already asked him if he knew where Kit had gone."

"Yeah," I said. "But sometimes people know things they don't think they know. Sometimes you need what they call a fresh perspective. So maybe you find him and we'll all talk together."

"And where you goin'?" Fearless asked.

"This address I found in BB's pocket. Maybe I can see who else these boys is messed up wit'."

Fearless shook his head.

"What?" I asked him.

"I'ont know, Paris. It's just that I'm used to you tellin' me how we should back up and stay away from trouble, and here you are jumpin' in wit' both feet."

Maybe drinking those sweet lime cocktails is what set my anger free.

"Listen here, asshole. I don't wanna be out here. I don't wanna be thinkin' about dead people and killers and stolen money. I don't wanna be runnin' out my back door when I hear a knock on the front. But I can't help it. I'm in trouble and never did nuthin' to cause it. It was you did it."

"Me?" Fearless protested.

"You. It was you came to me and asked for help. It was you that white man shot at us was lookin' for. It was you sent me lookin' for a man dead in his living room. This all started because you couldn't resist a pretty woman with a cryin' child askin' you for a favor. And now all I can do is try and keep my head above water." I remembered my dream of drowning in money.

"I'm sorry, Paris," Fearless and I said at the same time.

"That's what you always say when I'm under the gun," I added. "You're always sorry and I'm always up shit's creek. You're sorry and I'm in jail. You're sorry and, and . . ."

"You got a thousand dollars in your pocket," Fearless said, finishing my sentence.

I laughed then. What else could I do?

26 | FEARLESS DROVE ME to the bookstore and stood guard while I checked the place out. When I came back I put the thousand dollars that BB paid us plus seven of the nine hundred thirty I got from Miss Fine into the suitcase with my handmade book. I split the money left over with Fearless. After that I got into my car and Fearless followed me to make sure there was nobody else on our tail. After a few blocks he veered off to find Maynard Latrell. We'd made a plan to meet at Rob's All-Night Chili Burgers on Avalon at one in the morning. Rob's was a busy place after midnight and so our meeting wouldn't cause any suspicion. Neither Fearless nor I was ever late for meetings. His punctuality came from the military, while my nervousness kept me prompt.

I hit Olympic at San Pedro downtown and followed it westward, looking for the address I took from BB's pocket. I went past Vermont and Western, La Brea and Fairfax, beyond La Cienega and Robertson. I was four blocks west of Doheny when the number came up. It was a two-story stucco home in the Spanish style with a tiled roof and an eight-foot white plaster wall around it. The gate to the driveway was open and there was no car to be seen. Of course the garage door was closed, so someone might still be inside. But no lights were on in the house and there were six or seven newspapers on the other side of the wrought iron fence that guarded the path to the front door.

All of this I could see from the window of my car. It was just after ten. The street was almost empty of traffic. Now and then a car would rush past. But there was nothing to look at. My lights were off.

The leaves on the walkway to the front were in an undisturbed, haphazard pattern. Here and there in the iron fence there were delivery menus and supermarket ads that had been shoved in. No one was home, I was fairly sure of that. But who was that no one and why was this address in the pocket of a man who had just offered me and my friend eleven thousand dollars?

Man offer you a dollar for a day's labor, my mother used to tell me, *he's a man you could trust. But a man offer you a hundred dollars for a short night's work, you better run until you can't see him and then hide in amongst the trees.*

The eleven thousand dollars BB promised us had blood on it already. Anybody who wanted to earn it had to be ready to bleed. I didn't covet that money. I didn't care if it ever came my way. But I had to play along with the young Prince Perry, because as long as he thought I was in thrall to his riches he'd try to keep me in the game.

It was going on fifteen minutes that I had been watching the house. I had come all that way. It would be childish of me to leave empty-handed when all I had to do was walk up to the gate, at worst the door, and see whose name it was on the mailbox. There was no one home. Nobody had been there for days. I could trust my own logic on that score.

Even if the cops happened by and stopped me — it wasn't breaking and entering to ring somebody's bell.

The only thing to fear . . . they had said when I was a child.

I walked up to the gate and pushed it open. The rusty hinges let out a long screeching note that could have been heard three blocks away. I froze there, waiting for some punishment to descend. My heart was racing and my fingertips tingled. The chill of the desert night pricked at the sweat on my neck. My bowels rumbled but I still took a step onto the path of round stones that led to the front door.

A thick bundle of mail was jammed into the small box on the front door. The name of the addressee was Rikki Faison. Another name in the ever-growing cast of characters in the Fearless Jones Drama. I didn't try the knob. At least I'd learned that lesson.

I turned to leave and came face to face with fear itself. It was in the shape of a tall shadow, framed by darkness, with two glittering circles that took the place of eyes about a foot above my head.

Nigger, the eyes said, and then I felt a sharp pain on the left temple.

"NIGGAH TOLD ME that I had to come up wit' fi'e hunnert dollars if I wanted to see my farm again," a man said.

I knew him but couldn't recall his name.

"I will not discuss anything with you if you gonna use language like that," my mother replied.

"Language like what?" the man protested. "I done told you the niggah done stoled my farm. Went to county court and told them that I owed him money that he knows I'm gonna pay just as soon as the crop come in."

"I told you already that I will not listen to that kind of language."

I must have been very young, because my mother and the man she was refusing to talk to were giants. He was dressed in farmer's clothes and she had on her green Sunday dress with the white edges and seams. I was very upset because both of them were being so obstinate. The farmer was too angry to stop calling his nemesis a nigger, and my mother was too critical to break her rules long enough to understand his rage.

I wanted to talk but my voice was somehow silenced. I tried to think if I was too young to be able to speak, but it seemed to me that I was old enough — the words were in my head. But for some reason they refused to come out of my mouth.

I was so angry that I started hitting myself in the head so that my mother would look at me and both of them would agree on the rules of conversation. But they didn't notice and so I kept on hitting myself until it began to hurt.

That's when I woke up. I couldn't have been hitting myself, because my hands and feet were tied. The reason I couldn't speak was because of the gag in my mouth. My nose was partially stuffed up, and so I found it extremely difficult to breathe. I tried to spit out the gag but it was tied tight around my head. There were rags stuffed into my mouth. I got so frightened that breathing became even harder. That's when I started kicking and flailing around. I was in a tight space. There was the smell of gasoline and rubber around me. I was in the trunk of a car. This new bit of knowledge brought on my first-ever attack of claustrophobia. The word went through my mind, its definition and Latin root *claustrum,* a closed space, but that didn't keep the level of anxiety from rising to the color of red in my mind. I kicked and bucked and screamed silently.

The trunk came open and a tall man with thick glasses that had round lenses smiled down at me. I was writhing like an earthworm freshly exposed to air. The man grinned. All of his teeth had spaces between them. His lips quivered with amusement at my plight.

"Stuck?" he asked, and I stopped struggling.

He took out a large pistol and pointed it at my head.

"I'm going to untie you and take the gag out. But if you run or raise your voice I'm going to kill you with this here howitzer. You understand?"

I nodded as best I could and he pulled the gag from my mouth.

I gulped in air, realizing that it was the most precious commodity in all the world. Air. More valuable than gold or sex. It was delicious, rich. I lay there almost happy in spite of my predicament.

The white kidnapper had a thick mop of brown hair that seemed to grow only from the top of his head. He wore a blue suit on a long and elegant body that didn't belong to the big head and ugly face. He dragged me from the trunk and untied me. Then he pushed me so hard that I fell to the floor. He yanked me up and pushed me again, just as hard. I didn't fall that time because I was ready.

"Get moving, nigger."

The word brought back my dream.

We were in a cavernlike garage. The thug in the blue suit shoved me toward an external staircase that must have gone up at least two-and-a-half floors. At the top was a door. The goon pressed a jury-rigged button but I heard no ring.

"Louis?" a voice asked from the other side.

"Yeah."

The door opened inward. A small man was standing there. I say small because he was an inch or two shorter than I.

"You got somebody?" the short man said.

"Come on, Eric. You see him don't ya? He was sneakin' around the bitch's front door. I threw him in the trunk and brought him over. He up?"

"I woke him when you called. He's in the big room."

"Lead the way," Louis said.

Eric rubbed his hands together and led us through a maze of short hallways and across nondescript little rooms. We finally came to a broad corridor with thick burgundy carpeting and gold-and-yellow walls. This led into an antechamber whose only purpose was to bring many different hallways into the presence of a large, unfinished oaken door.

Eric allowed Louis and me to go ahead. I noticed that Louis hesitated before raising his knuckles to rap out our request for entry.

I was in a world that was completely strange to my experience. I understood men like Louis and Eric. I understood petit bourgeois pretenders like Bartholomew Perry. But that lobby was the largest room I had ever been in in a man's home, and it was just the appetizer for what was to come.

I realized that the main course in a house like this might well be a human life.

27

THE ROUGH-HEWN DOOR opened inward. The man standing there surprised me. He was a timid-looking guy in a shabby green suit. He looked like a bookkeeper or a door-to-door salesman — certainly not the monster that I felt must lay beyond that great door. The timid man stood aside and we entered a room that any king in Europe would have been at home in. There were rows of red velvet-covered chairs along the walls and an incredibly long and wide table, cut from a single great tree, down the center of the chamber. Above each chair hung an antique tapestry, each one depicting a different hunting tableau. At the far end of the table sat a throne. That's the only thing I can call it. You had to ascend three steps to get to it, and it was plush with golden velvet and ornately carved wood.

The man who sat there had a lean, leonine face and long, thick brown hair that flowed backward. He wore a red shirt and white trousers, no shoes or socks, rings or glasses. He was over forty and under sixty.

His eyes were mad.

"Who is this?" the king asked his vassals.

"The driver's license in his wallet says Paris Minton," Louis said.

"Where did you find him?"

"Checking out the mailbox at the Faison girl's house. I figured since it's niggers in this that you'd wanna see him."

The king looked at his lackey with something like disdain in his nutso gaze.

I wanted to scream.

"What's your name?" the king asked me.

"Paris, like the man said. What's yours?"

Louis's hand, which still gripped my biceps, tightened. The man on his throne sat up straighter. He frowned for a moment and then he laughed.

"They call me Maestro," he said, and my heart sank. "What were you doing at my daughter's sublet, Paris?"

"I don't know anything about your daughter, sir. All I knew was that it's an address that a man I'm looking for had left behind in his hideout."

"What man is that?"

"Young Negro name of Bartholomew Perry," I said as bravely as I could.

"And where was he?"

I gave the address, certain that the bookkeeper or Eric would write it down.

"But," I added, "he was already gone from those premises. We got there maybe three hours too late."

"We?"

"Me and Fearless. Fearless Jones." Just saying the name gave me hope and maybe even a tiny bit of nerve.

"And why were you and this Fearless looking for Mr. Perry?"

"A man named Milo Sweet was looking for him. He's a bail bondsman but sometimes he agrees to look for missing persons. Me and Fearless work for him now and then."

"What did he want with Perry?"

"He said that it was a missing person case. We figured that it was family lookin' for him."

I was walking a tightrope with the make-believe king and his subjects. I didn't know what they knew, so I decided to lie by leaving out any direct involvement we might have had with the Wexler clan. Fearless knew how to take care of himself and Milo was tucked away with Fearless's mother. The only person I had to worry about was Loretta Kuroko. But all I had to do was call her. That would be easy, if I lived to dial the number.

"How did you find Perry's hiding place?"

"Milo called me at my house and told me. He said that one of his informants had given him the tip."

"Who?"

"He didn't say."

"Didn't you wonder why he'd call you if he knew where his quarry was?"

"I was just happy to stay on the payroll, Maestro."

Louis's hand tightened again.

"Do you know who I am, Paris?"

"No sir. I mean, I figure you're rich and all, but I never heard'a you that I know."

"My last name is Wexler."

I squinted and then shrugged.

"No sir. I don't remember that name in any of this."

"My daughter and son have been murdered. I believe that this man you're chasing has something to do with the people who killed them. So you can see why I'm suspicious about anyone coming to her sublet home or anyone looking for Bartholomew Perry."

"Oh yeah."

"Do you have anything else to tell me?"

"No sir. All I know is that Milo Sweet hired me, then he told me where to find Bartholomew, I found what you tell me is your daughter's address and came to see if I could get a lead."

Silence filled the room. My ears got terribly hot, burning hot. I had spun my lie and now all I could do was hope the line would lead me out of there.

"How much is this Milo Sweet paying you?"

"Hundred and fifty if we find BB. Ten dollars a day for our trouble if we don't."

"I'll give you ten thousand dollars if you find him. Will you work for me?"

I looked over at Louis, then at his fist wrapped around my arm.

"Let him go, Louis," the king commanded.

The brute did as he was told.

"Sure," I said. "Yeah. Hell yeah."

"You would betray your employer?"

"The way I look at it, Milo gave up my trust when he didn't tell me how serious this problem was. He knows, I've told him before, that I never wanna get messed up with any problem got a killer in it somewhere."

"But you would do it for me?"

"The most money Milo ever offered me was for this job here. I'm already in it so why not go for the big payday?"

Maestro Wexler studied me then. He was a man who demanded allegiance from his employees and I was obviously not the faithful sort. But he needed me. Why harm me when I could still be of some use?

"Louis, give Mr. Minton your number and drive him back to his car."

"No," I said.

"What is it, Mr. Minton? Do you require a retainer?"

"A retainer sounds nice but that's not what I was talkin' about. I already been on a ride with this mothahfuckah right here. I don't need that again."

Maestro laughed.

"I've told you about your manner, Louis. Bradford."

"Yes sir," the bookkeeper intoned. He walked into my line of vision.

"This is Bradford," Maestro said. "He's my private secretary."

I nodded and so did the secretary. I liked him then. Maybe it was because he was the only man in the room who didn't seem to pose some kind of threat. But I also thought that he resembled me. Quiet and withdrawn from the brutish world. I was glad to have him in the room.

"Take Mr. Minton where he wants to go and give him a thousand dollars from petty cash."

"Yes sir," Bradford said. And then to me, "This way, Mr. Minton."

Eric piped up then.

"You want I should go with 'em?" the scrawny henchman asked.

"No, Eric. Mr. Minton works for me now."

I followed Bradford from the room, happy to leave the company of madmen.

IN THE LIGHT OF THE KITCHEN I could see that Bradford's pants and coat were darned here and there. His dress shoes had a high shine but they were shapeless from many years of use. His face was what I can only call a faded white. He had a long nose and an accent that wasn't quite English.

He entered a walk-in pantry and came out with a cardboard cigar box that held three stacks of cash. Half of one of these heaps was the thousand dollars the king had earmarked for me.

After paying me and returning the cash box to its unlocked closet, Bradford led me through a back door and down a series of stairs toward the vast garage. We got into an old Bentley and drove down a driveway that was a quarter mile or more.

We were on a mountain. I could see the lights of Los Angeles as we descended streets that had no sidewalks or curbs. That was how the rich lived in L.A. They didn't want people to be able to get to them easily, and once they got there they had to do their business and leave because there was no place to dawdle.

"Australia?" I asked after the view was gone.

"Yes. That's right," he replied. "You have a good ear."

"Bradford, isn't it?"

"Yes sir."

"You got anything to tell me, Bradford?"

"What do you mean?"

"I don't know. Maybe somethin' about what's goin' on. Why I was battered and kidnapped and dragged up here."

He drove a few more blocks and we entered upon Sunset Boulevard. There he turned left.

"I'm sorry you fell into this problem, Mr. Minton," Bradford said.

"I don't even understand it," I said, emphasizing my innocence with the tone of my voice. "What does a rich girl like Miss Wexler have to do with a buffoon like BB Perry?"

"She was the kind of girl who liked . . . what should I say? A certain type of man."

Like Fearless's rich girlfriend, I thought.

"What about that man shanghaied me? That Louis. What could your boss be thinkin' with a thug like that workin' for him?"

"Those men working for Mr. Wexler are criminals. I don't like having them in the house, and I certainly don't trust them," Bradford said. "He's a good man — Mr. Wexler is. But the deaths of his children have brought him to grief. He's used to being in charge and so the heartache makes him want to find the ones responsible for the murders."

"That makes sense," I said. "I know people who would have the same reaction."

"It would be better for all concerned if the police handled the matter, or if, if the culprits were never found. I mean to say that whoever gets involved with this fiasco will be the one most likely to pay a price."

I could see that Bradford was also a deep thinker. His take on the murder and revenge deserved a closer look.

"You mind if I smoke?" I asked.

"Not if you open your window."

I rolled down the window and set fire to a cigarette. I let the smoke drift up from my lips to be inhaled through my nostrils; that was my way of thinking and smoking at the same time.

"So you're tellin' me that I shouldn't be thinking about the ten thousand dollars," I said.

"Not unless you want to trust Louis and his friend," Bradford said. "They'll slaughter anyone to get their bonus from Mr. Wexler. And if you were the last man seen with the man killed, then you will be the one the police come after."

We were passing some pretty big houses going down Sunset but they were nothing compared to Maestro's palace.

"I guess me tellin' the cops about my visit to Maestro's house wouldn't get me very far," I added.

"Mr. Wexler is a strong supporter of the mayor and the chief of police. I doubt if you could find a single soul that would take your word above his."

"But wouldn't he get mad if I don't turn up something on BB?"

"All he has to think is that you're trying. You could keep the thousand you already have," he said, "keep it and stay out of the way."

"Excuse me, Bradford, but why would you care about me in all'a this? I mean, shouldn't you be more concerned with your boss?"

"It is in his interest that I speak to you. I have been with this family for many years, Mr. Minton. I've known all of Mr. Wexler's wives and children. Minna and Lance were bad from the start. Their mother was a dancer in San Francisco." He said the word *dancer* like it was a disease. "There was never any love in that union."

"Were the kids running some kind of scam?"

"I believe so. It had to do with a woman, a Miss Fine."

"What about her?"

"She has something that Mr. Wexler wants. I'm not sure exactly what it is, but it's property of some sort. Lance and Minna knew someone who was well acquainted with the woman. They were going to use him to get leverage on her."

"Bartholomew," I said.

"I believe so. Lance told his father that he could obtain some control over Miss Fine and now he, Mr. Wexler, feels responsible if indeed Lance's attempt got him and his sister killed."

"I guess he would be," I said. "Responsible, I mean."

"He didn't go to Lance," Bradford said. "The children were angry because their father had reduced them to a very low allowance. He wanted them to work hard to understand money. But all they wanted was to get rich quick. Mr. Wexler should cut his losses and move on. He has seven other children, all of whom are fine and upstanding."

We had worked our way down to Olympic by that part of our conversation. Bradford pulled up in front of the Faison house.

"So you think it would be better for all involved if I just dropped out?" I asked the Australian.

"You've seen his eyes," Bradford said.

"Yeah. I've also seen ten thousand acres of rice stooped over by just as many poor black Louisiana sharecroppers. You know ten thousand dollars sure enough might make that pain heal."

"Death is the only real cure to pain, Mr. Minton."

It might not have been a good argument but it was the truth still and all.

"I'm afraid," the male secretary continued, "that if you open a door for Mr. Wexler's revenge he will go so far that even his wealth will not protect him."

"I'll tell you what, Brad," I said. "You got a private line in that big house?"

"Yes," he said and gave me a card with only a number on it. "You can call me at that number any evening after nine."

"If I have any questions I'll call you first. How's that?"

"Better than nothing."

28

FEARLESS WAS EATING A CHILI BURGER at an outside counter by the time I made it to Rob's. The whole place was crowded with late-night customers. There were cops and cabbies, prostitutes and short-straw runners from a dozen companies that drew lots on the graveyard shift to see who had to take the drive for their burgers.

Fearless was talking to two young women who were looking him up and down, hoping that Rob would put something like that on the menu. It broke their hearts when I came up and Fearless shooed them off.

"You late, Paris," Fearless said. "I was gettin' worried."

"You should'a been. I got hit upside the head, hog-tied, kidnapped, threatened with a gun the size of a cannon, and questioned. I was in fear for my life."

"Well," my friend said dismissively. "I guess it didn't turn out too bad."

"I know it don't seem like it," I said. "Especially when it all ended up with me gettin' paid another thousand dollars and promised yet another nine."

"Damn, Paris. People just throwin' money at you."

"I don't like it, Fearless."

"Me neither, man. But we okay now. Ain't nobody after either one of us."

"What about Timmerman?"

"He probably dead by now. You know that brick hit him hard. Yeah. If he ain't dead he's outta play, that's for sure."

"Maybe," I said. "Maybe. But I'd like to know where all these players are before I can sleep comfortably in my bed. Did you find Maynard?"

"Yeah. I know where he's at. We could pick him off when he's goin' out to work. 'Bout eight o'clock."

"What we gonna do till then?"

Fearless nodded at an open-air counter across the parking lot from us. The two girls he had been talking to were standing there staring in our direction.

"Lisa and Joanelle," Fearless said. "I told 'em about your medical condition."

"What condition?"

"I told 'em I didn't know the right doctor's words for it, but down around where we were from they called it big-bone-itis." He slapped my shoulder and laughed. "They said we could go over to their place. It's just a few blocks from here."

I glanced across the lot again. One of them was pear-shaped

and the other skinny and short. But they were young and laughing. And I'd almost been killed two or three times already.

"Okay," I said. "Let's go."

THE EVENING WENT DIFFERENTLY than I had supposed it would.

When we got to the girls' apartment Fearless produced a pint bottle of blackberry brandy that he'd picked up somewhere. Joanelle, the pear-shaped, walnut-colored young woman, brought out a lump of ice with an ice pick. I chipped at the ice while Little Lisa, a name she answered to, cleared off a space on a traveling trunk that they used for a coffee table. They had paper cups for the brandy and potato chips for salt.

I was wondering how we were going to split up when Fearless said, "Paris, did I ever tell you about the time I crossed over into Germany with three white boys before our army invaded?"

"No," I said, wondering why he was addressing me as if we were alone.

"It was late in the evening and the CO told us that he didn't want to see us again until we had blowed up somebody's bomber planes. I was search and destroy," he added for the girls' benefit. "Usually I went out by myself, but because they wanted us to put a dent in an air base they had near the border, they sent two demolition men wit' us."

"Who was the third man?" Joanelle asked.

I could see by her face that Fearless had her complete attention with his tale of derring-do.

"He was the radioman," Fearless said. "If we came across

something that we couldn't attack properly, he was to call in for our bombers to take over. . . ."

The story went on for a long time. One of the demolition men had called Fearless a nigger before they went out. He told Fearless to stay away from him. But along the way the other two men were killed when they stumbled across a land mine. There were a few close calls and the surviving demolitionist was wounded in the leg. They found the secret air base, though, and Fearless was able to set the charges with the racist's help. He also dragged the wounded man all the way back to Allied territory.

"Why didn't you just let him die?" Little Lisa asked. She had her head on my lap but she kept awake for Fearless's story.

"I saved him because of the uniform," Fearless said. "He was my fellow American, and because'a that I had to save his butt."

"Did he change his opinion?" I asked, as rapt in the tale as those young women.

"I have no idea," Fearless said. "I dropped him off at the infirmary and never saw him again. You know he shouldn'ta said nothin' bad about me in the first place. What you want? I got to save every redneck's life in order for them to think I'm a man?"

Joanelle and Lisa had a thousand questions for Fearless. They'd never known a Negro who had autonomy in the war. Lisa pressed her head against my stomach and squeezed my hand. Joanelle had her head on Fearless's shoulder.

When I woke up at dawn we were all pretty much in the same positions. The chipped ice was nearly melted and the blackberry liquor was gone.

For a moment I regretted the missed opportunity but then I remembered how friendly the night had been. I could have slept with Charlotta for a year and never had the warmth or closeness I had with those girls. I sat there for over an hour with Lisa's hand between my thighs. I didn't move to wake them until seven-fifteen.

The good-bye kisses and hugs were warm, and they made us promise to come back when we were through with our business so that we could have another good time.

I FOLLOWED FEARLESS back to Ambrosia's house. We left my car in her garage and kept hers. I didn't want to be too far away from our money or my book. Then we drove over to a big apartment house on Alameda near Vernon. After a few minutes a tall man came out of a green door on the side.

Fearless stepped out and called, "Hey, Maynard!"

You could tell by the way the man looked at us he was considering escape. Fearless had a small limp that might have given Latrell the edge. Still, he would have to stay away from his own door if he ran.

He put on a smile and waved.

"Hey, Fearless. What you doin' here?"

"Lookin' for you, my man. Me an' my friend Paris here needed to know a thing or two."

"Maybe this afternoon. I got to get to work right now," Maynard said. He moved to walk away.

"Arthur North Construction let you slide fifteen minutes, brother," Fearless said, still friendly.

Maynard shook his head and then he nodded.

"Okay. All right. What you need?"

Fearless had walked up to Maynard by then. He shook the man's hand and guided him back to our car. He opened the passenger's door for Maynard and then climbed into the backseat.

"Okay, Paris," Fearless said. "There he is."

"We were wondering about Kit Mitchell," I said.

"You an' everybody else," Latrell replied.

"Everybody else?" Fearless said. "You didn't say that anybody else had said nuthin' when we talked."

"That's 'cause you talked to me five days ago. People been to see me ever since then."

"Who else?" I asked.

"White guy said he was in insurance, black guy said that they were old friends, a colored girl said that he was her husband, and the cops. The cops dropped on me only about a hour after you, Fearless. You know they had me down at the station for three hours. For a while there I thought they was gonna keep me."

"An' you told 'em that I been askin' about Kit?" Fearless asked in a too-neutral tone.

"Naw. Uh-uh. But when they asked me who knew Kit best I said it was you. Why not? I didn't think you was in any mess."

"What was the black guy's name?" I asked.

"Brown."

"Middle-sized guy?" I asked, thinking about my chess opponent at Miss Moore's rooming house. "Looks young at first but then you see that he's older?"

"That's him."

"What did he want?"

"He said that Kit owed him a thousand dollars, that I could have ten percent if I could tell him where Kit was."

"Did you?"

"I don't know where he is, man."

"So what did you give this dude?" Fearless asked. "'Cause I know you would'a tried to get in on that coin."

"I told him that Kit had that watermelon farm and that he made deliveries for that cosmetic line. That's all I knew."

"Not worth much," I said. "No hundred dollars there."

"He gimme twenty though," Maynard admitted.

"For what?"

"I'ont know. He didn't know what I told him. Maybe he might'a got to his man because'a what I said."

"The man I saw didn't have the kinda cash to be throwin' twenty dollars at somebody don't give him what he wants."

"Well he did," Maynard said.

"What else he give you?"

"Twenty dollars, like I said."

"No," I said. "Not money. He give you a way to get in touch with him."

Maynard shook his head and looked away. He wasn't a liar by nature and so found it hard to deny what he knew to be true.

I was sitting sidesaddle behind the wheel of Ambrosia Childress's Chrysler. Fearless was a shadow on my right and Maynard Latrell was in front of me with the key to a room full of money like an ocean waiting to drown some unsuspecting fool.

You too smart for your own good, my mother used to say to me. *You always askin' questions and lookin' for answers. You always actin' innocent, but that won't save a nosy nose or the curious cat.*

"He give you a number," I said in spite of my mother's advice. "He told you how to get in touch with him."

"No," Maynard said.

"Yeah, he did. But don't worry, Maynard, we ain't gonna jump you for it. 'Cause you see, Kit don't owe that Brown a thousand dollars."

"He don't?"

"No. If Brown find 'im he could get it. But so could me and Fearless. So I'll give you a hundred and ten dollars right here, right now, for that number he give you and anything else you got."

Maynard Latrell was a beautiful man. He had strong but not extreme features, bright eyes, and skin that almost glowed orange. His mouth curved into a smile, then a grin.

"Okay, men," he said. "I got it up in my room."

HIS STUDIO APARTMENT was on floor five of the gray building. There were gray carpets down the gray hall to his black door. The carpeting was the same in his one room but the walls had once been white. Now the dim green plaster was showing from under the thin coat of water-based paint.

The room was neat, though. The bed was up against the wall and covered with a printed yellow cloth. The pillows were set up like the bolsters of a couch. His chest of drawers had a bare top. And there was a chair next to a window that had a radio on its ledge. It was a room that a poor man could survive in, make plans in. One day, if the man was smart, he could move out of there and buy a small house with a backyard. He'd have to have a hardworking wife. They'd raise kids together, send them to college, and spend their twilight years happy in the knowledge that they'd made something out of nothing.

Maynard took two scraps of paper from the bottom drawer of the bureau. He held these in a clenched fist.

"Where the money?"

"You got ten dollars, Fearless?" I asked my friend.

He pulled out a fistful of ones and counted out the cash. I reached into my pocket and peeled five twenty-dollar bills off of the roll Bradford the secretary had given me. I was good at peeling off money from bills in my pocket. You learned to do that when you didn't want people around you to know just how big your wad was.

I handed the money over and Maynard happily gave me the crumpled snippets.

I read both numbers and asked, "What's this? Double vision?"

The numbers were University exchanges, both exactly the same.

"One was the girl," Maynard said, "and the other was that guy Brown."

"Girl called Leora Hartman?"

"Even if she is, I ain't givin' you no money back," Maynard said.

"Let's go, Fearless."

After we were just a few steps down the hall I could hear Maynard whoop for joy.

29

WE CALLED FEARLESS'S MOTHER'S HOUSE from a phone booth on the street. I told Milo to make sure that Loretta and her parents went up to visit their farmer relatives in Bakersfield — immediately. I wasn't worried about him taking my warning lightly. Loretta was the only person he loved in life. He might not have ever said anything, or even have bought her a present at Christmas, but Milo would have laid down his life to protect that woman.

The next thing I did was to call the Leora Hartman/Brown phone number.

"Hello?" a proper Negro voice queried.

"That you, Oscar?" I asked, trying to mask my surprise.

"To whom am I speaking?" he asked in return.

"It's Mr. Minton speaking. I, um, I wanted to speak to Miss Fine."

"Where did you get this number?" he asked suspiciously.

"This is the number I got, man. Something wrong?"

"This is my private line, not the house phone."

"What can I tell you, Oscar my man?"

Oscar paused long enough for a machination. Then he said, "She's still dressing, Mr. Minton. I'll see if she will return your call later."

"Don't bother. Just tell her that I'll be by in an hour or so. I have some reporting to do."

"I'm not sure if she'll be here. She said that she was going to do some shopping."

"Tell her that I have some hot news for her. She'll stick around for that."

"If you have something to tell her, I will be happy to pass it on."

I thought about Bradford, about how he was willing to filter the truth to and from his employer.

"No thanks, man. I better report to the one that's payin' me."

"I can't promise that she'll be here when you come."

"Just promise that you'll tell her what I said and we're jake." On that note I hung up the phone.

"Who was that?" Fearless asked.

"You in this with me now, aren't you, Fearless?"

"Yeah, Paris. You know it, man. You my boy."

"There's money here," I said. "Mr. Wexler plus BB is twenty thousand right there. Now Miss Fine might even be more than that. But I don't like all these other people involved."

"People come and go, Paris. They come and go. But you'n me be right here, baby. Don't you worry 'bout that."

His certainty almost made me confident.

I felt bad about the Wexler murders. Life is a precious thing.

But they were dead and I didn't know why. Maybe, if I found out what Kit had done to Miss Fine, I could solve the crime and retire too.

THE GATE TO THE FINE RESIDENCE was open when we got there. Oscar was waiting at the door by the time we reached the desolate front yard.

"Mr. Minton," he said. "Miss Fine is waiting for you in the study."

"Bring us to her," I said in a confident voice.

"Your friend will have to stay here," he informed me.

"The hell he will."

"Miss Fine is only expecting you."

Rose Fine, wearing a white satin gown and elbow-length black gloves, peeked around a corner down the hall from us. She snorted, then giggled and disappeared behind a pile of bound files.

"You tell Miss Fine that I'm here with my fellow investigator — Fearless Jones. If she wants to hear what I have to say, then she will have to talk to both of us."

Oscar was stuck. I had called him on his personal phone. He knew something was wrong and whatever it was it was bad news for him. If it was his house he would have ushered us out of the door and gone to hide under the bed.

But it wasn't his house.

He turned and walked through a scuffed-up lime-colored door. When he was gone Rose Fine poked her head out again.

"Hello, Miss Fine," I said.

"Do I know you gentlemen?" she asked me.

"Sure you do. Don't you remember? I sat on the wood bench and you took the barber's chair. Oscar got you a shot of whiskey."

"He wasn't here, though," she said, referring to Fearless.

"This is my friend. His name is Fearless. We're doing something for your sister."

"What?"

"Lookin' for a boy name of Bartholomew."

"Perry?"

"That's him. You know him?"

"Him and father — Esau. Bad relations is what I calls 'em. Definitely the colored side of the family."

"You don't like 'em?"

"They family so I have to put up with 'em on Christmas and Easter, but other than them days I wouldn't let them into my outhouse."

I liked her candor even if she was mad.

"What about a young woman named Leora Hartman?"

"Leora," Rose said. She grinned, showing us that she'd lost more teeth than she'd kept. "She's a feather bed in God's sanctuary."

"You know her?"

"Know her? She's my little girl. My baby."

"Your daughter?" I asked, surprised and a little confounded.

If Leora belonged to Rose, then the connection to the house was even stronger than it had seemed. Maybe I should have spent a little more time talking to the demure colored woman.

Rose didn't have many teeth but her hearing was better than mine. She made an unpleasant sound in her throat and darted back down the hall she'd come from. Two seconds after that the scuffed lime door came open.

"Miss Fine will see you both," Oscar informed us.

"Lead on, my man."

THE CURTAINS WERE already open when we entered Winifred Lucia Fine's study. Her nude image in the fountain was still attempting the impossible. My heart still skipped at the beauty.

It struck me that Maestro Wexler's home was much more opulent but somehow the beauty had gotten lost in all the majesty of his residence.

"Fearless Jones," my friend said, approaching the matriarch and holding out his hand.

I could see that she didn't want to shake, but the pressure of his friendliness got to her and she gave up a weak squeeze.

"Winifred Fine," she said.

"I had a aunt named Winfred," Fearless said. "She lived in Mississippi in a little cabin off 'a the Tickle River. Whenever anybody in my family got in trouble they'd go and hide at Aunt Winfred's. The house was built on a overhang and you could stay up under there catchin' and fryin' catfish until the law gave up and you could move on. She'd still be there except for a flood in 'fortyeight. Now she's up around St. Louis. She still gotta basement to hide in, the fishin's not too good though."

"My name is Winifred, not Winfred," Miss Fine said.

"She's a good woman," Fearless agreed.

"I need to ask you some questions, Miss Fine," I interjected.

"About what?"

"Me and Fearless found your nephew."

"Where is he?"

"You got to answer my questions first."

"Did I not pay you, sir?" she asked, using elocution that she probably learned at the same black college that her niece, Leora, attended.

"Question is, did you pay me to walk down the stairs or jump out the window?"

"What is all this?" she asked, waving both hands at the sides of her head. "River hideouts. Jumping out of windows."

"Fearless here is a rough customer, Miss Fine," I said. "He's a nice guy and fair but he's known around Watts as one of the two or three most dangerous men in the entire city."

"Are you trying to threaten me?"

"No ma'am. And it wouldn't matter even if I was, because Fearless would not hurt a woman no matter what I said. But when we broke in on your nephew, Fearless told him that he better act right or he might get hurt. BB was scared."

"I can imagine," Winifred said.

"That's right, ma'am. He was afraid of Fearless, but then, when we mentioned your name, he threw down and swung on Fearless like he was Sugar Ray Robinson up against a tomato can. Fearless had to knock your nephew out. Not only that. When he came to he begged us not to turn him over to you."

"I've already paid you."

"Not to bring a man to the slaughter."

"That's ridiculous. I would not harm my nephew."

"Somebody's been out there harmin' people," Fearless said. "Harmin' up a storm."

"What are you talking about?"

"Can we go out in your garden, Miss Fine?" I asked. "I mean, I like your room here, but I want to make sure that there aren't any ears to catch me in my report."

She cut her eyes at the far door and then toward the bookcase.

"Yes," she said. "That might be a good idea."

THE AIR IN HER GARDEN smelled richer than your everyday atmosphere. Big monarch butterflies and half a dozen other varieties wafted above our heads. There were two stone benches at the far side of the fountain. Miss Fine sat down and Fearless and I parked ourselves on either side of her.

"What do you have to say, Mr. Minton?"

"Do you know a man named Maestro Wexler?" I asked.

"Yes," she said. At first her expression was neutral, almost bland. But then a stitch of anxiety showed through.

"Do you have any business dealings with Wexler?"

"No. I mean . . . I don't have any dealings with him but . . ."

"But what?"

"Five years ago I began buying up corner lots in Compton, through a company owned by my cosmetics corporation. That way the people I bought from thought that I was the same color as the lawyer who brokered the purchases."

"And now Wexler wants those lots?"

"He wants to put in gas stations. He has a big contract for stations in Compton."

"You can't own all the corners of the whole town."

"I own enough to compete with him. I could put in forty or fifty stations myself."

Forty or fifty. I could see why Milo salivated whenever he spoke her name.

"You refused to sell?"

"I offered to go into business with him but he was too greedy. I decided to hold on to my property. Why not? I don't need him."

"Have you heard from him lately?"

"No. What is this about?"

"Two of his children have been murdered."

"Oh my God. That's terrible."

She seemed actually horrified. And I didn't believe that a woman of her caliber would put on an act for people like Fearless and me.

"Didn't you hear about it on the news?" I asked.

"I don't listen to the radio. Nor do I watch television."

"What about the papers?"

"I have Oscar read to me those stories that are salient to our concerns."

She was like a child. Completely cut off from the world, so that all that was important was her needs and her desires. In her world me and mine had never drawn a breath. The drama and tragedy of everyday people was invisible to her. In a way she was like Maestro Wexler sitting on his throne. I could see where money affected both of them more than race. It was the first time I had ever actually witnessed the power of money and class in forming character.

"I think his children's deaths have to do with something they were hatching up with BB," I said. "Him and Kit Mitchell."

Winifred had a poker face that could have broken the confidence of the most seasoned dealer. She might have been isolated but she knew how to play the game.

"I don't see what you mean, Mr. Minton."

"BB offered us ten thousand dollars to find Kit. He put a thousand down on that offer. Maestro offered me ten thousand to find BB. He also plunked down a grand. You already gave me near a thousand in five-dollar bills. That's three thousand that two poor black men have collected, and we haven't done a thing but ask questions and survive the answers."

"You want more money," Winifred Fine said.

"A white man says his name is Theodore Timmerman open fire on me and Fearless two mornings ago. All we did was call his name. He was willing to kill us and all he wanted to know was your identity."

"Me?"

"Yes ma'am," I said.

"And he was shooting at you?"

"Like it was the Fourth of July," Fearless said.

I glanced at my friend then. It was an unspoken rule we had that he would stay quiet when I was asking questions. He never understood the verbal nuances of complex discussions. I wondered why he wanted to be a part of our talk.

"What did he want with me?" Winifred asked.

"Milo sent him out lookin' for the man BB was workin' with. You know — Kit Mitchell. Somewhere out there he found out that he could make more money on his own. It's my bet that he figured the money would come from you but he didn't know your name. Fearless and me was just crows in the road."

"I, I, I'm sorry," she said.

"Sorry's all good and well," I replied. "But what I would like to know is what's goin' on?"

Miss Fine stood up. She walked toward a large rosebush until her face was in among the leaves.

She said something that only the flowers heard.

"What?" I asked.

"It was just a piece of colored crystal," she said, turning back to us. "Green. An emerald surrounded by white sapphires. Have you ever seen a white sapphire, Mr. Minton?"

"I can't say that I have."

"They look like diamonds only the glow is softer. They're beautiful. In the old days they used to give them for weddings. It meant good fortune and a happy life. My father got me a necklace with a single emerald surrounded by those sapphires."

"He must'a been rich as you," Fearless said.

"No. Not really. He had a farm. It was pretty large. But he sold a quarter of his acreage when he saw that pendant in a New Orleans jewelry store window." Winifred was far away in a dream of days gone by. "He loved me and he was superstitious too. He believed that if he made a sacrifice and gave me that gift that I would have a blessed life. He never saw that the real blessing was his love."

"So BB stole your father's dowry?"

"He got Oscar to hire this Kit Mitchell. Mr. Mitchell worked for three weeks and then he left — at our request. A few days after that, Oscar realized that the pendant was missing."

"And so," I said, "they intended to use that to make you give up on the property."

"I can't see how," she said. "I loved my father, not that piece of crystal. It's worth no more than ten or twelve thousand dollars. Maybe because BB knew the story he thought that I would be swayed. But I can assure you that nothing would make me give up on my Compton properties."

"Do you know a man named Brown?" I asked then.

"What is his first name?"

"I don't know. He calls himself Brown, and when he wanted someone to call him he gave out Oscar's number."

"Maybe he worked here," she said. "I wouldn't know."

"How about Oscar? Would he know?"

"Ask him."

"Why are you looking for your nephew?" It was my last attempt to decipher this straight-faced woman.

"When I found out that Bartholomew had suggested this Kit Mitchell for the job, I assumed that he would know where to find my necklace. That's why I need to talk to Bartholomew, to tell him to have my property returned."

"How would BB know where you kept the necklace?"

"He and my niece, Leora, used to play with it when they were children. They both knew where all my jewelry was."

"So what you want is the necklace and not your nephew at all."

"That's right. But I want to speak to Bartholomew, to tell him that I no longer consider him a member of our family."

"Uh-huh. So if me and Fearless get the necklace and make it so you have your chat with BB, then we're clear?"

"Certainly, Mr. Minton."

"BB seemed to think that you would be willing to commit violence against him if he didn't return your property," I said as a primer for further discussion.

"That is ridiculous," Winifred L. Fine said. "Violence is the last resort of the desperate."

"Okay," I said. "Let us go out there and see what we can see."

I touched Fearless's arm to indicate that it was time for our departure.

"One more thing," Winifred Fine said. "What about the man who shot at you? Is he still after me?"

"Don't you worry about him, ma'am," Fearless said. "He came down with a chest cold and now he's laid up for the season."

30 | FEARLESS DROVE US DOWN the dirt road toward the street.

"Where to now, Paris?" he asked me.

"I don't know. We could wait for BB to call us and then ask him how a twelve-thousand-dollar piece of jewelry's gonna be fifty thousand, or maybe what the Wexler kids had to do with it."

"You think he'd tell us that?"

"Maybe," I said. "Maybe if we threatened to drag him out here if he didn't."

We were approaching Baloona Creek when a woman dressed in a long formal gown and carrying a small brown bag ran in front of Ambrosia's car. Fearless hit the brakes and swerved to miss her. When she came up to the window I couldn't speak for a moment because of the shock of almost running Rose Fine down.

"You okay?" Fearless asked.

"Yeah," I said before realizing that he was talking to the crazy woman.

"Help me get away from here," she cried desperately.

"Hop in," Fearless said.

He jumped out and ushered her in through the rear door. Then he got back in the driver's seat and drove off as if he were a chauffeur and I was his assistant.

"Fearless?"

"Yeah, Paris?"

"What are we doin'?"

"I don't know. Where you wanna go, Miss Fine?"

"Anyplace not near that house, young man," she said. "Anywhere I can get away from them crazy people."

Fearless nodded slightly and continued on. I guess he figured that no matter which way he drove he'd be meeting her request.

"Miss Fine," I said.

"Yes, young man."

"I'm Paris. And I'd like to know why you want to run away from your own home."

"Because it's all gonna come out now. All of it. Winifred won't be able to stop the walls of Jericho. No she won't. But she's just willful enough to believe that she can."

"What's going to happen?"

"Everything we have will be squandered, stolen, and burned in hell," she said. "Too many secrets, too many lies."

"What kind of secrets?" I asked.

"I was a prisoner in there. No money and no car. And now not even no love."

I had very little confidence in the mad-eyed woman's ability to understand or communicate the truth. I had no idea what Fearless planned to do with her. But there we were, so I played the game as if I were privy to the rules.

"Who was Bartholomew's mother?" I asked.

"That would be Ethel," Rose said. She was staring out of the window, smiling at the passing strawberry farms as if they were strange new sights in a distant land.

"She's the one that started the beauty business?"

"No," Rose said, turning her cracked grin on me. "Our mother started the beauty product company. She named it after Ethel because Ethel was her firstborn and her favored girl. Ethel was the oldest, then came me, and then Winnie."

"And so you all owned the business equally?"

"Oh yes," Rose said. "Mama made sure that we were always equal. She had her favorites, but blood is blood."

"And Ethel was the favorite child?"

"Oh no," Rose assured me. "It's always a boy that has his mother's heart."

"You have a brother?"

"Of course we do. I thought you knew. Oscar is our brother."

"The butler?" Fearless asked.

"It's his own fault," she said, reciting a well-rehearsed speech. "When he was a young man he insisted to be paid for his part of the beauty supply company. We bought him out and he lost it all inside of three years. Winnie told him if he wanted to come back he had to work for us."

"She made him a butler?"

"That was his idea," Rose said. "Yes sir. He didn't want to

have anything else to do with the outside world. No business, no meetin's, no bein' in charge'a anything responsible. All he wanted was to work at home and hide away from how stupid he was. We didn't want him to be our servant, but Winnie said that he had to work if he wanted to eat our food."

"I know that," Fearless intoned.

"Why did you run away?" I asked, hoping the question would catch her by surprise.

"Because you had a car and kind eyes."

"You mean you've been waiting for a chance to get out of there?"

"Oscar thinks he's slick," Rose answered, "with all his sneakin' and overhearin'. But if you have a hidey-hole or a spare phone in the nook, then the spy might just be spied on. Yes sir."

"What did Oscar say to make you want to run away?"

"I'll never tell."

"What about a man named Brown?" I asked, switching tracks as fast as she.

"What about him?" Rose had no love lost there.

"Is he some other relation?"

"Oh no. No no no no. Brown is somethin' else altogether."

"And what is that, Miss Fine?"

The elder woman in the fine evening gown sat back and sighed. "I don't think I want to answer any more questions, young man."

"That's okay, ma'am," Fearless said. "You just sit back and I'll take you someplace where you can figure out what you want to do now that you're looking for a new home."

That stopped any more inquiries for a while. But I didn't

mind. Fearless was probably right. Rose Fine didn't have a strong grip on reality, and too many questions might have pushed her out of orbit completely.

The elder Fine sister stretched out on the backseat and was snoring quicker than Fearless Jones.

I DIDN'T WANT TO TALK on the drive because I worried that Rose Fine might have just been pretending to sleep. Fearless, I was sure, remained silent to let her catch up on her rest.

"Must be hard livin' someplace you hate," he whispered after quite a while. "That's why I'm never jealous'a what another man got."

"Where are you plannin' to go, Fearless?"

"I figure out to Mama's," he said. "You know Milo might be some help askin' Miss Fine questions."

"I can ask questions with the best of 'em, Fearless. We don't need Milo."

"You ask okay but you don't have the kinda manners that refined women like Winifred and Rose is used to," Fearless informed me. "Your questions sound like sandpaper but Milo feel like shammy cloth up in their ears."

I didn't argue. If Fearless and I worked for a corporation I would have been his boss's boss's boss. But in the world of hearts and minds I was more like his dog.

"TRISTAN," HIS MOTHER SQUEALED. We had come to her little home on Elm off Paulsen. "And Paris. Oh, baby, it's so good to see you."

Gina Jones was almost as tall as her son and twice his girth. She wrapped me in an embrace that was somewhat like the ocean — she rocked back and forth and buoyed me up on soft strength that could crush stone, given time.

"Hi, Mama Jones," I said.

Fearless kissed his mother and said, "This here is Rose Fine, Mama. She had to leave her home and we didn't know where to take her so we brought her here."

"Isn't that a beautiful gown?" Gina said.

Rose grinned broadly and clasped her gloved hands together. Fearless carried her tiny suitcase.

"Come in, everybody," Gina said.

She led us into a small parlor that had been set up to make the most possible out of the space she had. Against adjoining walls were two coral-colored sofas that came together at a right angle, with an extremely small walnut table set where they met. There were two wooden chairs near the door to the kitchen and an overhead light with a blue-and-yellow shade instead of a lamp that might take up table or floor space.

Milo Sweet — fully dressed in tan suit, blue vest, and red tie — was seated in one of the chairs holding a small china cup in one hand and an equally delicate saucer in the other. He stood up, put the cup and saucer on the chair, and then approached us.

"Paris, Fearless," he said. Then he laid eyes upon our Victorian charge.

"Miss Fine," she said. "Rose Fine."

She held out the back of her hand and Milo actually kissed the glove.

"Milo," Fearless said.

"We have things to talk about," I added.

"Not until you all come into the kitchen and sit for something to drink and eat," Gina Jones said.

She was from another era, a time in the country when people traveled by foot or horse-drawn buggy. Whenever anyone showed up at the door, it had to be after a long and dusty journey.

I felt like I had been a long way. A drink and some lunch sounded like just the right thing.

31 | THE KITCHEN WAS A BIG SQUARE ROOM with a small stove and an icebox set in the corner next to a big-basin sink. The rest of the room was dominated by a large square table with a yellow linoleum top. There were more than enough chrome chairs with red vinyl cushions for Gina's guests. After hefty meatloaf sandwiches she served us lemonade and pound cake with marmalade and strawberry preserves.

Milo brought out a flask of vodka for the men to lace their drinks. Rose and Gina spoke for a long time about things like silver thread and salad spoons, rhubarb pie and quilting circles. Every time Milo or I tried to bring up business we were gently shushed by Fearless's mother.

After forty-five minutes or so Rose asked if she could take a short nap. Gina led the millionaire off to her bedroom and stayed with her for a while.

"What you boys got?" Milo said as soon as they were gone.

I told him almost everything except about the money we'd been paid already. Milo hadn't really hired us and so I didn't see why he should be cut in on our gain.

"So all you got to do is get the pendant and Miss Fine will be happy," Milo said, finishing our story with his own happy ending.

"Milo," I said. "People are dead here. Big-time people. People who don't give a shit about some Negro farmer's treasure. It don't make sense."

"Who cares?" he said. "We didn't kill anybody. We weren't anywhere near it. All we got to worry about is keepin' Winifred Fine happy."

"That's all *you* got to care about, man," I said. "I'm worried about sleepin' in my bed without somebody waitin' outside in the street with a pistol in his hand."

"Don't be a fool, Paris. Nobody cares about some niggah own a used-book bookstore. They worried about property and money. White-people money, not your little change."

"Maybe that man beatin' on your ass didn't get through to you, Miles," I said. "But these people serious out here. They will hurt anybody that might even be a little bit in the way. That white man lost his children. I wouldn't be too quick to mess in with the man he think killed 'em."

Milo's eyes were glazed over by the hope for money and power. He wasn't listening to me. Neither was Fearless as far as I could see. The World War II killer was leaning back in his chair with a smile on his face.

"What you grinnin' at, fool?" I asked him.

"It's nice to see Mama with a lady her own age. They could sit and talk all day long, I bet. That's real nice."

"Fearless, we got trouble here."

"What you want to do about it, Paris?" He wasn't being negative. It was just a question. If I said to go out and roll a stone up a hill he would have pushed up his sleeves and done so, smiling about his mother all the way.

"Milo, you could help," I said.

"How?" he asked.

"Me and Fearless got a spy might know a guy knows Kit. His name is Honeyboy, and we told him to call your answerin' service to tell us where we could catch up with him."

Milo called his service. Honeyboy had left a message earlier in the day. He said that we could find him at an address on Downey Road in East L.A.

Milo had no idea that Honeyboy was really Bartholomew Perry, the man he was looking for. It gave me a great deal of pleasure fooling him like that.

THE ADDRESS THAT BB LEFT FOR US was across the street from the New Calvary Cemetery, a fairly big graveyard in the middle of East L.A. By the time we got there it was closing in on five-thirty. The house was large and painted blue-green with a dark green trim. There were eighteen stairs to a front porch that ran the whole length of the front of the house.

Fearless took the stairs three at a time, so I lagged behind him. At least that's what I pretended. New places in serious times always slowed my pace.

Fearless was knocking by the time I had reached him. With all those strange stairs and a graveyard at my back, I felt a shiver as I caught up. So I wasn't surprised when the door opened and a man pointed a gun at us.

I wasn't surprised, but I was terrified enough to lose my senses.

I fell hard to the floor, rolled, and then tried to rise to my feet. But the fear in my heart was like in one of those dreams where you try to run but you can't do it, you can't run because the fear is an anchor in your chest. I rolled on my back and put up my hands, hoping that somehow I could survive the barrage. But what I saw was that Fearless had moved in the opposite direction, grabbed hold of Theodore Timmerman's gun hand, and delivered a devastating right hook to the jaw of the man who had tried to kill us two times in three days.

Timmerman went down and Fearless disarmed him. Then my friend turned to me, smiling and holding out a helping hand.

"I, I'm sorry, Fearless," I said.

"For what, boy?"

"I didn't mean to run. I didn't even know that I was doin' it till I was on my back."

"Lucky you did, Paris. Teddy here thought you had somethin', so he turned your way. And you know, baby, you better not ever turn away from me if you wanna live."

TIMMERMAN WASN'T DEAD — at least not quite. His shirt was open, so we could see the nasty bruise on his chest from the brick Fearless had thrown. His jaw was swelling now too.

The house had a professional look to it. There was a living

room to the left that might well have been an office. There were dark-stained oak furnishings and white curtains that were closed. Fearless set Timmerman down in a padded oak chair.

"Why ain't you in a hospital, man?" he asked Ted.

"Fuck you," the would-be killer replied.

"No, really, man," Fearless went on. "You got somethin' wrong there. It ain't gonna heal without some help."

The white man's sallow chest was bruised blue, green, and black. It was like a large dark cloud hovering under his pale skin.

"What you doin' here?" I asked.

"Fuck you."

"Where's BB?"

Timmerman said nothing.

There came a rumble that might have been pounding and a voice that made sounds but no discernible words.

"Go on, Paris," Fearless said. "I'll stay with your friend."

There was a hallway at the back of the room. It was long and also more professional looking than homey. There were no paintings or any sign of somebody living there. After going twenty feet or so I came to a door. The sounds were coming from there.

Still it was just muffled pounding and a muffled voice.

I turned to go back to Fearless. I was going to tell him that I found the door where the noise was coming from. But I stopped halfway. Looking back at the door, I finally convinced myself to do something to redeem my pride after panicking on the front porch.

I went to the door and quickly pulled it open so as not to lose heart.

Opening doors wasn't lucky for me during that period.

I thought it was the Mummy who fell out on top of me — if the Mummy weighed two hundred and twenty-five pounds. All tied up in sheets, bleeding, and yelling through the gag he wore. It took me a few moments to realize that the monster wasn't attacking me but struggling to get free from the bonds. It took a moment more to recognize Bartholomew thrashing and screaming under the knots of gauze.

Before I grasped the situation I yelped. It wasn't a scream of terror or even a shout. At least I could be proud of my reserve.

Regardless of the dignity I maintained in my mind, Fearless came running with the wounded white man in tow. I looked up at him, on my back for the second time in less than ten minutes, and said, "I found him."

"MOTHAHFUCKAH COME UP TO MY DOOR and pointed his gun at me," Bartholomew was telling us.

The skin over both eyes was so swollen from the beatings that he was barely recognizable. He was bleeding and had lost a tooth. Timmerman might have been hurting but he was still dangerous.

"He kept askin' who was lookin' for me. I didn't say nuthin' and he just started beatin' on my ass."

"And so you give us up so he could beat on us too," I added.

"No I didn't. I had already called that number, all I said was that you was gonna call me. That's all," BB said. "You know he had me so tied up I couldn't even breathe in there."

I wanted to sneer but then I remembered choking in the trunk of Louis's car. I would have given up the secrets of the atom bomb to get out of there.

• • •

"WHAT ELSE YOU TELL HIM?" Fearless asked.

We were back in the sterile living room. Ted was tied up with the same sheets that had bound BB.

"I, I told him I didn't know why you were lookin' for me," BB said. "And then he beat me so bad that I had to give him something. I had to."

The expression on my friend's face was impossible to read. BB saw something there that scared him, because he shrank in his chair.

"Who you tell about bein' here?" Fearless asked at last.

"Nobody."

"You already give us up to a killer, brother. Don't lie too."

"I just told him that you was gonna call. If I didn't he would'a killed me."

"That's what you told him," Fearless said. "Who did you tell that you'd be here?"

"Nobody, man. Nobody at all."

"Uh-uh." Fearless shook his head. "And you know how I know that?"

BB shook his head too.

"Because this white man come up in here after you. He wasn't goin' door to door lookin'. He knew right where you were."

"What is this place?" I asked.

"It's a house my father's church bought as a home for some of its old people. It's a church house."

"And how'd you get here?"

"I went to my father after you found me. I told him that I needed to hide. He had the keys and gave them to me."

Fearless glanced at me and smirked. There was too much blood and pain in the room for me to share his humor, but I knew what he meant. We had a path to follow now. And following was always better than being stalked.

"What about you?" Fearless asked Theodore Timmerman.

"Fuck you."

"That's all right, brother. Yeah. You just keep on sayin' that. But I'm sure your mama don't want them to be the last words on your lips before you die."

"You're not gonna kill me," Teddy said, I thought rather hopefully.

"No," Fearless agreed.

He crouched down next to the chair Teddy was tied to. Then he took a long finger and jabbed it lightly in the center of that dark cloud in Timmerman's chest. The pain shuddered through Milo's ex-agent like a quake through a dying engine. He tried to inhale but his lungs stalled and a dribble of blood appeared at the corner of his mouth.

"You taste that?" Fearless asked. "That's the end comin' up outta you. All I got to do is leave you here, man. That's all, and you'll be dead before sunrise."

Timmerman was still trying to recover from the deep hurt that Fearless had pointed out. He took small breaths, jammed his eyes closed, and clenched his jaw tightly.

After a few moments of this agony he looked up and said, "Fuck you."

My friend laughed and shook his head.

Ted Timmerman had won Fearless Jones's respect.

32

FEARLESS REMOVED TIMMERMAN'S shoes and pants, gagged him, and bound his hands behind his back. I drove Ambrosia's Chrysler up the driveway next to the big impersonal house and Fearless took our captive and pushed him on the floor of the backseat.

"You better not let nobody but Jesus know where you light next time, Barty," Fearless suggested at the back door.

"What you gonna do wit' him?" BB asked.

"Don't worry 'bout him. Worry 'bout yo'self, man."

I opened the door to the car but then I closed it again.

"BB."

"Yeah, Paris?"

"Tell me about Rikki Faison's house."

"What?" he asked with a weak grin and slight shrug.

"Don't fuck with us, BB. Tell me about that house and what you were doin' there."

"You got to go, Paris," Bartholomew complained.

"Fearless," I said.

"Uh-huh," he replied. He got in behind the wheel and I ushered young Prince Perry back inside the church house.

"Tell me about Minna, man," I said after the door was closed behind us.

"She was my girlfriend, that's all. We been messin' around for three, four months."

"And?"

"And . . . well. One night she said that her brother heard that I was related to Aunt Winnie. She said that we could get a hold on her that we'd be able to make a big payday. Big."

"So what you do?"

"I got together with Kit and we hatched up a plan."

"What plan?"

Bartholomew stared into my eyes. His visage was a rueful one. I think he wanted to unburden his heart.

He shook his head instead.

"No, man. You might find out along the way, but if Aunt Winnie ask you you tell her you ain't heard it from me."

"I hope you know what you doin', brother," I said. "Call Milo's number when you know where you gonna be. And don't forget to use the name Honeyboy. Don't use your own name."

You could see that he didn't want me to leave him alone there. Being tortured will bring out the communal spirit in most men. But he didn't want to beg. At least he had that much pride.

• • •

WE DROVE TO GENERAL HOSPITAL and pulled into an alley across the street. It was closing in on seven-thirty by then and so the alley was empty. Fearless untied Timmerman, took him out of the car, and set him up against a wall.

"You can come after us or sign yourself into the emergency room across the street," my friend advised.

Then he climbed back into the car and we drove off. Through the back window I could see the white man struggling down the alley. I wondered what his decision would be.

"That boy got some nuts on him," Fearless said as we cruised down State Street.

"In his head."

"Well," Fearless opined. "Yeah. Most'a your brave men is a little bit crazy. Either that or they pushed up against a wall. But I got to hand it to your boy there — he not backin' down for nuthin'."

We got the home address of Esau Perry from his son. We told BB that it would be better if we found out from his father that night who he had spoken to about his whereabouts.

Esau's house was on Piru Street, not far from his car lot. It was a rare brick home, with a fireplace and patch of lawn not even big enough to sun on.

Fearless knocked on the door and we heard a young child squealing from inside. A few moments went by. It was almost fully night by then. The last shreds of daylight were far off on the western horizon, a jarring combination of ember-orange and deep blue.

The door opened and Esau stood there, still in his coveralls. The child chirped out a glad note from somewhere in the house.

"Yes?"

"Mr. Perry," I said. "Sorry to bother you at night, sir. But we have a problem that we thought you might want to know about."

He knew something was up. He knew that he was involved too. That's why he didn't slam the door on us or at least ask me more about what I meant. Instead of a challenge he stood aside for us to enter.

He led us into a kitchen that was painted and furnished all in yellow, under a yellow light. There was a large young Mexican woman sitting on a small chair playing with a little brown boy who resembled Henry from the comic strips.

"Hey, Son," Fearless said.

The boy looked up at my friend with a sense of confusion and wonder and said, "Hi."

"Take him up to his bed, Trini," Esau said to the woman.

"Okay, baby," she replied, speaking volumes about their relationship with two small words.

The boy protested verbally but he let Trini pick him up and carry him out of a back doorway. As they left, Son held out his arms toward Esau. The older man's arms moved toward the boy, saying good-bye and reaching too.

"How's BB?" Esau asked after Trini and Son were gone.

"He might be dead if Fearless here wasn't faster than Jesse Owens at a Nazi barbecue."

"That white man hurt him?"

"Oh yeah," I said. "He installed a sun visor over his eyes."

"Shut up, Paris," Fearless said.

"No. No. I wanna know why a father would send a man like that out to kill his own son."

Esau went to the kitchen counter and poured himself a shot from a quart bottle there. He downed the drink and poured another.

"He took Son."

"What?"

"He come out here and took Son."

"Kidnapped him?" Fearless asked.

"Yes sir. Took him right off the front lawn when Trini's back was turned. Called me up and said that he wanted to know where BB was."

"And you turned him over," I said in a voice that I didn't mean to be so damning.

"Yes I did. Really he did it to himself. He got himself into all this trouble."

"What trouble?" I asked. "You mean that pendant?"

"Pendant?"

"Yeah. Emerald job that Winifred's father bought for her."

"That piece'a green glass?" Esau said. "No. That's a trinket compared to what BB and his friend did."

"You mean Kit?"

"Yeah. That's who I mean."

"You got a phone, Mr. Perry?" Fearless asked.

"Right through this door," Esau said. "Right on the right."

Fearless walked out and I continued my interrogation.

"Do you know where we can find Kit?"

"No," Esau said. "I don't wanna have nuthin' to do wit' that man. Him and BB likely to bring that whole family to misery."

"How's that?"

Esau gauged me for a moment. I have no idea what he saw but he said, "Son used to stay with his auntie."

"Winifred?" I asked, and then I remembered the toy gyroscope in her drawing room.

"Yeah. She got him from his mother when she was havin' problems with her husband, but when Leora wanted him back Winifred said that he'd be better off there with her. She wanted to bring him up herself."

"Could she get away with that?"

"She did," Esau said. "That is, until BB got that Kit Mitchell to go up in there pretendin' he worked with fancy gardens and shit. He took the boy and give him to his mother, but then he told some rich white man that he could tell Winifred that he kidnapped the boy and that she either had to play ball wit' him or Son would die."

I liked the shape of the scheme. There was no real crime, at least not that could be proven. The boy was with his mother and safe, the threat would have been vague enough that a prosecutor might not even be able to prove extortion.

"That was the Wexler kids did that?"

"Yes sir."

"You know they're dead, right?"

Fearless walked back in then. I wondered who he could have called so quickly.

"Yeah," Esau said. "That's why when that white man gave me the choice between Son and BB, I made up my mind on the innocent. He wanted to trade BB's hidin' place for Son and I agreed."

"What's Son to you?" Fearless asked.

"He's Leora's boy. My nephew by law and by love. She brought him here to me while she tried to fix the damage that Kit and BB had done."

"What damage?" I asked. "She got her boy. What's wrong with that?"

"BB and Kit took somethin' else," Esau said.

"Necklace?" asked Fearless.

"Naw. I don't know what it was, but Leora was real upset about it. That's why she said that she had to find Kit."

"Why didn't you just call the cops?" I asked.

"Because this is beyond the police. White man came here to me. White man got his kids killed. Rich white man. All I could do was hope that BB could dig his own way out the hole he dug."

The pain in Esau's words was almost a physical thing.

"So," I said, "Kit took Son out from Winifred's house."

"That's right."

"Is he in bed yet?"

Esau glanced at the back wall and cocked his ear. At that moment I heard the weak cry of water running through pipes in the wall.

"He's in the tub by now," Esau said.

LITTLE CHILDREN IN BATHTUBS must be the same all over the world. More like tadpoles than humans, they kick and slide and laugh at the pleasure of warm water and their own nakedness. Trini was smiling down on her little charge.

"Hey, Son," Fearless said as we three men entered the bathroom.

When he stared up at us his mouth fell open.

"We need to find somebody," Fearless continued.

"My daddy?" the child asked.

"No, uh-uh. Not right now. But do you remember a man name of Kit?"

The boy shook his head no.

"One of his teeth is silver like."

"Oh yeah. That's the man took me out from my auntie's house and give me to my mama."

"Do you know where we could find him?"

"Where the big wheel is," Son said with a nod.

I was ready to jump in and ask as many questions as necessary to find Kit but Fearless just said, "Thanks, boy," and turned to walk away.

I put a hand on his arm and asked, "Where you goin'?"

"To get Kit. You comin'?"

WHERE TWEEDY BOULEVARD MEETS Santa
Fe there was a garage that specialized in all problems associated with car tires. Inner tubes, retreads,
patches, and even axles — they had everything. Their insignia was
a gigantic transport plane landing tire. It must have been fifteen
feet in diameter. Add that to the fact that it stood upon a twenty-
foot pylon and you had a strong symbol of your business. It made
sense that that tire would dominate Son's imagination. It also made
sense that Fearless would have known immediately what Son had
meant, because he had a deep affinity with the wonder of children.

"But suppose it was some other big tire?" I asked. "They got
one out in the valley."

"I don't think Kit would be hidin' in the valley, would you,
Paris?"

"Might not even be a wheel," I said. "Maybe it's something else."

"Like what?"

"Like a Ferris wheel for instance," I said.

"Ain't no circus or carnival down around Watts right now, Paris. And Watts is all Kit knows. Uh-uh, man. We might as well look here."

I hated when Fearless's logic defeated me.

"Where we gonna look?" I asked.

There were three apartment buildings and half a dozen small homes across the street from the garage. Behind there was a very large apartment structure, like a lodge, and there were various other domiciles up and down the block.

"He could be anywhere around here," I said.

"Let's go get some wine," Fearless replied.

Diagonally across from the garage was a small banana-colored bodega. The sign above the front door read BRUCE'S STORE.

The Mexican behind the counter had sad eyes and a drooping mustache. But he was smiling still and all. It wasn't a friendly smile, more like the secure sneer of a man who's got a shotgun under the counter.

"You Bruce?" Fearless asked right off.

"No. Brucey owns the store. He don't work at night."

"He a white guy?"

"No. Like me."

"Then how he gonna have a name like Bruce?"

"His name was Guillermo when he was born in Ensenada. But he came here to pick lemons and stayed to open this store. He said he didn't want just our people to come here, that he wanted everybody to be welcome, so he changed his name to Bruce."

The shopkeeper's smile warmed while he spoke.

"Legally?" I asked.

"Yes. It's on his driver's license. Do you need something?"

The little market was set up like a California liquor store. At the back was a coffin-shaped, glass-doored refrigerator filled with juices, milk, sodas, and beer. The aisles had mostly snack food. Behind the counter were rows of cheap wine.

"Gimme a bottle'a that Thunderbird, will ya?" Fearless said.

The clerk, who was trim and fifty, pulled down a pint bottle, slipping it into a brown paper bag that seemed fitted to our purchase.

"Forty-nine cents," the clerk said.

Fearless paid with a five-dollar bill. While he was receiving the change he said, "Maybe you could help me out."

The chill returned to the man's smile.

"Oh?"

"Yeah. I'm lookin' for my cousin Kit. Brown like Paris here and he got a silver tooth up front." Fearless pointed at one of his own teeth with a baby finger. "And he drink this here Thunderbird like it was orange juice."

"Oh yes. I know him. Kit? He never said his name. But I seen him go into that big gray building behind the garage."

WE CROSSED THE STREET and went up the block to the front of the big building. I was wondering as we went how we could search for Kit while keeping a low profile. After all, the police rousted Fearless for just knowing the Watermelon Man.

As we neared the double doors that gave entrée to the monolithic building, Fearless touched my shoulder.

"Look over there," he said, pointing to the street.

"At what?" I asked.

"That gray Rambler over there."

"What about it?"

"That there is Leora Hartman's car, I bet."

Not only was it her car but she was in it, laid up against the steering wheel and crying like her own son.

Fearless opened the driver's door and helped her out. She fell into his arms and cried in utter despair.

I looked around, hoping that no one saw us. In my experience people always remember a woman's tears. But no one was out on their porches or strolling down the street. L.A. has never been a pedestrian's town, I thanked the Lord for that.

"He's dead," Leora whimpered. "He's dead. He's dead. He's dead."

"Who?" Fearless asked.

"I think it's Kit Mitchell."

"Don't you know?"

"I never met him before." She took in a large gulp of air and made a strangled sound.

"Take us to him," Fearless said. It was an order and not a request.

Leora led us into the big building and up to the sixth floor. The door to 6R was unlocked.

When I got into the room I closed the door quickly. Mainly because of the breaking and entering and because the man lying on the floor was at a most uncomfortable angle.

Leora Hartman cried on Fearless's shoulder.

I went to the man. He was definitely dead. He'd been dead for a while, probably as long as the Wexlers.

"We've got to get out of here," Leora was saying.

"Is it him?" I asked.

"Yeah," Fearless said. "Damn."

"I didn't kill him," Leora said as if we were cops.

His face was brutalized, his left arm likely broken.

"No," I said. "Not unless you Superman under that dress and you like livin' with the dead for a few days."

Leora began to cry harder. Fearless embraced her as a father would his child. From around the corner of his shoulder she stared at the Watermelon Man's corpse. There was terror in her eyes.

"What were you doing here?" I asked.

She couldn't tear her eyes away from Death.

I put my head between her and eternity and asked my question again.

"Oscar told me he was here."

"How did he know?"

"There's a woman on the first floor who has a cousin that works for Madame Ethel's Beauty Supply. Oscar had sent out the word to all the people work for us to look for Kit Mitchell. The employee, her name's Bell Britton, asked her cousin if she knew Kit, and she finally got the word today."

"And why did Oscar tell you?"

"So I could come by and talk to him." Leora's eyes widened and she began to cry again.

"Why would he —"

"Paris," Fearless said. "Let her get it out first, will ya?"

"I came here," she continued, "the door was unlocked."

"What were you looking for?"

"I, I . . ."

"Leave her alone, Paris."

"Shut up, Fearless."

It was one of the few times I told Fearless to be quiet. He knew enough to listen.

"Talk to me, Leora."

"He kidnapped my son."

"Son is with Esau. You already knew that. What did Kit have that you wanted?"

Leora started gasping and then panting. She was at some early stage of shock. I knew that Fearless wouldn't let me continue, so I said, "Damn!"

"We better get outta here, Paris," Fearless said. The worry in his voice was for Leora.

"In a minute," I said.

I launched into a quick search of the apartment. I went through drawers, closets, bedclothes, cereal boxes, the refrigerator and icebox, and the medicine cabinet in the bathroom.

Following my lead, Fearless searched the dead man.

"Here it is," he said.

Next to the Watermelon Man's right ankle, under the sock, was the emerald pendant. Kit must have hidden it before answering the door for the last time.

"I'll put it with the money," Fearless said.

I wondered if I'd be toting that bag on my journey down into hell.

WE MADE IT OUT of the building without too many people marking our passage. But every eye turned my way felt like a gun sight following me across an open field.

"I can drive myself," Leora said when we tried to guide her to Fearless's ride.

"I'll drive her," I said.

"No, Paris. You have her jumpin' out the window with all

your questions and shit." With that Fearless handed me the keys to Ambrosia's car.

"Okay," I said. "You right. But where do we meet? Your mother's?"

"Naw. I don't wanna be talkin' 'bout no murders in my mama's house. No. You know where Milo leave his key, right?"

"Yeah, in a hole in the wall behind his mailbox. But what about Timmerman?"

"I ain't worried about him. He ain't got no pants, no shoes, no money, no car keys. Anyway, he admitted himself to the hospital."

"You don't know that."

"Sure I do. Remember when I made that call from Esau's?"

"You called the hospital?"

"Yeah, man. I knew he'd probably come after you so I wanted to make sure his butt was in the sling."

"Why come after me?" I asked. "You the one that hurt him."

"Yeah," Fearless said, nodding. "That's why he gonna leave me alone."

ON THE RIDE BACK TOWARD MILO'S OFFICE I tried to make sense out of death. Anybody I'd come across could have killed Kit or the Wexlers. Even Timmerman had been in the mix long enough. And what was Leora after? I didn't doubt that she was innocent of Kit's murder, but why come after him if she already had her son?

And why wouldn't the man who killed Kit have searched him? Because he was looking for something particular, something that could not be hidden in a sock.

34

LORETTA KUROKO'S OFFICE had more room than Milo's. She also had a small canvas cot in a closet behind her desk — kept there for any client who had to make an early-morning court date. Leora Hartman was reclining on the cot by the time I made it to Milo's place.

She and Fearless were talking when I got there. That was good, because Fearless had a way of making people trust him, even those who thought that he was dumb.

"How you feelin', Miss Hartman?" I asked when I came in.

"Fine."

"Is that what I call you? Miss? Or is it Missus?"

"Missus. But my last name isn't Hartman — it's Brown."

I knew a dozen people who went by that name. You met a new one every day or two. It was as common as Smith or Jones — more so among colored people. But still . . .

"Your husband's not a chess player, is he?"

"He is. How would you know that?"

"And he's from Illinois but he was born in Mississippi?"

"Where is he, Mr. Minton?" Leora sat up, her sorrow dissipating by the moment.

"No, uh-uh," I said. "You tell us what's goin' on first."

"Brown is my husband," Leora said, "but you already know that."

"You call your husband by his last name?" That was Fearless.

"Everybody does," I said before Leora could get it out.

"Have you seen him, Mr. Minton?"

"I thought you and he were havin' problems?"

"Yes, but not like you think," she said. "He was a gardener at Hampton College when I went there. Nobody liked Brown very much but I loved him and we were married after I graduated. We had Son and moved back to Illinois. But Brown had a, a . . . he had a medical condition but we didn't know it, not then. At first I just thought that he was just getting used to being married and a father. But . . . He was offensive and rough at times, but then he'd be wonderful. Finally, one day he turned on Son. We decided to put him in a hospital where I could be with him. I sent Son to stay with my mother —"

"Rose," I said.

"You've met her, so you know that she isn't able to give the twenty-four-hour care that a young child needs."

"But Aunt Winnie could," I said.

"Paris, will you let the lady finish?" Fearless chided.

"Yeah. Go on."

"Well, you know most of it. I mean, you may have heard about Brown but you don't know him. He's the most amazing man I've ever met. He's funny and smarter than anybody I ever knew at Hampton, even among the professors. He's great with his hands. . . . He was in the asylum for a year and a half. I worked full-time to pay the expenses. I only got to see Son once a month or so, I was working so much. Finally we heard about a juju woman down in Louisiana. We were told by a white doctor that he had seen great improvement in a Negro patient who went down to her.

"We went and she treated him with herbs and the like, and there was enough of a change that we could start our life over again. I went to Aunt Winifred then, but she refused to give Son back. She said that Brown was crazy and violent and that she wouldn't put her nephew into harm's way like that. Here he's my son and she had the nerve to question me bringing him to harm."

"Why didn't you and Brown just go get him?" Fearless asked.

"I told Brown to stay back in Illinois," Leora said. "He's bet-ter . . . but even a sane man might come to violence if someone tried to keep him from his son. I thought he was still back home until you just said —"

"So Winifred refused to let Son go back to you," I said. "Then what?"

"She said that she was going to raise him. I tried to reason with her and she went to a lawyer, Lewis Martini. He's the one that put my mother's wealth into Winifred's hands."

"Winnie got the power of attorney on Rose?" I asked.

"Yes."

"Damn. She got you comin' and goin'. Use your own family's money to keep everybody in line."

"She thinks that she knows best so there's no arguing about it."

"In steps Bartholomew Perry, son of the dear departed Ethel Fine Perry," I said.

"Yes. Esau had my cousin BB working at the car lot and he didn't like the work. So he told me that he'd take Son out of there for ten thousand dollars. Once I got him I could go back to Illinois, and Winnie would have a lot of trouble trying to take a child from his mother and father across state lines."

"I thought you were broke?" I asked.

"He said that I could pay over time," she said. There was a slight catch in her throat, though. The lie couldn't make it out of her mouth unscathed.

"I bet he did. So then BB hires Kit to get in there as a gardener," I said. "Kit takes Son and brings him to BB. How does Maestro Wexler get in with it?"

"You know about that?"

"When Paris digs his claws into a problem he find out everything," Fearless said. "I told you that."

"BB was going out with Minna at the time. He told her about what he was doing, because he didn't realize that she had any interest in his aunt."

"So it's just coincidence that she's in his bed when he plans a kidnapping from the woman her father wants to get the reins on?"

"Yes," Leora said, and I'm sure she believed it. Why would she think that she was the perfect pawn for the machinations of the white siblings?

"And how does Kit know BB?"

"BB sold some trucks to Kit."

"So Kit knew BB from the used car business?" I asked.

"BB moved stolen cars," Leora said. "That's how he made money on the side."

"But not no ten thousand dollars," I said. "And surely not no fifty grand."

Fearless spread a blanket out over the distraught woman.

"Maybe we should let her sleep," he suggested.

"Yeah, yeah," I said. "But lemme ask you just two more questions."

"Yes?"

"Did Kit bring Son to you after he took him out from your aunt's house?"

"No, it was like you said before. Kit brought Son to BB and BB turned him over to me. I was so happy to see him. All he wanted was to go see his father."

"Then why you wanna go and ask Fearless to look for Kit? You already had what you wanted. You had your son. And why would somebody wanna kill the Wexlers?"

Leora turned on her back and stared at the ceiling. Maybe she had hoped that the question wouldn't come, that we'd overlook the obvious. I wanted to press Leora but I didn't think that Fearless would stand for it. He was a gentleman and would never allow a lady to be tormented except in the most extreme circumstances.

"Son wasn't all Kit took out of Aunt Winnie's house."

"No? What else he take?" I knew she was going to mention the pendant, and I was ready to argue about the worth of the stone and the fact that Winnie didn't seem that worried about it.

"A book," she said, and a whole section of my logic and my mind collapsed.

"What book?"

"A handmade book," she said. "Bound in leather with sheets of goatskin instead of paper. Handwritten and dating from the early part of the eighteenth century."

My heart was beating fast enough to burst. I glanced at Fearless. He didn't seem to have any reaction at all. Maybe he didn't connect my prize with Winifred's loss.

"Why would he take that? Was it valuable?"

"It's a treasure," Leora assured me. "More valuable than all the other riches of my family put together."

I really didn't want to hear any more. I stood up and went to the door. I pushed it open and looked outside as if maybe I had heard something. I was looking for cool air to clear my head but the night was still hot.

". . . IT'S A FAMILY HEIRLOOM," Leora was saying to Fearless when I turned back into the room.

My mind was racing for an answer while she spoke. I didn't want to give up the book. I wouldn't give up the book. It was mine. I found it.

". . . for more than two centuries," Leora said. "The first woman to write in it was Gheeza Manli, the first woman of the Fine family born here in America. From her time until now our family has kept a diary of our American experience."

"You say it was started in about seventeen hundred?" I asked.

"No, she said eighteen hundred," Fearless said.

"Eighteenth century," Leora corrected.

Fearless didn't know what she meant so he sat back and let us talk.

"So you sayin' that you got a goatskin book that couldn't have more than a hundred fifty, two hundred pages that's got two hundred fifty years of family entries?"

"Three hundred pages," she said. "And there are four books.

They've been in our family for generations. The book that was stolen was the first one, the one that Gheeza Manli wrote in. Winifred's the current keeper. She was going to teach Son to do it."

"Why not you?"

"I didn't want to live at home, and Aunt Winnie wouldn't let the books out of the house. Anyway, she detested Brown because he always stood up to her."

"And that's what Kit stoled?" Fearless asked.

"Yes. BB told him about it. When we were kids Aunt Winnie would take us to her secret library and tell us about our family history. BB was never very interested but he knew where it was."

"Did the Wexlers know?"

"I don't think so."

"What about Oscar?"

"What about him?"

"Where does he come into the story?"

"He's the one who told me about the book being missing."

"Does Winnie know about it?"

"Not yet. The only reason Oscar knows is that it just happened to be time for him to clean out that little room. Aunt Winnie calls it a shrine."

My respect for Bartholomew Perry's intelligence rose then. He sent in a thief to grab his family's most precious treasure, and if the thief got caught he could say that he was there trying to get a mother back together with her son. If he was lucky Winifred would be so distracted by the loss of Son that she wouldn't know about the real theft until Maestro Wexler called.

Just about smart enough to get himself hung, my mother always says.

35 FEARLESS ELECTED TO TAKE LEORA to Esau's. I stayed behind in Milo's office. It was my time to shine. I knew almost everything, even what people didn't know. The one piece that was missing was the identity of the man who had killed the Wexlers and Kit. I would have liked to know that man's face and name for my own security and peace of mind.

But the biggest problem was Winifred Fine's family journal. That was what everyone was after. That's why people were getting killed. And I wanted that book for myself. The only thing I had ever wanted more was the ability to read. When I was a child I fantasized about a book like that, a book written by intelligent Negro minds that told the truth about some shred of our history. I didn't care so much about slavery or racism. I didn't want to know about abuses as much as I wanted to know what people were thinking, my people. Everybody else had it: the English, Irish, French, and Russians; the Chinese, Indians, Tibetans, and Jews; even the Mayans and Egyptians had hieroglyphics, and the Australian Aborigines had paintings that went back before all of them. The stolen book was all of that and more for me.

Was it worth my life? No, but maybe I wouldn't die. There was no one except possibly Fearless who knew I had the book. He wouldn't turn me over. All I had to do was make sure I knew who the threat was. If I knew the threat I could avoid the problem. That's what I told myself.

Greed will make even a meek man into a fool.

I CALLED A NUMBER and a man I knew answered, "Fine residence."

"Tell me about Brown."

"Excuse me? Who is this speaking?"

"You know who I am, Oscar, and you know what I'm talkin' about too. So let's not be stupid this late in the game."

"Are you crazy, man?" the once-rich butler asked.

"I got this number from a man that got it from Brown. You're the only one in the house he'd be callin', and that's because you brought him out here to find that book before Winifred found out it was gone."

Silence is almost always an admission, usually of guilt. When you run out of retorts, replies, rejoinders, and responses there must be truth on the table with you out of money and cards.

"What do you want?" Oscar asked.

"Why did you send Brown after those white people?"

"I did no such thing. If he went after them that was his decision. I only told him about that Kit Mitchell. I told him that Kit
stole the book, that if he found it he could keep Winifred from
ever threatening to take his son again."

"And what you supposed to get out of all that?"

"That book means more than the life of any member of this
family. We must have it."

"You could give Maestro what he wants," I suggested.

"He doesn't have the book. I've already spoken to his agent.
What is it that you want, Mr. Minton?"

It was a good question, a very good question.

"I don't know, Oscar. I really don't. Did Leora know that you
had gotten in touch with Brown?"

"No. I called him because I knew that he would do anything
to protect his family. She wanted him to stay away for the same
reason."

"Why did you give Leora Kit Mitchell's address instead of
Brown?" I asked. And then, "Or did you tell him too?"

"I did not," Oscar said. "I told Leora because she's reasonable.
If Kit had the book she could at least start to discuss terms with
him. Who can tell what a man like Brown might have done?"

"You think he killed the Wexlers?"

"I wouldn't know."

"What do you know?" I asked.

"That Kit Mitchell came in here and stole our family history.
He acted as if it was Son he was after but the book was his real
intent. I didn't mind about the child. A boy should be with his
parents."

"And what about the book?"

"Do you know what it contains?" Oscar asked.

"Yeah. It's a diary. A family history."

Oscar grunted at my quaint understatement. "We are the only Negroes in all the New World who can follow our heritage back to the beginning, back to Africa. I know of six generations of my African heritage across a dozen different nations."

"Shouldn't something like that be in a museum?" I asked. "Or maybe the Library of Congress?"

"It's ours. Our history, not theirs. The Negro population isn't ready yet to receive it. They wouldn't know the value of such a treasure — not yet."

"I see. And you think it's worth the multimillion-dollar deal Maestro Wexler wants to make."

"It's worth everything."

From what Rose had said, Oscar was a man who had thrown away everything once already. I wondered if Winifred was of the same opinion.

"What will you give me if I can get the book?" I asked. "I mean, I hear that Maestro Wexler is willing to pay fifty grand."

"We will double the offer."

"You talkin' for Winifred?"

"She will do what is necessary."

"Well, I ain't seen a book like that. But I'll put it up on the top of my list. I sure will."

I put the receiver in the cradle and sat back in Loretta's swivel chair. Milo's hunger for money was worming in my gut. At the same time I wanted to steal the Fine family chronicle for myself.

I had about twenty-five hundred dollars left from the money I'd been given. Twenty-five hundred was good money in 1955. Even if I had to share it with Fearless it meant a year of easy living and no worries.

But a hundred thousand dollars was a whole lifetime. I could buy a house, build my business, and be set for life. And I had the book right in the trunk of Ambrosia's car, with Fearless Jones as my Cerberus standing guard.

Those were the most sublime moments of my life. Sitting there in the lap of possible riches and treasure, plotting out a future that no poor man I ever knew had attained, and with none of the responsibilities that come with such gifts.

It was like that span of time when you've just met a woman that you want more than anything. She wants you too but you have to wait a day or two so as not to seem improper and tactless. You sleep alone but she's there with you. You never speak but you know every word that would come out of her mouth. And when she finally does say, *I'll be seeing you,* you know the deeper implications, the heat of her desire to give and take everything you both have.

As time has gone by I've come to realize that those moments of anticipation are always the high points. Love fades and money squanders itself. Familiarity, even with riches, comes to boredom, and a fly on angel's food cake or a fly on shit is still just a fly after all.

There came a knock at the door that jarred me awake.

"Paris," Fearless Jones called, and my anticipation turned once more to fear.

36 | IT WAS CLOSE TO ELEVEN-THIRTY when we drove off in Ambrosia's Chrysler.

"How'd you make it back here?" I asked Fearless.

"Drove Leora's car. I told her uncle where I'd leave the keys. He said they'd come by and get it in the morning."

Fearless was in a lighthearted mood. He told bad jokes and laughed at them too.

"What is it?" I asked him after three stories about the war.

"What?"

"Why are you so happy?"

"Oh, I don't know. Mama really likes havin' Rose in the house with her. Son's a good kid and so's Leora. You know I was worried there a while because I thought she had fooled me. But now I see that she really needed help and she wasn't tryin' to bring me grief."

"That's like you and me," I said. "You my friend and you never mean to get me in trouble. But here I am, with you, in the crosshairs."

This also made Fearless laugh.

"I'd tell ya I'm sorry, Paris. But you know I needed you in this one here."

"Yeah."

"Hey, Paris," Fearless said. "Where's that guy you always play chess wit'?"

"What guy?"

"You know that sneak thief so smart."

"You mean Jackson Blue?"

"That's him. You know they got him for takin' money out the contribution basket at Second Avenue Baptist."

"I think he's in one'a Mofass's illegal places on Hester," I said.

"That yellah buildin'?"

"Uh-huh. What you want with Jackson Blue?"

"He the one got that camera equipment, right?"

"Yeah."

"I wanna take some pictures of Mama and Miss Fine. Maybe Jackson lemme borrah his cameras. You know I can snap some shots. They had me doin' that in the war too. Called it reconnaissance."

"Man, all you need is a Brownie to take home pictures. You don't need Jackson's fancy jive. Anyway, that stuff he got might be stolen."

"Might be?" Fearless joked. "Shoot. Naw, baby. I wanna take some high-quality pictures. Yes I do."

* * *

WE GOT TO VICTORIA MOORE'S ROOMING HOUSE near midnight. The dining room was dark but there was a light on in the sitting room. Big, yellowy Melvin Conroy was sitting on the couch with a buxom girl who was less than half his age. They were talking while she had her hand on his knee. There was no love or romance in the young woman's eyes, so I decided that they were working out the details of a business transaction. That didn't bother me. He was getting on in age and obviously down on his luck. She was just trying to pay the rent, I imagined, and was probably supporting some child fathered by another man like Melvin.

"Hey, DeLois," Fearless said as we entered.

The young woman took her hand off Conroy's knee and lowered her eyes.

"Hi, Fearless," she said. "You livin' here?"

"No, uh-uh. Me and Paris got some things we need to do. You okay, honey?"

"Fine," she said tentatively.

"Sure she's okay," Melvin said. "Why you wanna go and ask that?"

"I'm not talkin' to you, big man," Fearless said. "I'm just askin' my friend a question."

Melvin sized up my friend and understood immediately the implications of any loud protest.

While they regarded each other my eyes met with the young DeLois. The smile she had hidden from Melvin came out for me. She stood up from the couch and walked over to us.

"I was just gettin' ready to leave," she said.

Her brown skin shone and her eyes did too.

"Let's walk her outside, Paris."

Melvin's shoulders got all tight but he didn't say anything.

At the car DeLois told us that she lived some miles away. Fearless said that if she waited in the car we'd drive her home after we finished our business.

Melvin Conroy was gone from the sitting room when we returned. His door was closed when we passed it going down the back hall. We went up to the second floor and down to number twelve, the room Charlotta had told me was hers.

That door was open wide.

Brown was kneeling over the battered and bruised Charlotta.

"What the hell?" Fearless said, and I knew the trouble was about to begin. Fearless never cursed unless he was truly outraged.

He stalked into the room and Brown rose up in a crouch.

"Hold up, man," Brown said.

But he was too late. Fearless threw a hard and fast right that the smaller Brown somehow avoided. He stood up to his full height, connecting with an uppercut that would have rendered anyone but Fearless unconscious. Fearless just moved with the blow and connected with a left hook against Brown's jaw. That collision sounded like two stones being slammed together. Brown hit Fearless in the gut with both hands. I knew that they were hard punches because I heard Fearless grunt. But he didn't slow down. He hit Brown twice, hard enough to send my chess partner staggering back a whole half step.

There were very few men who could stand toe to toe with Fearless Jones.

I looked down and saw that there was a large white-enameled pitcher filled with water next to the unconscious, or dead, Charlotta. I picked up the jug and splashed the two titans. Surprisingly this had the desired effect.

Both men turned toward me.

"It's okay, Fearless. He's tryin' to help her. You too, Brown. We're not here to hurt nobody."

The men looked at me a moment. Then Brown went down on one knee. I was even more impressed that he had absorbed so much punishment without showing how badly he was hurt until the bout was called.

I closed the door.

Fearless and Brown knelt on either side of Charlotta.

"She come staggering in about forty-five minutes ago," Brown was saying. "She said that a white man had beat her, and then she fainted. I brought her up here and tried to make her comfortable."

"I need a first aid kit and some ice water," Fearless said.

Brown was up and out of the door before I had taken the words in.

Fearless unbuttoned Charlotta's blouse and took it off. He scanned her flesh, prodding here and there. I supposed that he was looking for wounds or deep bruises. It was odd looking at the body I had spent so much time with. There was no allure left, only tight little bruises and slack muscles.

"She gonna be all right?" I asked Fearless.

"Yeah," he said. "I think so. Her head ain't hurt except for some hard slaps, and these bruises ain't deep. It's just some arm punches. First she fainted, then she passed into sleep."

Fearless pinched her cheek hard and Charlotta opened her eyes.

"What?" she said, and then she sat up.

She realized she was half-naked but that didn't seem to bother her, at least not at first.

"Paris, what happened?"

"Brown said that you came in and said a white man beat you."

She gasped with the memory. "Yeah. Yeah. Bastard beat me like a rug."

"Who?"

"Some man left a message for me. I called him back and he said that he needed to talk about Kit."

"Did you know him?" I asked.

"Uh-uh. He called Miss Moore and told her that he owned a restaurant that Kit had been in with his girlfriend and that he left somethin' behind. He gave her his number and she give it to me. She was all mad, sayin' that if I talked to Kit she wanted her twelve dollars."

"And you called the man?"

"Yeah. I didn't know what he was talkin' about but I was, you know, curious."

"And so he met you here?"

"Yeah." Charlotta picked up her blouse and swaddled her breasts with it. "He met me out front at about ten. At first he was nice, but then when I didn't know what he was talkin' about he started beatin' me."

Charlotta began to cry.

"What did he want from you, baby?" I asked softly.

Brown came back with a blue pitcher and a drab green first aid kit.

Fearless went to work on the bruises of Charlotta's lumpy face.

"He wanted to know if Kit had a old book and who was Kit workin' with."

"What did you tell him?" I asked for more than one reason.

"I don't know nuthin' 'bout no book or nobody he been workin' with except for BB. I told him all that, and he beat me anyway and then threw me out the car. Ow!" This last was because Fearless was putting iodine on a cut above her left eye.

"Did he ask you where he could find Kit?"

"No."

"What did he look like?" I asked.

"Like a white man," she said as if that explained everything.

"Was he fat?"

"No. He was slender-like."

"Ugly?"

"Plain."

"What color hair?"

"It was nighttime, Paris. I didn't see no color but white."

"Was there anything strange about him?"

"He talked like a Mexican."

"He had a Spanish accent?"

"Uh-huh. Yeah."

"You gonna have two shiners by mornin', girl," Fearless told her.

"Oh Lord," she said. "Why they always pickin' on me?"

Fearless lifted her in his arms and then put her down on the bed. He took off her shoes and skirt, her stockings, and even took away the blouse she still had clutched to her chest. Then he covered her and ran his fingers over her head.

"You should take some'a this aspirin," he said. "'Cause them bruises gonna hurt in the mornin'."

Charlotta loved the attention she was getting. I think if they were alone she would have asked him to stay.

"Charlotta?" I said.

"Yeah, Paris?"

"Do you still have the number that man left?"

"No. It was in my bag. But I dropped that in his car."

"What kinda car was it?"

"A red Ford."

37 FEARLESS, BROWN, AND I WENT UP to my room for a powwow.

"We know about Son and Leora," I said right off. "And that Oscar called you to come out here and help them with the book that white man was after."

"You know everything then," Brown replied. He was getting fidgety, tapping his left foot and looking around.

"No," I said. "Not everything. Not where the book is or who killed the Wexlers and Kit."

"Kit's dead? Since when?"

"Probably the same time the white folks got it."

Brown's cheek jumped from an involuntary tic, but that seemed to come from the nervousness descending on him and not guilt.

"I need some water," he said.

I poured a glass from my private sink and handed it to him. He took a wax paper packet from his pants pocket and poured a foul-looking powder into the glass. He drank it down in one big gulp, after which he grimaced and coughed.

"What's that?" Fearless asked.

"Medicine," Brown said.

"Doctor give you that? In wax paper?"

"No. Witch woman from down in Louisiana."

"Not Mama Jo?" Fearless asked.

"Yeah. How you know that?"

"Jo's famous, man. She got people comin' all the way from South America to get her cures."

In just the few moments it took them to speak Brown began to calm down.

"Yeah," he said. "I got this nerves thing that fucks me up. Sometimes I get so crazy that I could put my fist through a brick wall, and then sometimes I might be so sad that all I can do is cry and sleep. Doctors couldn't do a thing. But Mama Jo had me out there in her swamp house for three days, and when I left she give me these packets and says take one if I feel the lows comin' on. I could still feel it for a while but it don't get to me."

"About the book," I said.

"Yeah. Yeah. I found out that Kit was stayin' here, so I moved in hopin' to get a hint about where he put it."

"Why's he holdin' on to it in the first place?"

"I don't know for sure but the best bet's money," Brown said. "BB said too much about what that book was worth, so Kit decided that he didn't need no partner."

"And what about you?" Fearless asked.

"What about me?"

"Are you crazy or what? Are you workin' with that white man worked over Charlotta and tryin' to put it over on us too?"

Fearless was dumb as a post when it came to letters and other intellectual concerns. He couldn't follow an eighth-grade fairy tale. But he knew people, at least most people. He understood the workings of the heart. But his greatest knowledge was at those moments when he was aware of what he didn't know, when he looked into a darkness that even his bright soul could not illuminate. Brown was such an anomaly. He was a cipher, a man without even a proper name.

Brown grinned, then he chuckled. He was used to hiding when he was standing in plain sight. I felt then that I was seeing him for the first time.

"I've done some bad things, Fearless," Brown said. "Things I'm not proud of and things could put me under the jailhouse. But since I been takin' these herbs and whatnot I haven't lost control for a moment. And you know I'd have to be crazy to be killin' white people ain't done nuthin' to me."

You could have spent a year interpreting Brown's simple declaration. There was a Bedlam and an Alcatraz, maybe even a gallows, woven in between the lines. But all of that was unnecessary, because Fearless listened to him and then nodded as if to say, *This man has got the job.*

"So what do you know that we don't?" I asked.

"What's your business in this first?" Brown asked back.

"We have been offered a lot of money," I said. "But mainly I just wanna know that I'm not gonna get squashed by some man thinks I've done him harm."

"Well, that last part is okay," Brown said. "But I don't know about the money. What I plan to do is get the book and give it to Leora so that she can work out a deal to keep her aunt off our back."

"We might could work that together," I said. "We take a little less money and Miss Fine gets her prized possession."

"I don't know," Brown said. "I don't think I could go along with that. I mean, what if Miss Fine does business with you and then give us the shaft?"

"What if we find the book and you didn't wanna work with us?" I replied. "This way we both got coverage. Me and Fearless get some money and peace'a mind and you get a happy family."

"But how do we trust each other, man?"

"You can trust me," Fearless said. "Whatever it is Paris says, I'll make sure that it's true."

Brown's smile made it to his eyes for the first time.

"Okay, Brother Fearless. All right. You give me your word and I'll take it. But you know I don't know a whole lot. Oscar called me a week ago and said that he needed my help. Leora was already out here to get Son back from Winifred. At first I was worried that somethin' happened to her or Son, but then Oscar told me that Bartholomew had sent some man in to kidnap Son, that he knew about it because he was in it with Leora. But then the man took Son also stoled their family book. Now he was callin' and sayin' that he wanted fifty thousand dollars for it."

"Kit?"

"Yeah. BB had been in it but Kit cut him out."

"What about the Wexlers?"

"Kit told Oscar that he had a white man wanted to buy the book already. He was ready to spend almost fifty. He told

Oscar that he had to have the money in three days or the white man was gonna get the book and Winifred would come down on everybody."

"What'd he mean by that?"

"Oscar was in it with BB and Kit in the first place. He set it up so that Kit could take Son. But he didn't know about the rest."

"And you run down here from Chi?" Fearless asked.

"Yeah. I was waitin' for Leora and Son. But she didn't come because Oscar had called her too. I took the train and started lookin' for Kit. I heard that he was at this rooming house, so I came here. They told me about him and Charlotta, so I kept my eye on her."

"Don't make no sense," I said.

"What?"

"Why would Kit waste his time on Oscar if there was somebody wanted to buy the book already? I mean, the white man had to be Maestro Wexler or his son. They got almost fifty thousand dollars layin' around in the closet. Why give Oscar time to raise the money?"

"Maybe because he killed the kids," Fearless said.

"Kit's been dead too long for that," I said. "Same man killed him probably killed them too."

"You right, Thad — I mean Paris," Brown said. "Why would Kit waste time with Oscar? I mean, Winifred had already went to the police because'a the necklace."

"She didn't tell the cops about Son?" I asked our new ally.

"No. She was afraid that the cops would wanna know where his parents were."

"I don't get it," Fearless said. "If this book is the big thing, why Kit wanna mess around with a hot necklace?"

It was a good question, reminding me that Fearless was a thinker too.

"Oscar let Kit take the necklace. That was what they agreed on to pay Kit for his taking Son."

"So Kit had to take the choker in order to keep Oscar and Leora from suspecting about the book," I said.

"Yeah. Oscar promised to pretend that the emerald got misplaced," Brown added. "But once he realized about the book, he told Winifred that Kit stole the necklace."

"Somethin' must'a gone wrong on Kit's side," I said. "Somehow Lance was in trouble and Kit needed to get his money fast. He leaned on Oscar but instead Oscar put you and Leora on the case. Maybe he was thinkin' that Leora could set him up and then he'd send you in to take him down."

"Yeah," Brown said. "That was it. And Oscar told Winnie what he wanted her to know. That way she could get after them without knowing about the book."

"And that's where Milo comes in," I said.

"Who?" asked Brown.

"A man we know that Winifred hired."

"Who do you think it was beat up Charlotta?" Brown asked me.

"He doesn't sound like one of Wexler's men," I said. "But I don't know. Wexler could have a hundred men workin' for him. I guess it could be that Oscar is lyin' to us. He lied to his sister."

"So you think he took the book?"

"Naw. That wouldn't make any sense," I said, knowing that I had the book in the trunk of Fearless's car.

"You guys finished yammerin'?" Fearless asked with a yawn. "'Cause you know I'm tired."

We broke up then. Brown went to his room and we went down to the car.

DeLois was asleep in the backseat.

She looked so peaceful there with her hands folded together under her cheek, her breath coming slowly and deep. She might have been a troubled child but sleep came to her, a gift from a milder deity than the one that governed my fitful world.

38 FEARLESS DROVE US to Ambrosia's house. DeLois slept the whole way. I told Fearless that I'd drive her home because he'd been nodding at the wheel. But when he wanted me to take my car I balked.

"Why bother taking my car outta the garage?" I reasoned. "I could just hold on to yours."

"Not mine, Paris — Ambrosia's. Don't worry, man. I ain't gonna lose the money. And sure as hell ain't nobody gonna take it from me."

He was right. The money and the book would be safer with him.

I woke DeLois up and led her to my car. She was groggy but trusting. Fearless kissed her on the cheek and told her that I'd drive her home.

In my car again I opened the window so that DeLois would wake up with the fresh air.

"Where you live exactly?" I asked her when she finally sat upright.

"Over near Adams and Hoover."

I guided the car in that direction.

"You got a cigarette, Mr. Minton?"

I fished out two and handed them to her.

"Light me one too," I said.

There's nothing quite like a woman lighting your cigarette for the immediate feeling of intimacy. Putting the filtered tip in my mouth she touched my lower lip with her fingertips.

"What you and Fearless doin' in Miss Moore's house?" she asked me.

"Gettin' into trouble I guess."

"I guess if you gonna get into trouble you might as well do it with Fearless Jones," she said and then giggled. "He sure did make that fat man sweat."

"What were *you* doin' in Miss Moore's place?"

"Maybe I live there."

"Maybe," I said. "But you don't."

"How you know I don't?"

"Because I took a room there a few days ago and I had dinner with the whole houseful. You weren't there. And if you did live there, then why am I driving you home?"

DeLois's face wasn't small but it was petite. She pouted and then brought the cigarette to her lips.

"You know," she said.

"Somebody send you in there to Melvin?"

"Naw. It's just this bar I go to sometimes where he go too.

He always tryin' to mess wit' me, but you know I always tell 'im to go on."

"But not tonight."

DeLois took another drag and turned to the window.

"How do you know Fearless?" I asked to ease her discomfort.

"He used to live in the apartment upstairs from me. He's a real nice man. One time I had this boyfriend wanna try and beat on me. Fearless come down and asked him if he wanted to leave. It was funny. Richard started blusterin' about how he was gonna kick Fearless' ass. But the whole time he was talkin' he was movin' backwards and pickin' up his things. Finally he shouted some curse or sumpin' when he was at the door and then he ran." DeLois laughed. I did too.

We drove a few more blocks.

"So what were you doin' at Miss Moore's?" I asked again.

"I cain't make my rent and I got my little sister wit' me. I got fifteen dollars but they want thirty."

"You could slide a week or two."

"I done slid a month already."

We came to the small aqua-colored building on a street named Orchard. I stopped the car but neither of us moved or said anything.

I was closer to Fearless than to anyone except my mother. He had expectations of me that he never had to put into words. The fact that he took DeLois out of that rooming house was him saying that he wanted me to finish the job.

"So how come you left wit' us?" I asked.

"I didn't wanna fuck that man," she said. "I don't wanna fuck the landlord neither, but at least he don't weigh five hundred pounds."

I reached into my pocket and peeled off four twenty-dollar

bills. I handed the money over. She didn't take it at first. Instead she looked me up and down.

"What?" I asked.

"Nuthin'. It's just that you even skinnier than my landlord and you the right color too."

I took her hand and folded it around the money.

"No, DeLois. It ain't like that. People been throwin' money at me and Fearless the last couple'a days now. And my mama always told me to keep what I earn but to share good fortune. This is just for you and your sister."

DeLois's jaw dropped. "You mean you just givin' me this money?"

"That's right."

"And you don't want nuthin'?"

"I want you to have it."

The young woman's face turned serious then. In some other circumstance I might have been afraid of her pulling out a razor. When she put her free hand on my wrist I believe that she meant to give it a gentle caress, but her feelings made it like a vise.

"You could come upstairs, Paris," she said. "I want you to."

And there it was again: that moment of anticipation. That offer of something I wanted — and deserved too.

"No, baby. You take that money, pay your rent, buy some breakfast, and go out and find a good job. After you do all that and you been workin' a month or two, if you still wanna see me ask Fearless for my number."

She smiled and kissed me twice. The first kiss was a thank you, the second was a promise.

I drove off thinking that I had done the right thing for the first time since Fearless came banging on my door.

• • •

I GOT TO MY HOUSE at about one, still happy over those two wet kisses. I was still in a good position. Wexler thought I was working for him and Timmerman was in a hospital bed. Brown seemed to be on our side and Oscar wasn't any threat. BB was in hiding somewhere, but he thought that I was on his side too. I parked in front of my place and skipped up the front stairs. In a week or two I'd begin to wonder if DeLois would ever call me. In a month I'd worry that she had moved on. But at least that one night I was a knight in shining armor and the princess had only me in her thoughts.

I opened the front door and received what seemed to be my nightly knock in the head. I fell to the floor and heard the door slam. A light came on simultaneously with the sudden deep ache in my head.

I turned on my back and looked up but all I could see for the moment was a looming shadow.

"Surprised to see me, nigger?" the shadow asked.

Nigger? Louis? I had a dozen one-word questions but neither my mind nor my ears were clear enough to provide an answer. The man lifted me by the lapels of my shirt. His breath was rank but unfamiliar. His skin, where it touched mine, was hot.

"Wake up!" he shouted.

The stinging slap across my cheek brought Theodore Timmerman's face into clarity. He still wore the brown jacket he'd had on the first day he showed up at my door. But now he was wearing green trousers that didn't cover his ankles. He had the beginnings of a beard around his chin. And his breath smelled like a disease.

"What you want, man?"

"Where's the book?"

"Fearless got it."

He slapped me again.

"You think you can fool me? Where is it, bastard?"

"Fearless got it. He does. I'm not lyin'."

He threw me against the wall. My feet actually left the floor before I struck. I felt the pain in my lungs.

"Where is he?" Timmerman bellowed.

I gave up Ambrosia's address without even a second's hesitation. Everything I did for DeLois was washed away in one cowardly moment. Deep in my mind, though, I didn't believe that Timmerman would ever get the upper hand on my friend.

Then he fell on me. His hands wrapped around my throat and my eyes felt as if they were going to pop out of my head. The pressure increased, and for the first time in the thirty years I had been alive fear left me. I was dying and there were no words to dissuade my killer. There was no Fearless Jones to break in at the last moment. There was nothing but death yawning out under me.

My ears were on fire and my heart was exploding. I started pounding with both of my fists at the point Fearless had tapped Theodore in the chest. There were bandages there now but I was striking him with strength I'd never known before or since. Timmerman released me and fell backwards. I went after him, hitting that bull's eye again and again until finally I collapsed.

My foeman fell on top of me and I knew that I'd soon be dead. I struggled for a moment, trying to breathe, hurting from my throat. And then I faded into unconsciousness, knowing that I would never awaken again.

39 FEELING AS IF I HAD BEEN TRAMPLED by some prehistoric wooly rhino, I tried to look around. I couldn't open my eyes all the way, and the light I managed to see was a dingy blue-brown glow. I could barely breathe, feeling as though there was a great stone on my chest. I tried to pry my eyes wider. The world was small and crazy. It was as if maybe a lead blanket had been draped over me and it was slowly pressing the life from my lungs.

Suddenly I came fully awake. I yelled and bucked, rolling the body from on top of me.

Theodore Timmerman, who probably never worked for an insurance company, was lying next to me on his back — wide-eyed and dead. I was on my side thinking about standing up but unable to make the right moves in order to achieve that goal. All I could do was lie there next to a dead man who had come close to killing me. My bones were jelly and my mind was a dull thud. All sensation had fled my body. Only breath remained. Sweet, sweet breath. Breath and death and every once in a while some sound like the house settling or the waterlike whoosh of a car passing down Jefferson.

There were also gurgling sounds emanating from within the corpse that lay mere inches from my ear. The body fluids settling down, headed back for the ground that they rose from. A motor started humming somewhere on the side of the building. A cat yowled and I felt a sharp pain in my left hand.

The fingernail of my ring finger was bleeding, half torn off in the struggle with the big white man. I concentrated on that pain, realizing somehow that if I didn't I might lose consciousness again or I might even lose my senses completely and lie there until someone found me and called the police, who would then cart me off to prison.

I got up on one elbow, stayed there for what felt like a month, then I rocked up into a sitting position. I was moving fast by then. It took me no longer than five minutes to remember my legs and feet and the possibility of walking.

I stared at the phone for a long time, I have no idea how long, trying to remember Ambrosia's number and how to dial it. I knew I had tucked it away on a slip of paper someplace but it was beyond me to think of where.

What I did think of was my little cousin Aster, a young girl, not yet five, who died in a flash flood when I was six. She was my best friend, and when my mother took me to her parents' house to help with the preparations we found them washing the body before putting her in her Sunday dress. I asked could I wash her feet, and I remember her mother, a big West Indian woman, cried and wrapped me in her arms. My mother wouldn't let me wash Asty's feet, but that night I dreamt that I washed her soles and between her toes with a real sea sponge and perfumed soap.

Looking down at the phone, with Theodore's corpse in the periphery, and thinking about dreaming about washing my dead playmate's feet, I suddenly remembered Ambrosia's number.

"Hello," she said without the slightest shred of civility.

"Fearless there?" I asked in a voice that belonged to a dead man.

"Do you know what time it is, Paris Minton? It's three in the mornin'. First Fearless don't get in till two and I just fall asleep again, and then —"

"Get him for me, Ambrosia," I said. "I don't have time to play."

Maybe she could hear the stress in my voice. Maybe Fearless had talked to her about me being his closest friend. Whatever it was, she stopped her complaints and a moment later Fearless was on the line.

"What's up, Paris?"

"I just killed Theodore Timmerman."

"I'll be right there," he said.

He hung up the phone in my ear, leaving me holding on to the receiver and thinking about how Aster would scream and giggle when I tickled her.

"HE'S SURE ENOUGH DEAD," Fearless was saying. "No doubt about that at all."

I had pulled up a chair next to the corpse while Fearless examined the body.

"I didn't mean it," I said.

I had been saying things like that since Fearless got there. I said I was sorry. I said I didn't mean to kill him. I asked Fearless why did he have to try and hurt me like that.

"You didn't kill him," Fearless said.

"What you talkin' 'bout, man. I hit and hit and hit and hit, and he fell dead."

"If anybody killed him," Fearless said, "I'm the one. I'm the one threw that stone. I'm the one threw him down and tied him up. But Paris, we took him to the hospital. We called to make sure he got a bed. What else could we do? And what was you supposed to do wit' him stranglin' you like that? I mean, if there was ever a case of self-defense in Los Angeles, it's this right here."

"Yeah I . . . Yeah I . . . guess."

Fearless put his hand on my neck. I thought he was trying to console me, but then I felt a pinch on a muscle next to the big vertebra. A pain went down my back and up into my head that was beyond any physical hurt I had ever known. I cried out and tried to get away from the hold but Fearless would not let go. It seemed as if he had taken up Timmerman's job and planned to kill me too.

Finally he released his grip and I fell to the floor writhing. Fearless picked me up and carried me to the bathroom in the back of the store. He turned on the shower I had installed over the bathtub and threw me in, clothes and all.

The water was freezing!

I tried to climb out but Fearless wouldn't let me. He held on to my arms and legs until I was almost numb with the cold. After long minutes he pulled me out and said, "Dry off and then go upstairs and change, Paris. We got business to take care of here."

"Man, what the fuck you do that to me for?" I shouted, sputtering with rage.

"You was slippin', Paris," he said, giving me a one-shoulder shrug. "Shock, man. You know I been on the front lines. I seen boys experience death for the first time. And here you think you killed that man. We ain't got time for no sanitarium, so I just put you through the crash course."

I was so cold that I was shivering. The quavering in my chest and Fearless's offhanded manner made me laugh. I did that a bit and then stopped for fear that my friend might throw me back in the shower.

It was at that moment that I accepted myself as a killer.

40

I CHANGED CLOTHES QUICKLY, not thinking about the dead white man downstairs at all. Fearless had been busy too. He'd found two old blankets and some rope and trussed the body up so that now it looked like an oversized, unfinished doll.

"Here, Paris, let me take care of that finger."

While he bandaged up my torn nail he kept talking. "I emptied his pockets. It's all on the table in your kitchen. Now I'm gonna take him out somewhere and get rid of him."

"Don't you think we should call the cops?" I asked.

Fearless just shook his head.

"I, I'll go with you, though," I offered.

"No, Paris. I don't need you and it'a be bad enough if one of us is found wit' a dead man in the trunk. I know what I'm doin', brother. You just do what you do with his things."

I watched as Fearless carried the man-doll down to the street and dumped him in the trunk. I didn't worry about the money or even my book in there. I was a new man, at least for the moment, concentrated on the task at hand.

ALL THEODORE TIMMERMAN LEFT in the world was a package of mint gum, a roll of nickels, one of his own fake insurance cards with *Craighton at pull lay 10:30* scrawled on it, and a ring of three keys. The keys were probably to his apartment, but the address would have been in the wallet that Fearless had confiscated before taking him to the hospital. We'd tossed the man's pants, wallet, and shoes in a bin downtown. There was no finding his address.

And why would I still be chasing him down anyway? He tried to kill me three times already. There was no reason for me to put us into further jeopardy. The one real threat to me was dead. I had killed him with my own two hands.

The memory of the fight flooded my mind. For my entire life I had imagined what it would be like if I would fight to the death against some tough and come out victorious. But the reality was empty. I still felt guilty, even though he was a bully and white and had intentions of killing me. I felt I owed something to the world because I was a murderer and Fearless Jones was out covering my tracks.

I GOT TO MILO'S OFFICE at about four in the morning. The streets were empty of traffic. It didn't take me long to locate Milo's operatives file. The problem was that it was in one of the cabinets that Timmerman had overturned when he went after Milo to find out Winifred Fine's identity.

Hindered by my sore finger, I took a while to flip the metal cabinet, but I finally got it.

Timmerman had his checks mailed to an address on Ogden Drive just north of Venice Boulevard.

IT WAS A HOUSE, not an apartment, on a street that was empty of any potential witnesses. The first key I tried in the lock fit. The numbness of my near-death experience kept me from fear or common sense. I went inside without even knocking. What if he had a girlfriend or a roommate? But those thoughts didn't cross my mind until weeks later. At that moment I was a fool on a mission. And all the bricks of the road to hell were falling right into place at my feet.

The house was dark and so I ran my hand along the wall until I found the switch.

Mr. Timmerman hadn't cleaned up once since the day he had moved in. The sink and tables were full of crusty dishes. The garbage stank and he had forgotten to flush the toilet before leaving his house to hunt down Bartholomew Perry, Kit Mitchell, and me. There was a rug in the bathtub, I never did figure out why. His bed was littered with half-filled potato chip bags and magazines with pictures of nude Negro women on every page. The floor was his hamper and every shade and curtain in the house was drawn.

Sherlock Holmes would have been at sea in that grubby hole. The skip tracer's papers were in among the dishes and newspapers and scattered with coffee grounds.

Some mothers think they're showing love by cleaning up after their sons, but in the long run they make them into feral things, growing bacteria in their bedrooms and filling the air with fungus and dust.

I looked around aimlessly for a while and then concentrated my search. I figured that even a slob like Timmerman would have a special place for important papers and projects. I was looking for a trunk or a briefcase, a filing cabinet, or maybe just a corner of a closet that didn't have the clutter of the rest of his house.

Over an hour later I hadn't found a thing.

The back door of his kitchen led to a small walkway in a yard overgrown with weeds and the branches of an untrimmed oak. Through the leaves and boughs I found another door. This one opened into his garage.

I knew from the moment I flipped the light switch that Theodore Timmerman was insane. The garage was neat as a pin. The floor was tiled with black and white squares that had been perfectly laid. He had three different desks, a telephone, one white upright filing cabinet, and over four thousand watts of light to illuminate every corner.

The life of his mind was in the garage, whereas his house was a trough where he ate and masturbated. Looking over his files I could see that he was a man of many faces. He used jobs like Milo's to worm his way into more lucrative, if less legal, activities. He had files on dozens of men and women he had chased down, and scams that he ran through the mail on a regular basis. There was one whole file of photographs. Most of these were of the incriminating variety: people in places they shouldn't have been, men and women making love, grinning so wide that you just knew they weren't married — at least not to each other. But then there were other pictures that were more disturbing: men in sexual situations with young boys, over two dozen photographs of corpses, with detailed notes about the circumstances of their deaths. One photograph was of a young woman who I had first read about in the *L.A. Times*. Minna Wexler was stripped to the waist. One of her large breasts had been marred, maybe burned. Lance Wexler looked just as he had when I came across him in his apartment. Kit Mitchell was also pretty much the same as I had found him.

Timmerman had killed them all.

Theodore Timmerman was a pornographer, murderer, extortionist, and blackmailer. And Milo had been working with him for years. I didn't think that Milo knew what this man was up to, but just the fact that he didn't suspect him put the bail bondsman in a whole new light for me. I would never again trust his estimation of people or situations. And there was another thing . . .

At the back of the top drawer of his center desk I found a tiny leather notebook like the one Sergeant Rawlway took notes in. The notebook had page after page of handwriting that covered every detail of the cases that Timmerman was covering. His descriptions were cruel and humiliating, but they also served the purpose of obscuring the identities of the people he stalked. Toward the end of the little book there began the entries about Bartholomew Perry. The most important segment read:

> . . . *Watermelon Man must have had a weak heart . . . he had a telephone number that Craighton answered . . . Craighton made Mr. Sweet's salary look like chump change . . . Craighton sent me after Titty mama and Strong boy but they didn't know shit . . . it was the nigger who knew but he died before he could*

*even tell me where the car salesman lived . . . but I got some
leads . . . pretty soon Mr. Sweet will have to get me into that
rich woman's house . . .*

I read everything he had to say about Bartholomew and Kit
and Milo. It seemed that somewhere along the way he became
aware of the book. It was probably the man Craighton who told
him. But there was no information about who this Craighton
might be. It was clear that the mystery man was the mastermind
behind Timmerman and that he was willing to pay big money
for Winifred Fine's book.

There was no more information on Craighton. A new player
with no face or even a race. He had to be rich, that's all I knew for
sure.

Later entries were about Fearless and me. I ripped out those
pages and returned the book to its place in the drawer.

I spent another hour searching the garage-office. Under a loose
tile I found a rusty metal toolbox that had stacks of twenty- and
fifty-dollar bills in it. It was a lot of money but I didn't have my
usual sticky-fingered reaction. When I looked at that money all I
could think of was those pictures of perverts and corpses. Blood
money was one thing but Ted Timmerman's money was drenched
in filth. Try as I might, I couldn't bring myself to touch it.

I left the house of evil at about eight forty-five.

41

WHEN I GOT BACK HOME I cleaned my place from top to bottom. I washed the floors and windows and walls. I dusted and scrubbed until the whole place smelled of cleaning fluid. By four that afternoon I was exhausted.

It might seem that I had wasted the day on trivial matters, but that's not true. While I mopped and swept I was thinking and plotting. The murder of the Wexler kids was ordered by an enemy of Maestro Wexler, of that much I was sure. This faceless foe, named only Craighton, had hired Timmerman to take out the kids and steal the book. With the book this new player — also a millionaire, I surmised — would shake down Winifred and get control of the prime property in Compton.

All I had to do was figure out who it was that stood to gain from the loss of both Wexler and Fine. That might have been an impossible task, but I had one advantage: Bradford, the personal secretary and self-styled mother hen of the Wexler clan.

I had to wait until nine that evening to use the number the personal secretary had given me, but that was fine. I spent a couple of hours rereading the poem "Little Gidding" from the *Four Quartets* by T. S. Eliot. The language swept me away until six, when the phone rang.

"Hello," I said, with a fair certainty that it would be Fearless on the other end of the line.

"Paris?" she asked. "Have you heard from Fearless?"

"Hey, Ambrosia. No, I ain't seen 'im since early this morning."

"What you call him for anyway? You know he ain't been back here since then."

"He said that he had some business with a man he wanted me to introduce him to. Probably they got down to some work." I was pleased being obscure with the taciturn Ambrosia.

"I'm worried about him, Paris. He said that we were gonna go to Big Mama's Bar-B-Q Pit tonight."

"It's okay, honey. You know Fearless is the last man on earth you gotta worry about. John D. Rockefeller got more to worry about than Fearless Jones."

"I know you right," she said. "But I just get worried and I can't stop myself."

"Well all right then," I said. "I'll go out and see if I can find him. The minute I see him I'll make sure he calls your number."

"Thank you, Paris," she said sweetly. "I'm sorry I cussed at you before. You know I get kinda surly when people mess up my plans."

"And I'm sorry I bothered you, baby. But you got to know that I just called 'cause Fearless wanted me to help him."

"With what?"

"I'd like to tell ya, Ambrosia. I truly would, but you know Fearless don't like his business out the box."

"Okay then," she said. "You tell him to call me, though."

"I will."

I also wondered where Fearless could be. Had he been found with the corpse? I turned on the radio and listened to three newscasts, but none of them said anything about a gold Chrysler, a black man named Tristan, or the recently deceased Theodore Timmerman.

BY NINE NO ONE ELSE had called or dropped by. I dialed Bradford's number and he answered a quarter of the way into the first ring.

"Yes?"

"Bradford, it's Paris Minton calling."

"Mr. Minton. How can I be of service?"

"It's me can help you," I said. "I think I have some information that you might want to have. It has to do with your boss, his kids, and some fellah that's been pulling the strings from behind the scene."

"Who is that?"

"Why don't we get together?" I suggested. "Then maybe we can share information and come to some kind of agreement that will make everybody as happy as they can be."

"All right. There's a little park off Lucile Avenue near Hoover," Bradford said. "Do you know it?"

"No. But I can find it."

"Why don't we meet there now?"

"No thanks," I said. "You know my score on nighttime meetings ain't too good."

"I can promise you that Louis won't be there."

"Promise me that you'll meet me at nine tomorrow morning and I'll be a happy man."

"All right," Bradford said in a resigned tone. "Tomorrow at nine. There's a bench near the sidewalk, across from a French café."

"I'll be there."

I WENT TO BED but not to sleep. I just lay there in the dark thinking about how I'd almost died and how I took a man's life. I had never killed before. Many a time I had been in the room where people had expired violently, but I never pulled the trigger or drove the blade. Theodore Timmerman's files and his own rank breath clung to me in the darkened room. The depravity and certainty of death created a sad conviction in my heart.

At ten minutes to four Fearless knocked at the door. I knew it was him because I was awake and when I'm conscious I know Fearless's knock.

"Hey, Paris," was all he said when I admitted him.

"How are you?" I asked. "Ambrosia was so worried that she called me."

"I was doin' things that we don't need to talk about, man. But you don't have to worry about Teddy no more."

I told Fearless about the killer's house and the obscure notes on the murders.

"Damn that's cold," Fearless said after taking it all in. "Sometime people get like that. I seen boys in the war would line up prisoners for target practice. Sometimes they raped and killed more than they fought the enemy. And it wasn't just the Germans or the Russians. Sometimes you had blue-blood American rich boys rollin' in the blood. I think there's just some kinda men made for killin' and hurtin'. Just one little scratch and they like to go off."

"Well at least we don't have to worry about Timmerman anymore," I said, and then I told Fearless that I was going to meet Bradford, to find out who our friend Mr. Craighton might be.

"Hey," Fearless said. "That's a helluva lot easier than makin' a man disappear from the face of the earth."

I didn't ask about what he meant. I didn't want to know.

"You know I gave you up to him, Fearless."

"And then you beat him to death. That's okay."

"No, man. You shouldn't put your trust in me. I was so scared when he grabbed me that I told him where you were in a second. Even Milo lied to the man when asked to give up Winifred Fine."

"Milo lied to save his chance at kissin' millionaire butt," Fearless said.

"That doesn't absolve me."

"Paris, when I got in trouble I came to you. And you agreed to help me. Now if while you helpin' me some man says he's gonna take your life, you *should* give me up. Don't worry, baby. You'n me is tight."

42 I GOT TO THE PARK on Lucile Avenue at eight-fifteen. I like to be early to potentially clandestine meetings. That way I can scout out all the exits and escape routes before it's too late.

There was a French café across the street. Instead of a name there was the picture of a fat chicken wearing a beret as the sign. I moved over toward an alley and took out a newspaper that I pretended to read while waiting for the private secretary to arrive.

I wasn't worried about Bradford. He seemed like a good guy, a concerned employee. We were the same kind, he and I, thinkers. I would have bet that he was a reader. He was satisfied with his position in life. So was I.

At least I had been until people started talking about hundred-thousand-dollar books. At first I wanted the Fine family diary for myself, but as time had gone by I had begun to crave the money. I had never known a Negro who had a hundred thousand dollars before the day I met Winifred Fine. That kind of money could make a whole new life for me. Even if I had to share it with Fearless I'd still be rich. I could open a bookstore down by the ocean and have the two things I loved most in life: reading and the sea.

Bradford arrived at ten to nine. He wore a simple gray suit that had seen its day of wear. He looked around and then sat on a park bench perched at the edge of the grassy lawn and facing out across the street. Bradford was erect and expectant. He was my doorway to riches. He would know the identity of Maestro Wexler's nemesis. Wexler's enemy was mine because he was after the book that was going to make me a rich man. After dealing with him I could sell the book back to Oscar or, if he couldn't make the grade, I could sell it to Maestro and he could close the deal with Winifred Fine directly. Either way I'd get paid for my services and the world of Theodore Timmerman would slowly fade from my mind.

At three minutes after nine I crossed the street to Bradford. Looking both ways many times before reaching the opposite side, I noticed the French café twice. The second view of the silhouetted chicken set off a bell in my head.

"Mr. Minton," Bradford said, rising as I approached him.

"Mr. Bradford." I stuck out my hand.

We shook and sat down side by side on the park bench.

There was the café again.

"So, Mr. Minton," Bradford said. "You have information for me."

"It's a nice morning, isn't it?" I said.

"Why yes," he replied with a friendly smile.

I'm sure he thought that I wanted to impose some decorum on our meeting, when really I was stalling for time. The café disturbed me, though I had no idea why. I had never been on that street as far as I remembered. But still there was a vague apprehension.

"I like this spot," Bradford continued. "It reminds me of my younger days in Paris, before the war."

It was him saying my name, that's what did it. My name, the capital of France, the country where people spoke French, where the term *chicken* would be translated *poulet* — or to the unenlightened, *pull lay*.

"You lived in Europe?" I asked.

"Yes. I was the assistant to Parnell Wexler, Maestro's uncle, in the thirties. I had a small apartment on the Left Bank and walked down the Seine to work every morning."

"I hear that the weather is terrible in Paris," I said. "My friend Fearless spent six months there, on and off, after they threw out the Germans. He said that he didn't see the sunshine again until he was back in the U.S."

"It's a glorious town," Bradford said, the nostalgia in his voice deepening his Australian accent. "Beyond weather concerns. The art and architecture, the people and the language, are the very top of human potential."

He was a white man and he had an accent. Maybe Charlotta didn't know any accents but the ones that Mexicans had. Maybe the word Mexican meant accent to her.

"What's your first name, Bradford? You know, if we're going to be working together. We might as well be on a first-name basis. You can call me Paris."

"Bradford *is* my first name, Paris," he said easily. "Bradford Craighton."

"Well, Brad, I can hear how much you love Paris, not me but the city," I said. "Must be great now you're goin' back there in style."

Bradford turned his head slowly, as if he really didn't want to see what I had become there next to him.

"Come again?"

"You ever meet a guy named Timmerman?" I asked.

"Timmerman? What is his first name?"

"Theodore."

"No. I don't think so. Why do you ask?"

"Think hard, Brad. He's the man that called you after he pulled your number off a man that he had just gave a heart attack. He didn't know it, but he really wanted to speak to Maestro, but it was your number he called, your private line."

"I, I, I don't know what you're talking about."

"Tall white guy, ugly, likes the color brown in his wardrobe," I said, pretending to jog his memory. "You sent him off to look for a book."

"What book is that?"

When he didn't want more details about the murder I knew my suspicions were true.

"I don't know what it's about but it's real old, over two hundred years. Winifred's family prizes that one handwritten manuscript over all their other possessions."

"I don't know anything about what you're saying," Bradford said.

"Yes you do. I know it. You know it. So let's stop playin' and get down to brass tacks."

"I have no idea what you're talking about. Does this have anything to do with Lance or Minna?"

"Late last night, after I talked to you, this Timmerman snatched me and my friend Fearless. When he had the upper hand he let it slip about the book and a fellah named Craighton that he met on a park bench in front of a French café. He even told us the time you guys met. Ten-thirty."

"That's ridiculous. Why would he tell you all that?"

"Because I'm not a brave man, Mr. Craighton. He asked me what I knew and I threw your name at him, hoping to save myself from a beating."

"You say that he had the upper hand?"

"My friend is tough. Theodore let his guard down and Fearless laid him low."

"Where is this Timmerman now?"

"They admitted him to the hospital this morning. Fearless busted his leg for sure. His jaw too."

"Why was he after you?"

"He wanted me to bring him to Winifred Fine. I think he had something for her."

"What, what was that?"

"That's enough from me for the moment," I said. "That's all I got to say until I hear somethin' from you."

"I already told you," Bradford Craighton said, sounding almost like an Englishman, "I don't know this Theodore Timmerman."

"You ain't never gonna get that book lyin' like that, man. If you want to stay in the game you got to share."

"What do you mean?"

"I got some information. You got some too. We share, and then once we trust each other, maybe then we can make a money deal."

Bradford must have loved Paris more than he loved life and liberty. Paris was whispering in his ear, sweating through his pores. He stared at me so hard maybe he saw his beloved city in my stead.

"Timmerman called me," he said at last. "Like you said."

"Uh-huh. But Kit called you first, right?"

"Yes."

"He said that he had the book," I prompted.

"Yes."

"Come on, Bradford. Don't make this be like the dentist's chair."

"Mr. Mitchell called and said that he had the book, like you said. He wanted, he wanted money. Money I didn't have."

"Now how does a colored farmer come up with the private number of the personal secretary of one of the richest men in L.A.?"

Bradford wasn't about to answer that question, so I did myself.

"Because," I said, "Lance and Minna told you about the book. They came to you to get to their father. You were the go-between. But Kit fucked you up. He took the book for Bartholomew Perry and then kept it. BB was too conceited and gave Kit so much information that he thought that he could go out on his own. He cut out BB and Lance and Minna. But what he didn't know was that cuttin' them out put a definite crimp on you retiring to France."

"You seem to know everything already," Bradford said.

"Not why your boy Timmerman killed the Wexler kids," I said. "Did you tell him to do that?"

"Certainly not."

"Then why?"

"Do you have the book, Mr. Minton?"

"I don't say a thing until you explain these murders to me," I replied.

"Why? Why do you need to know?"

"There's a legal term, Brad. It's called accessory after the fact. If I try and make money from a crime I know has happened, then they can put me in jail for that crime."

Our eyes met then. Two men, one white and one black, one an Australian and the other almost an American. Both of us aging a day for every minute that passed.

"I asked Timmerman to search Mr. Mitchell's apartment for the book. He did not find it. Then we had the meeting here on this bench. He told me that he had been searching for Bartholomew Perry. I told him that Mr. Perry probably had the book or at least he had knowledge of where the book could be found. . . ." Bradford's words trailed off there. He had taken me up to the door and now he was afraid to go through.

"So you sent Timmerman after Lance and Minna to try and get through to BB. You thought that maybe they were going to go to Winifred directly." It was all supposition by then. I just needed to keep him talking.

"I didn't know that he was going to kill them. I didn't know what kind of man he was," Bradford said, practicing for the trial. "I just told him to get in touch with them, to offer to help and see what they said."

"Instead he tortured them to find out what the book was worth and then killed 'em to cut down on the number of potential partners in the crime." I was flying by then.

"Now you know what I do," Bradford said. "Can you help get the book?"

"I believe I can, my man. I believe I can."

"How?"

"I'm pretty sure that Timmerman got the book somewhere on the way. When Fearless knocked him down I got his address and the key to his door. Fearless is there right now, lookin' for the book. When he gets it I might consider sellin' it to you."

"Why?" Craighton asked suspiciously. "You could go to Maestro or Miss Fine yourself."

"Oh yeah," I said. "I could tie the noose for the hangman too. No, no, brother. You find twenty-five thousand dollars and I'll let you decide how to make money on the book."

The light of hope was shining in Bradford Craighton's eyes.

"That's a lot of money," he said.

"I bet you could pick it up in that pantry you paid me from," I said. "Sell the book to whoever pays the most, return the loan, and fly off to gay Paree."

"I'll tell you the same thing I told Mitchell," the private secretary said. "I can raise seventy-five hundred dollars. That's all I can lay my hands on."

"I'll meet you halfway and take twelve thousand five hundred."

"Mr. Minton," Bradford said with great reserve. "I have what I said. Take it and you will be safe and quite a bit richer. . . . Or take your chances with Mr. Wexler and his thugs."

I stayed silent for a long moment to make him think that I was considering the options he presented. I wanted him to believe I might leave him hanging.

"Okay," I said. "All right. I'll take the seventy-five hundred, but you got to promise to keep my name out of it."

"You have my word."

Words: from the Emancipation Proclamation to the names on the ballots every election day, they had a life of their own and precious little to do with the truth.

43 IT'S FUNNY HOW YOU START OUT trying to help somebody else and end up in business for yourself. Fearless had come to me to find out why the cops were after him and what was going on with Leora and Son. That was all behind us, but there I was, still hanging in there, trying to make money out of thin air.

Bradford Craighton had gone into business for himself. Minna and Lance had come to him, the trusted family employee, and asked him to help make Maestro pay them for their crime. Bradford saw his chance. All those years working for the big man made him hungry for the real thing.

Paris is even more beautiful when you don't have to walk to work every morning of your life.

But Kit took the book and called asking for more money than the down-at-heel secretary could raise. When Kit said that he'd go directly to the Fine family, Craighton thought that he'd lost his one chance. Then came Teddy Timmerman. But Timmerman also betrayed him. He killed the kids, killed Kit, and now Bradford was out on a limb. But there was the slight hope that he could still get the book.

The last two threats to my security were Maestro Wexler and the weasel Bradford. The master wanted to find the killer of his children and he looked to me as a guide. Of course I couldn't very well turn over his secretary, because then I could be implicated in the secretary's crime. And Bradford would need me out of the way sooner or later because I knew about his crimes.

I called the Seventy-seventh Street Precinct from a phone booth on Central Avenue.

"Police department," a white woman answered.

"Sergeant Rawlway, please."

"One moment."

I waited through a series of clicks and buzzes. Finally there came another ring.

"Sergeant Rawlway speaking."

"Good morning, sergeant. This is Paris Minton."

"Oh. Hello, Mr. Minton. You're a little late if you wanted to turn in your friend. We already found him."

"It's not that, sir. I know you talked to Fearless because he told me about it. He said that you were looking for a man named Kit Mitchell."

"Mr. Jones really shouldn't be discussing police business."

"Maybe not, sir, but do you think it's a coincidence that another man showed up at my door just yesterday asking me if I knew the whereabouts of Fearless or Kit?"

"What man?"

"A guy named Theodore Timmerman. At least that's what he said his name was. He gave me a card with a number on it. Do you think that's important?"

FEARLESS WAS AT MY HOUSE when I got there, shuffling a deck of cards. He was stretched out on the front room sofa — playing solitaire in a room full of books.

"Hey, Fearless —"

"I got bad news, Paris," he said. "Somebody stole our money, man."

"What money?"

"That we had in the trunk'a her car."

"What about the book?"

"Book? Who cares about a book when we lost almost three thousand dollars and that emerald necklace?"

"Did they leave the book?"

"It was in the same bag as the money, man," Fearless said. "They took it all."

I sat down. If there hadn't been a chair behind me I would have fallen to the floor.

"No," was all I said.

"I know, Paris," Fearless said. "I know."

"Who would have known to take the money?"

"Ambrosia took the car to Tito's Car Wash. I had driven it up into the Santa Monica mountains and it got kinda streaked. She was just gettin' it clean if I wanted to drive around some more. You know at Tito's they do the whole car. The trunk was wide open the whole time. They got at least twenty people workin' there. And there's a big sign sayin' not to leave no valuables in the trunk."

Up to that moment the loss of the Fine family chronicle was the worst defeat in my life. I forgot about the man who died at my hands and even the danger still posed by Maestro and his scheming secretary. I forgot about the police and their constant threat to my liberty. All that was left was the loss of more money than most Negro families made in an entire life of labor.

"Paris?"

"I'm goin' to bed, Fearless," I said.

He said something but I didn't hear it. I scaled the stairs to my illegal loft. I don't even remember getting into the bed. And I didn't have one dream that I can remember. It was just as if I had died. That's how far I'd fallen.

I DIDN'T FEEL HIM SHAKE ME but he must have. He'd stayed downstairs for nearly twenty hours, standing guard over my despair. When I opened my eyes Fearless was just sitting there in a chair beside my bed. He'd undressed me and covered me with blankets and a sheet.

"Hey, Paris. Feel better?"

"Ungh," I said. "Ugh."

A wave of nausea went through me and I got out of the bed and rushed down to the toilet. My head was aching and one of my nostrils was clogged. I'd lost a fortune because of a car wash attendant who would never know the value of the book he stole.

Fearless was at the kitchen table when I got there. He'd made pancakes with hot maple syrup and country sausage.

"Anybody call?" I asked.

"I took the phone off the hook, man. You needed your sleep."

"Well, I better put it back. I got work to do."

My first job was to read the morning paper.

Kit Mitchell had been found. He'd been dead for at least a week. There were signs that he'd been tortured before he died, but the cause of death was not immediately known.

Maybe, after I died and if I went to heaven, the celestial host would give me a medal for ending Theodore Timmerman's rampage on earth.

RAWLWAY AND MORRAIN CAME BY at about five. Fearless went upstairs before I answered the door.

"Sergeant, officer," I said in greeting at the door.

"May we come in, Mr. Minton?" Sergeant Rawlway asked.

"Sure can."

They took seats this time and sat forward with clasped hands and elbows on their knees.

"We found some suspicious evidence at the house of the man you called us about," Rawlway said.

"Oh yeah? What about him?"

The hairy cop just shook his head.

"Well," I said, hesitating, "was there something else I could do for you?"

"What did you say his name was again?" Morrain asked in a surprisingly deferential tone.

"Timmerman," I said. "Theodore Timmerman. Why?"

"His phone records and other papers seem to be a bit confused."

"How do you mean?"

"He went by half a dozen names. And there were some very incriminating materials in his garage."

"Really?"

"Just what did he say to you when he was here?" Rawlway asked. He took out the tiny notebook and small ballpoint pen made to scale.

"He asked if I knew a man named Fearless," I said, looking up at the ceiling as if I had to think about my answer. "Then he asked about Kit. I told him that I didn't know but I heard that Fearless worked for a man named Kit for a while but that was over now. He wanted to know Fearless's address and I told him that I didn't know. That's when it got kinda strange."

"How do you mean strange?"

"He put his hand on my forearm and squeezed it hard. Then he asked about Fearless again. It was as if he was testin' me. You know his eyes were scary, and so I was happy that I passed."

"Did he say anything else?" Morrain asked.

"No. He let me go and left."

"How long ago was that?"

"Day before yesterday."

"And you waited a whole day to call?" Rawlway asked.

"Yeah. Well, you know I didn't wanna get involved. But then I woke up yesterday morning and I got worried. I tried to get in touch with Fearless but he'd gone somewhere. So then I called you guys because I don't want my friend to get hurt."

"It's unusual for Negroes to willingly give up information to the cops," Morrain speculated.

"Maybe about other Negroes, but Timmerman or whatever his name is is a white man." *Who died three feet from where you're sitting,* went through my mind.

"If Timmerman calls you again you should call us," Rawlway was saying.

"You mean you didn't catch him yet?" I said, putting a little fear in my voice. "I mean, what if he figures to come back here?"

"Don't worry," Morrain said. "We got his house covered. We'll get him."

"How can we get in touch with Fearless?" Rawlway wanted to know.

I gave them Ambrosia's phone number and address. Fearless would call her and make sure she wasn't helpful. Sooner or later he'd have to talk to the cops, but not before we finished our business.

AT NINE EXACTLY I called Bradford Craighton. He answered even before I heard the ring.

"Mr. Minton?"

"Hello, Bradford. I got what you wanted. I got even more than that."

"Where?"

"Right here at Timmerman's house. Fearless found the book and left it. He said that he didn't see any reason to go runnin' around with Timmerman in the hospital and the police lookin' into three murders. You just bring my money here. Bring it and we'll turn over the book to you."

I never expected to see that money or anything else that was promised to me, but I had to act like I did. I gave him the Ogden address and he hung up the phone without even a good-bye.

44

THINGS FELL INTO PLACE QUICKLY after that. Bradford Craighton was arrested at Timmerman's house on charges of attempted breaking and entering. Maestro Wexler had him out of jail before noon. The private secretary immediately fled the state, which set off a nationwide search. Over the next days there were a series of articles about the conspiracy between Minna Wexler, her brother, and Bradford Craighton to extort money from an unnamed millionaire. It was also believed that, with the help of an as yet unnamed accomplice, Bradford ordered the deaths of the brother and sister.

Three days later it all came to naught. Bradford Craighton hung himself in a three-dollar-a-night room in Toledo, Ohio.

A long way from the Left Bank.

Maybe a week after that a couple camping in the Santa Monica mountain range found the desiccated body of a tall white man. The corpse had no hands and had also been beheaded. Nearby there had been a fire that contained the remains of human bone.

I PUT IT ALL OUT OF MY MIND: the one unbroken thread of African history as it bled into the world of slavery; the possibility of being a rich man with a house near the shore; the first, and hopefully the last, killing my hands would ever commit. I forgot about everything and went back to my spotty life of book sales and reading.

Rose Fine moved in with Fearless's mother. Son, Brown, and Leora decided to stay in L.A. to be near her. The cops picked up Fearless but he played ignorant and they soon let him go. The information I found in Timmerman's files never made it to the news. Neither did the money he had in that rusty box.

A few weeks later I was lamenting not taking at least a few dollars for the trouble Timmerman had caused me. The dread of his evil files and photographs had worn off but the mailman was still delivering the bills. I was having those thoughts when my telephone rang.

"Mr. Minton?"

"Oscar?"

"My sister would appreciate it if you could come to the house this afternoon. Shall we say four-thirty?"

• • •

THE HOUSE WAS GOING THROUGH a major renovation. The lawn had been cleared of the junk that had been rusting there. The façade was being painted. Hard-muscled men of every race were straining and struggling to make the Fine house into the mansion it could be.

I felt guilty as I approached the front door. I'd lost the greatest fortune this family owned, maybe the greatest treasure for American Negroes. Maybe, I thought, Winifred now knew about the loss and she wanted to hire me to search down the book. I had decided that I wouldn't take her money. It would just be the wrong thing to do.

SHE WAS SITTING AT HER DESK with the curtains open on the Eden behind her. She wore a pink dress that was cut low enough to show the pendant against her chest. It was a large emerald surrounded by white stones that looked like diamonds but which were really white sapphires.

"You got it back," I said.

"As if you didn't know," she replied. "Have a seat, Mr. Minton."

"What do you mean?"

"Do I have to explain the word seat?"

"I mean about the pendant."

"It's okay, Mr. Minton. Your friend Fearless brought it back to me of his own free will."

"Oh," I said as I lowered into the soft chair. "I see."

"He also returned my family book. When I spoke to you I didn't even know that it was missing. With Son being taken from me and the pendant too I was distracted."

"I imagine so," I said pleasantly. But inside I was boiling. Fearless had done it to me again. He knew that I planned either to keep the book or to sell it, and he made the decision that either act would have been wrong. He stole the book from me and gave it back to Winifred. I silently swore never to help him again.

"He told me," she was saying, "that you found the book and turned it over to him so that he could protect it until you gave it to the rightful owner."

"Well, that's how it was, I guess. What is it you wanted today?"

"I've already made my allowances for Fearless," she said as if I should have understood. "And now all I have to do is meet your request."

"I see," I said. There were prickles now working their way up my spine.

"I have an offer that you may or may not be interested in."

"And what's that?"

There was a black-and-yellow garden spider sitting in the middle of her web in the window. She was a behemoth. Near the web a tiger swallowtail butterfly, also yellow and black, fluttered haplessly looking for pollen and a place to lay her eggs. I began to be afraid for the butterfly. I wanted more than anything for her to go the other way.

"I could give you the ten thousand that Fearless said you wanted," Winifred Fine said. "But —"

I forgot the butterfly then.

"But what?"

"I also have in my possession the same amount of money in a stock that I intended for Son's education. I'll get more stocks in the future, and I'd like to hold on to as much cash as possible because I'm about to embark on a new gas station business in Compton."

"I'll take the money, ma'am."

"Are you sure? The stocks might make a great surge and you can always sell them."

"No ma'am. I'm just a poor shopkeeper. I don't know about finance. You got the money here?"

"It's in the briefcase next to your chair."

I looked down to see a slender alligator skin case on the right side of my chair. When I looked up the spider was wrapping the butterfly and Winifred L. Fine was smiling.

"I see that you're fixing up around the front of the house," I said to make a little conversation before running out of the door with my loot.

"As I told you, the front of the house was Rose's domain. Now that she has left us I have taken over that responsibility."

Which one was crazier? I wondered.

"Tell Mr. Jones that I met my end of the bargain," she said.

I nodded and stood, my treasure in tow. I turned to leave and then turned back.

"What was the name of the stock you wanted to give me?"

"International Business Machines," she said. "They make typewriters."

I smiled and wandered out of the house, not a rich man, but certainly not poor.

45

"YEAH, PARIS, you know I had to give that lady back her book. It was a family heirloom."

It was a week later. I had eaten steak every night, wondering what I should say to Fearless when I saw him. He had dropped by after eight carrying a large brown paper shopping bag.

"You had no right to take that book without talking to me first, Fearless. I could have made a hundred thousand dollars on that motherfucker."

"It wasn't yours, man."

"I found it."

"And you got ten thousand dollars plus the twenty-five hundred was in with the book."

"Where's that?"

"In this here bag," he said.

"What? You turn it into quarters?"

Fearless grinned then, and I knew he had done something else, something that he thought I'd like.

"What I got in here is seventy-two rolls of thirty-five-millimeter film, what they call archival quality."

"No."

"Jackson had lent his camera equipment to a white girl he know goes to UCLA. I went over to her place and we took the pictures in her basement."

If I had been with anyone but Fearless I would have broken down into tears.

"I know how much you love that book, Paris," he said. "And I know it's important too. There shouldn't be just one copy, and Miss Fine's gonna have to get up off it one day and share it with the world. But until she do at least you got somethin' to build a darkroom over and then somethin' to read in the middle'a the night.

"You know it's not just that money neither. She promised to leave Son and his parents alone and leave Rose to live with Mama. That way everybody's happy. Everybody, that is, except that poor Mr. Wexler. It's really a shame about his children."

FEARLESS HAS ALWAYS COME THROUGH for me. He's always been a better man than I am and smarter than I am too. I've been studying photography lately and spending time in the darkroom at LACC. Pretty soon I'll have my own copy of the Fine family story. That and ten thousand dollars and all the air I can breathe.